The Poison In His Veins

A Detective Inspector Benedict Paige Novel:
Book 2

Joshua Black

Rathbone Publishing

Joshua Black

Joshua Black is the pen name of Rupert Colley.

Rupert is the author of ten historical novels, all set during the 20th century.

The Love and War Series
The Lost Daughter
Song of Sorrow
The White Venus
The Woman on the Train
My Brother the Enemy
The Black Maria
Anastasia

The Searight Saga
This Time Tomorrow
The Unforgiving Sea
The Red Oak

rupertcolley.com

The Poison In His Veins

R
Rathbone
Publishing

rupertcolley.com/joshua-black/

Prologue

There's only one thing worse than losing your dog on a walk, and that's losing someone else's dog on a walk. Rita Nandi and her partner, Liam, were currently suffering from such stress. You always feel doubly responsible when something in your charge isn't actually yours – a friend's car, their child, their bloody dog. The time was approaching eight on a cold February morning and, to make matters worse, they both had to get to work soon and not stressing over a bloody Jack Russell gone AWOL in Greenfield Park. 'Why did you let her off the lead, anyway?' snapped Liam.

'Because I was told I could, that she always comes back when you call for her.'

'Yeah, right. Not exactly working now, though, is it? Betty? Here, Betty!'

They'd walked around the park and had been enjoying the novelty of the early morning exercise and fresh air, and the little dog's excitement. They laughed at her antics and the way she ran and ran and interacted with other dogs and the way she chased after a squirrel, barking in frustration when

1

the little rodent scarpered up a tree. They exchanged pleasantries with fellow dog walkers and generally felt better with life. Not so joyful was the moment when Betty did her first shit of the morning.

'Just leave it,' said Liam.

'Oh, this from the man who just last week stepped in some shit and declared that all dog owners who didn't clear up after should be publicly hanged from the nearest lamppost and left to rot for a week?'

'But we're in the park now.'

'No, people are looking, Liam.'

'Oh, sod it. Here, I'll do it.'

'You're so gallant, my love.'

'Yeah, right.'

That was until they entered the woods and Betty dashed off. Rita and Liam hadn't even noticed at first, so wrapped up in their discussion about who to invite to their upcoming engagement party. They rented a one-bedroom flat three minutes from the park, and feared the landlord wouldn't approve of a massive party, so Liam was currently getting quotes on hiring a space in a pub. Who to invite, who they couldn't afford *not* to invite, and the cost of the whole shebang were, of course, completely intertwined, and this had been the first time they'd discussed it without falling out and having a huge row about it. Rita put it down to the fresh air and the dog.

When Rita's friend asked if they'd look after the dog for a week, she jumped at the chance. They'd been thinking of getting a dog, especially now that Rita worked from home, and this seemed like an ideal dry run. Rita asked a fellow dog walker if they'd seen a small, white Jack Russell on their travels. They hadn't.

They called out Betty's name repeatedly. Rather quietly at first, as if not wanting to alert the dog walking community to their failure. But now, with the minutes ticking by and the desperation kicking in, they'd already lost that inhibition and were openly yelling Betty's name for the whole park to hear and damn the silent disapprobation.

'Bloody dog. It's too bloody cold for this,' said Liam, blowing into his hands, as if emphasising the point.

'We should've brought treats or something,' said Rita. 'But, honestly, Liam, I wasn't told this would be a problem. Betty? Good dog, Betty?'

'Wait.' Liam stopped in his tracks. 'Listen.'

Yes, somewhere in the distance, they could hear the yap yap of a small dog. 'That's her!'

'How do you know it is?'

'It's got to be.'

With renewed vigour, the couple began marching up the hill following a path that meandered through the trees, calling the dog's name. 'We're not getting a dog,' announced Liam out in front.

'Oh, that's decided then, is it?'

'I can't be arsed with this every morning.'

'It'd be me doing the majority of the work, Liam.'

'Yeah, and I'm saving you the work, we're not getting a dog.'

'No, it doesn't work like that,' she said, trying to keep up. 'You don't unilaterally make the decisions now.'

'Hurry up, she's up here somewhere.'

'No, Liam, this is important–'

'No, Rita, finding this stupid dog and getting to work is important right now. Betty! Betty.'

'There she is,' said Rita, pointing up the hill.

Liam charged ahead, gently calling out. Betty was clearly agitated, alternatively growling and barking so hard, her feet lifted off the ground, stepping back, then inching forward again, her tail erect.

'What's she barking at?' asked Rita.

'Don't know. I can't see.' Liam strode up the incline. He stopped. 'Fuck!'

'What? What is it?'

He glanced back at her and she saw he'd turned pale. 'Liam?'

She caught up with him and followed his gaze. Her legs wobbled beneath her. 'Oh my God.'

A man, entirely naked, sat at the base of a tree, his legs splayed out, his head drooped to one side, a gag over his mouth, the whiteness of his flesh stark against the dark bark of the tree trunk.

'Is he dead?' she whispered.

'No, look, he's still breathing.'

They took tentative steps towards him, fearing, perhaps, a trick of some sort or a trap.

'He's been tied up.'

Sure enough, Rita could see now that his arms were pulled back either side of the trunk.

'Should we take the gag off?'

'Of course.' Liam approached and removed the strip of cloth over the man's mouth. 'You OK, mate?'

The man groaned but didn't answer.

'What's your name?'

Still no answer.

'Give him your coat,' ordered Liam.

'Me? Give him your coat.'

'Oh, for fuck's sake, Rita.' But he took his coat off and

4

approached. 'Get the dog out of the way, will you? You alright, mate?' He placed his coat over the man in an attempt to preserve his modesty and provide some heat. 'Christ, he's been beaten up.'

Yes, Rita could see it now, the bruising on his face, the black eye, the cut lip. Betty had quietened now and ran around the tree, slowly losing interest in the naked man. Liam tried to untie the man's hands at the other side of the trunk while Rita rang 999 and, asking for police and ambulance, gave the operator directions to the small car park on this side of the hill. 'Five to seven minutes,' she told Liam.

'I can't do it. They've used those plastic ties, you know?'

'Can you hear me?' asked Rita, not expecting a response. 'What's your name? Someone's on their way. Won't be long now.'

She touched the man's shoulder and was shocked by how cold he was to the touch. This man was almost dead; he needed more warmth. She removed her jumper, grimacing as the cold wind bit into her, and tied it around him, beneath Liam's coat. Liam, without being asked, did likewise. A spiel of bloody spittle dropped from his mouth. 'I think he's coming round.' said Rita, more in hope than expectation.

'I wonder how long he's been here,' said Liam. 'I mean, he could have been here all night.'

'No, he'd be dead by now, surely.'

'He almost is, Rita.'

'And who did this to him?'

'Don't know but they must have planned it unless they happened to be walking around with ties in their pockets.'

Finally, they could hear the welcoming sound of a siren fast approaching, swiftly followed by a second set.

'Help is on its way, love,' said Rita.

5

'I'll go wave at them from the bottom of the hill.' Liam rushed off. Betty, happy to see some action at last, followed and quickly overtook him.

He looked about thirty, thought Rita, five years older than she and Liam. Dark, lanky hair, and, on his left shoulder, a large tattoo of an eagle, its wings spread wide. But nothing else around – no clothes, no phone, no bag, nothing to tell anyone who this unfortunate man was. Whoever he was, he had a tale to tell, and someone, some sick bastard, needed to be punished for this. She just hoped the poor man lived long enough to find his voice and bring the bastard to justice.

Chapter 1: Benedict

Today was the first day of the school half term, and Detective Inspector Benedict Paige and his wife, Sonia, got up to an unusually quiet household: no kids arguing over breakfast cereals, complaining that the other was spending too long in the shower, and demanding where certain items of their PE kit were. They both tiptoed around and spoke quietly, as if any noise might awaken their sleeping children while knowing that, in reality, a herd of rampaging elephants would fail to disturb them from their deep slumber.

Sonia worked as an architect for Camden council and was telling him about the string of meetings she had today in, he thought, rather too much detail. Words like 'procurement', 'consultation', 'supply chain' and 'health and safety' cropped up at regular intervals. While she appreciated that Benedict's job could, at times, present its own challenges and that, occasionally, he had to come up close and personal to life's grimier aspects, he always felt that she considered his job a breeze in comparison. He wasn't tied to a computer or a succession of unending meetings every minute of his working day, didn't have to worry about compliance to anywhere the same degree and that, on the whole, his job was *fun*. Sonia's job could never be described as fun. 'And you meet such interesting people.' Yes, if you really want to describe the assortment of murderers, pimps and rapists 'interesting'. 'While, I just get to meet middle-aged white men in suits,' she added, as her middle-aged white husband stood at the mirror hoping his jacket hadn't become too small for him. 'Yes, dear.'

An hour later, Benedict walked into the office he shared with his small but dedicated team of police officers. Although quite where Detective Constables Jamie Kelly and Andrew Prowse were, he didn't know. He exchanged pleasantries with his new Detective Sergeant, Jessica Gardiner, who, on transferring to Camden's CID a fortnight ago from her previous job in Manchester, had already been involved in her first murder case.

His boss, DCI George Lincoln, called Jessica and him through for a 'short briefing.' To be fair to the man, 'short' always meant 'short'. Unlike architects, police officers were people of few words, and that's the way Benedict liked it.

'Where are DCs Kelly and Prowse, sir?'

'Have you forgotten, Ben? They're on an hour-long manual handling refresher training.'

'A manual handling refresher training? Jeez, have you seen the size of DC Prowse, sir? He's a gym bunny, lifting weights every morning before work. I reckon he can handle lifting the printer from A to B.'

'Do you feel the need to attend a refresher on manual handling, Ben?'

'No, sir, indeed I do not.'

'Be quiet then.'

He sensed Jessica chortling in the chair next to him.

'So, something rather unusual for you to start the day off. I need you both to go to a scene in the woods next to Greenfield Park. There's a small car park on the north side on Greenfield Street.'

'I know it.'

'A couple of dog walkers found an unconscious man, gagged, and tied to an elm tree. Uniform and ambulance are already on their way. The man was found entirely naked.'

'Whoa,' said Jessica. 'In this weather? Amazed he survived.'

'He might not, DS Gardiner. So, get a squad car and get there pronto. Time is of the essence here. If the paramedics can revive him, it might be our only chance to question him. But keep it brief. I don't want anyone accusing us of harassing the man in his final moments.'

'We're on it, sir.'

*

Using the squad car, as DCI Lincoln had suggested, DI Paige and DS Gardiner were at Greenfield Street in a matter of minutes. Benedict parked up next to another squad car and an ambulance, their sirens flashing but now silenced.

'It's bloody cold,' said Jessica, buttoning her coat as she got out of the car. 'I wouldn't fancy being tied to a tree in this weather.'

'Without a stitch on.'

'Exactly.'

They took the only clear path up a short but steep hill to the top where they could see, through the trees, a gathering of uniforms and activity. A PCSO advanced towards them. The woman welcomed them as if they'd just arrived at a social gathering and not the scene of an attempted murder,

9

and introduced them to Rita Nandi and Liam Naylor, the young couple who found the unfortunate man. They were being looked after by PC Stevens, a familiar face at the station. But first, Benedict wanted to see the victim. Two paramedics were about to close the ambulance doors when Benedict called over. 'Do you mind if I quickly say hello?' he said, showing them his ID.

'He's conscious,' said the female paramedic. 'But not making any sense.'

'Classic signs of hypothermia,' said her male colleague. 'Go ahead though. But don't be too long, he needs proper attention.'

'Any name?'

'Not yet.'

Benedict jumped into the ambulance while Jessica talked to the paramedics. The man was covered neck to toe in a foil blanket. Only his extremely white face showed, although his cheeks were bright red, which, thought Benedict, was probably a good sign, it meant he was warming up from the inside. He was breathing heavily, moving his head slightly from left to right and back. His eyes were closed, although one involuntarily so as a result of a black eye. His blue lips were swollen, but whether that was through injury or the cold, Benedict didn't know. 'Hello, sir,' he said loudly. 'Can you hear me?'

No answer.

He jumped back outside. 'Thanks,' he said to the paramedics.

'Oh, by the way,' said the female paramedic. 'He's got a rather distinctive tattoo of an eagle on his shoulder. I took the liberty of taking a photo of it. Do you want it?'

'Wow, yes, that'd be super useful. Thank you.' He gave her

his business card. 'Mobile number's there.'

The woman nodded. 'Sure.'

Benedict called PC Stevens over.

'Good morning, sir.'

'Stevens, good to see you. So, what's going down?' He cringed inwardly at his abysmal use of the vernacular. 'He was found naked then?'

'Yes, sir. We have no clue as to who he is. We had a preliminary search of the immediate area and found nothing of interest. But forensics are on their way.'

'Did he say anything to you?'

'No. Just groaned a bit.'

Jessica cleared her throat. 'He'd been beaten up but has he been mutilated?'

'Mutilated?'

'His genitals. Were they still intact?'

'I didn't look too closely, ma'am, but as far as I can tell, then yes, they were fine, if rather shrivelled.'

Benedict's phone pinged. It was the paramedic's photo of the tattoo, nice and clear. 'Yes, that is rather distinctive.' He showed it to Jessica and PC Stevens.

'Certainly big enough,' said Stevens.

'And certainly a one-off, I'd say,' added Jessica.

'This is the thing that will identify him. Stevens—'

'I know, sir, circulate posters and all that, social media included.'

'You're a good man, Stevens.'

Stevens smiled, perhaps despite himself.

'Right,' said Benedict. 'Let's go see the couple here.'

Benedict was too slow to prevent a Jack Russell jumping up at him and leaving its muddy paw prints on his hitherto pristine trousers.

11

The woman, Rita, apologised. 'She's not ours,' she said, despite having the dog on a lead. 'But, in fact, it was Betty who found him.'

'Go on.'

'We're dog sitting for the week. Today's our first full day with her, and she ran off, didn't she, Liam?'

'That's right, and we couldn't find her for ages–'

'And when we did–'

'She was barking at this bloke.'

They took turns describing the man with his hands tied together at the back of the tree trunk. They'd covered him as best as they could and called emergency services. They also hadn't found any trace of his belongings, not a shred of his clothing. And no, they hadn't seen anyone else in the immediate vicinity.

'Look, I don't want to appear rude or anything,' said Liam. 'Can we go home now? We've been out for an hour and I'm freezing standing around.'

'Sure. You've left us with your details?'

Benedict and Jessica watched as the couple made their way back down the hill towards the park, the Jack Russell pulling on its lead.

'So, what do you think, Jessica? What's going on here?'

'He could have been raped, maybe several times over.'

'It's a definite possibility,' agreed Benedict. 'Or he's the victim of some bizarre ritual, or maybe…'

'Boss?'

'I don't know. I reckon this is a punishment for something.'

'That's quite some punishment. He almost died up here.'

'Indeed. Whatever the reason, I reckon we'll know soon enough.'

Chapter 2: Elise

Elise Tanner woke with a smile on her lips. Outside, dawn was just breaking and it was dark, and drizzly and grizzly. But she didn't care. Next to her, her naked, gorgeous boyfriend, now officially her fiancé. She couldn't have been happier. He was still fast asleep. She stretched. Last night, their engagement party was perhaps the happiest night of her life. She couldn't remember a time when she'd laughed or danced so much. Phil was her man now; it was official. And nothing but nothing would drive them apart. Meeting Phil six months ago had been one of those life-changing moments, one of those "you had me at hello" moments. She knew straight away, as soon as he opened his mouth, that he was the one for her. And, it seemed, the feeling was mutual.

She hadn't even drunk that much last night, a couple glasses of champagne, a couple more of Prosecco, and that was it. But boy, had she danced. She danced with everyone, even her seventy-year-old grandfather and grandmother. And she'd danced a slow dance with Dad, Coldplay's *Yellow*, and both of them had cried. It'd been a tough few years for the family.

Phil stirred and opened his eyes. He smiled on seeing her. 'Hello, gorgeous.'

'Good morning, darling. How are you feeling?'

He put his hand to his brow. 'I may have had a couple too many but apart from that…'

'We've got the whole day to ourselves. We could spend all day in bed, if you like.'

'Oh really? Now, you're talking,' he said, with a salacious grin.

'Oh, Phil, I would've thought you had enough after last night.'

'Enough? Baby, I'll never get enough of you.' He inched closer to her, enclosing her into his arms.

'Phil, we can't; Mum and Dad are downstairs. They'll hear.'

'Doh, you spoil sport. This time next week though.'

'Yes, I can't wait.'

They'd laid a deposit on a one-bedroom flat nearer the centre of Camden, nothing special, but it was a start and it meant the world to her. It meant a new start with the man she intended to spend the rest of her life with. She held up her hand and twisted it left and right, allowing the light, such as it was, to catch the small diamond on her ring finger. 'I'm sorry it's so small,' said Phil.

'No, don't say that. I love it. It could be ten times the size and it still wouldn't mean any more to me.'

'I'm going to have a shower,' said Phil. 'Is that OK?'

'Go for it, my love.'

He got out of bed and Elise couldn't help but admire his firm buttocks before they disappeared under his dressing gown. 'You OK?' he asked.

'Never better, darling.' She smiled and he knew.

'Won't be long.'

She lay back in bed, her arms behind her head and sighed with contentment. Looking back, she couldn't believe how worried she'd been about introducing Phil to her parents; after all, she'd never had a black boyfriend before. But her concerns had proved totally unfounded; they took to him immediately. She knew why, as long as he was decent and devoted to their daughter, they were happy. They'd seen how miserable she'd been in the past, and her happiness was all that mattered. And they knew straight away that Phil made her happy and would always make her happy. Yesterday morning, she'd even rang the registry office and made a date for their wedding. Short notice too – just two months away. Which meant so much to get organised in so little time; why, she hadn't even decided on her bridesmaids yet, she had so many friends she could ask and that, in itself, was proving stressful. She was tempted to ask Phil's sister, thereby upsetting everyone and no one at the same time. Ultimately, she realised having too many friends whom she could ask was a nice problem to have, a first-world problem, as her dad often said whenever Elise was complaining about something. Such a dad-thing to say.

She heard the doorbell ring and wondered who could be calling so early on a Sunday morning. Straining her ears, it sounded like a delivery.

Phil came out from the shower, a towel wrapped around him. She watched him dressed, admiring his torso, smiling to herself.

'What's so amusing?' he asked.

'I was just thinking what a lucky girl I am.'

'And why's that?'

'You're fishing for compliments. I'm not going to tell you.'

He threw his damp towel at her. She screeched and laughed.

Her Alexa speaker made an announcement – it was her mother's voice ringing up from the kitchen: 'Would you lovebirds fancy a big English breakfast? Dad's doing the full works just for you.'

Elise answered in the affirmative, the thought of one of her dad's infamous fry-ups appealed greatly right at that moment. Phil, now dressed, sauntered downstairs. She jumped out of bed and threw on some scruffy, Sunday-esque clothes and brushed her hair.

She joined Phil downstairs in the dining room, greeted with a kiss from her mother. Ten minutes later, Dad appeared bearing two plates of bacon, eggs, tomatoes, mushrooms and more. He'd forgotten that Phil didn't like mushrooms, but that was OK; she'd sneak them off his plate.

The four of them talked animatedly about the party. Phil had been the first man Elise had allowed into her life since her experience. She hadn't had a boyfriend for years; too mentally scarred by what had happened. There had been one but he didn't last long. He called her 'damaged goods', and she knew it to be true – but it'd hardly been her fault.

And then she met Phil, and it was like a light bulb illuminating her life in a flash. Everything changed. Life suddenly had a future and a meaning. She met his sister and she was lovely, and she met his parents, Michael and Phyllis, and although nice enough, she'd always suspected his mother didn't think much of her. The woman never said anything negative but she always seemed aloof, as if she didn't quite approve of her son's choice of a future wife.

Then, just four months ago, the other piece of good news – her father being released from prison. He'd done three years out of a five-year sentence. He'd hit a teenager on a bicycle while driving slightly over the limit. He held up his hands immediately, apologised and took his sentence on the chin. Every day her father spent incarcerated had been torture for Elise.

'What a great night, last night,' said Dad, pouring everyone a round of tea. 'Just what this family needed.'

'You've got some good moves there, Hans,' said Phil.

'Natural Austrian rhythm, I'll have you know.'

'Who knew there was such a thing?'

'Everyone is so happy for you, darling,' said Mum, reaching over the table and squeezing Elise's hand. 'No one deserves it more than you. I'm so proud of you, my little petal, so proud my heart could burst.'

'All right, Nicola,' said Hans. 'Don't embarrass the girl.'

'I'm just saying, thank you. Why can't I be proud of our baby?'

'I know. Thanks, Mum.' Her father was right, though; why did her mother always have to go overboard?

'Now, after breakfast, you can open all your presents,' said her father.

The engagement presents were piled up in the living room, dozens of them. 'Wow,' said Elise. 'Look at them all. This beats Christmas.'

'People have been very generous to you both,' said Mum. 'And you so deserve it, what with–'

'Yeah, yeah, I know, Mum.'

'Crack on then,' said Dad. 'I'll keep a list so you know who to thank after.'

And indeed, it was like Christmas – one present after another from various relatives and friends: champagne flutes engraved with their names, scented candles with their initials writ large, an intricately-designed stainless steel salad bowl, a forty-centimetre high silver sculpture of two entwined hearts, a pair of glass tumblers, one engraved Mr Right, the other with Mrs Always Right, two cushions with their names stitched in large, bright letters, and much more. It took them twenty whole minutes to complete the task, and afterward Elise and Phil sat back and considered their haul with quiet satisfaction.

'People are so generous, aren't they?' said Mum. 'It's because–'

'Mum, please. I know. You don't have to say it.'

'I'm sorry, my love.'

'You're going to have to start writing those thank you letters,' said Dad, taking yet another photograph of the happy couple on his phone. He must have taken a hundred at the party.

'Oh, we almost forgot, Hans,' said Mum. 'What about that one that arrived earlier?'

Hans slapped his forehead. 'Of course. I slid it behind the settee, it was so big. Here...' He reached for it and pulled out a large flat package, some three foot by two.

'My word, what is that?' said Phil.

'A painting, maybe?' said Elise.

'Open it and see,' said Mum, rubbing her hands together.

'You do the honours, darling,' said Phil.

With a pair of scissors, Elise ripped open the packaging, followed by the blue and pink wrapping underneath. 'Nice paper,' she said. 'Oh look, I was right, it *is* a painting. Look, it's got a title – it's called 'Country Dawn' by Justin Travers.'

'Who's it from?' asked Dad.

'There was a tag attached to it by string and Sellotape. Elise read the message aloud: *'To Elise and Philip, Congratulations on your engagement.*' Flipping the tag, she looked puzzled. 'Doesn't say who it's from.'

'You sure?' asked Dad.

'Maybe there's another tag,' said Mum.

Elise looked but no, nothing else, no clue as to who it was from.

Resting it against the settee, the four of them stood back to admire it. 'God, it's beautiful,' said Elise. It showed a bucolic sunny countryside scene, a dry muddied path leading into the distance, greenery and bushes either side, a sturdy elm tree to the right in full foliage. The distance a haze through which one could make out a church spire. Birds flew towards the sun and, to the left, three brightly coloured butterflies.

Dad looked at the back. 'It's numbered. Number eighty-six out of five hundred.'

'Oh, so that's rare then,' said Mum.

'Must be worth something,' said Phil. 'But who'd buy us such a thing? It's lovely. Do you like it, El?'

Elise didn't answer, her attention focused on the butterflies, two red admirals and a honey blue. She knew her butterflies, had done so since she was a small girl. *He* knew that; he always bought her gifts featuring butterflies.

'It'll look great in the flat, don't you reckon, Else? Thank you whoever sent it to us. Elise, are you alright, love?'

She knew exactly who'd sent it. And why. It was a message. He was telling her *I'm watching you; I've not gone away; I'm still here.*

Chapter 3: Dominic

Monday morning. Dominic Woods sat in his office at Safe Hands Trading plc overlooking the city, not that one could see much of it on this grey, overcast day. He had a number of phone calls to make although nothing unusual about that – he spent most of his working day drumming up new business, mainly for Safe Hands but also for the benefit of his lucrative side hustle, Hadley Investments.

His was a bare office, just the essentials with four white walls and frosted glass in the door, no ornaments here, no photos on his desk. Dominic Woods liked things sparse, business-like. He started his day, as always, with a coffee and an apple and checked his emails. The emails never stopped coming but that was fine – the more emails, the greater the number of prospects. And Dominic liked prospects; he needed them simply to survive and build. He responded to them one by one, usually with a holding response, promising that he'd call them back and suggesting a time, which, on receiving confirmation, he marked in the diary. And today, he decided with some satisfaction, was going to be a particularly busy day. Fine by him.

He was about to make his first call of the day, when there

was a knock on his door. Anthony Browning. 'You alright, Dom?' Browning was a pretty-boy with plenty of old-world charm but, considering his experience, astonishingly naive. The man had the backbone of a trout and the bite of a Chihuahua. 'Did you complete the McCory account?'

'Sure did. Finished it last night.' Why was he even asking; what business was it of his?

'Has O'Brian okayed it?'

'Not yet but why wouldn't he? I can't envisage there being a problem. Has there ever been?'

'No,' said Anthony, having to concede the point, much to Dominic's satisfaction. Anthony slipped away.

'Shut the door behind you, please.'

Anthony returned and did as asked. Dominic could see the annoyance on his face. People didn't like it when their colleagues were successful *and* bragged about it. That's why he liked working in the States – there people respected success and respected people who celebrated their own successes. It only served to make everyone aim higher, and everyone benefited from that. Here, in Britain, if one was successful, one had to hide it under a bushel, no one liked to see people boast of their success. People grew resentful, and Anthony definitely fell under that category. He was an OK trader but lacked the thrust and guile to really make a success of it. He was too honest with people, too transparent. God, Dominic hated that word: *transparent*. It was a word politicians and businesspeople held up as a virtue, something to aspire to. But to Dominic the word signalled weakness, a lack of faith in what one was trying to achieve. If it took a degree of subterfuge, if it meant cutting the occasional corner, then so what? As long as the customer got his / her return, and as long as he got his hefty commission, then *transparency* could go hang.

'Right then,' he said aloud. First call of the day – a Mrs Hernández.

'Mrs Hernández? Hello. Dominic Woods of Hadley Investments here. Is now a good time? Excellent, excellent.'

So, Dominic ran through his usual spiel, one he could recite like a stage actor reciting the same lines several times a day, day in, day out. Hadley's was, he told her, an expert cryptocurrency trader, with a specialty in trading Bitcoin derivatives and with many years' experience behind them. The technology they used was without rival here in the UK, utilising sophisticated lending software to trade the funds. He always referred to Hadley's in the plural while, in truth, it was a one-man operation – him.

'Nothing in this business is guaranteed, Mrs Hernández. If anyone tells you their scheme is one hundred per cent guaranteed to provide fantastic returns, tread carefully, in fact, I'd suggest you run a mile because they're lying to you. We don't make such guarantees because no such thing exists. However, saying all of that, I, personally, have yet to fail. Every account I look after, be it big or small, there's always a very satisfied customer at the other end, and today, Mrs Hernández, that customer could be you.'

He could tell he was impressing her, although he always did. Then came the first question – and that was fine; potential customers needed to ask questions. And Mrs Hernández's first question was the obvious one people always asked – was now, what with the current economic climate, a good time to invest?

'A perfectly reasonable question, Mrs Hernández, and I'm pleased you asked it.' He trotted out his next spiel – about how traditional investments could indeed be seen as potentially risky ventures, but things were different in the world of cryptocurrency. Here, yes, there were dips but it had proved, over the years of its existence, remarkably robust and resilient to the slings and arrows of the national and international economies.

'At the moment, Mrs Hernández, with things as they are, you're looking at achieving monthly yields of up to one hundred and twenty-five per cent per year. Now, we do ask you to commit for a whole year but it is a request, if you like, a suggestion, one which you can ignore at any time you wish. Then, with every month you complete, you're earning compound interest. So success builds on success and so it goes on. We find that our longest-serving account holders are our happiest ones. They're in it for the long haul, Mrs Hernández; they're thinking of their retirement, they're thinking of their grandchildren. I'm sure you understand.'

She certainly did.

He saw a shadow on the other side of the frosted door. Was that someone listening in? These were fire doors, so being so thick they provided good sound insulation, still, he paused until the figure moved away.

'The thing you have to understand, Mrs Hernández, is that my personal benefit is directly tied to yours. You see, I work on commission, so if the account yields a good return, which I highly anticipate it will, then I too will benefit. If, on the other hand, your account returns nothing, then I get nothing.'

She liked that; he could tell. They always did – they were in it together.

'Now, like I said in my email, we do ask for a minimal investment of four thousand pounds, ideally more. But that amount should set you up nicely. It may seem a lot to dish out in one hit, and I appreciate that, but I reckon this time next year, you'll be thanking me. So, what do you say, Mrs Hernández?'

Mrs Hernández was keen. The four thousand pound initial investment was not an issue, she had her savings accrued after working over thirty-five years for local government.

Within half an hour of finishing the conversation, Dominic Woods had Mrs Hernández' four thousand pounds in his account. Job done. Now, to the next call…

But first, Anthony Browning returned. 'Hey, Dom, fancy a drink later.'

'Not really.' Dominic never socialised with his work colleagues, the less he had to do with them, the better.

'No, really, I insist. My shout. You see, there's something we need to discuss—'

'Is there? What is it?'

'I think it'd be better if we were away from work, somewhere more neutral. Shall we say the Davenport at half six?'

Browning was smiling but Dominic could sense his tension; something was off about this; he didn't like it one bit. Whatever it was, he might as well get it over and done with. 'OK. Half six.'

'Great. See you then, Dom.'

The little guttersnipe, he was up to something; he had that look about him. He put such thoughts aside as he reached for his phone and made his second call of the day.

Seven hours later, Dominic Woods had finished for the day. He'd deposited almost seventeen thousand pounds into the company's accounts and over six thousand into his personal account.

Not bad for a day's work.

Chapter 4: Elise, 2018
Five years earlier

Saturday night. Elise Tanner was running late. She knew by the time she got to the Three Bells pub, her friends would already be halfway to being two sheets to the wind, in other words, half drunk. And it was only eight. A long night stretched ahead. She didn't expect to get into bed until the new day was rising. Bring it on!

She opened the pub door and was assaulted by the noise and mayhem. She immediately caught sight of her friend, Sharon, the birthday girl. Pushing through the hordes, she shouted Sharon's name.

'Elise,' screamed Sharon, on seeing her. 'You made it!'

'Of course I bloody made it. I was hardly likely to miss this, was I, you dipstick?'

'Oh my God, El, everyone's here.'

'You're a popular girl, Shaz! You look fucking hot, by the way.'

She removed her coat and scarf. 'Jesus, El, you're not looking too shabby yourself. Love your lippy. And where did you get that steaming dress, girl?'

Elise had opted for a short dark green dress with glittery diagonal stripes and the highest heels she could get away with and still walk – just about. She knew that if William, her boyfriend, saw her in this, he wouldn't be impressed; he'd think it too revealing, the neckline too plunging. 'New Year sales in TopShop.'

'You'll pull in that; you'll have them flocking, babes.'

The music was loud, the alcohol flowing, the atmosphere electric. Sharon and her friends had taken over a large section of the pub, and were, by far, making the most noise. Elise reckoned Sharon had invited every female she'd ever met. Elise didn't know that many of them but that was fine; once she'd had a couple of drinks, she could talk to anyone. There were no boys in their group, this was a strictly girls' night out, just a huge bunch of raucous girls out on the tiles. From the Three Bells, they were heading into town to dance the night away at The Keys, Sharon's favourite nightclub.

Sharon had ordered several bottles of sparkling white wine, and, pouring a large glass, passed one to Elise. 'Bloody brilliant, this place, isn't it? Some fit fellas, Jesus, El. We could do all right here.'

Their friend Amara overheard. 'Hey, I thought tonight was a no-boy zone.' Elise always considered Amara to be one gorgeous Asian babe.

'Yeah, bloody right,' said Sharon. 'No boys, fuck 'em; they're all a waste of space. Girls only tonight.'

'I'll drink to that!' shrieked Amara.

Elise lifted her glass. 'Happy birthday, Shaz.'

Several of Sharon's friends joined in with the toast, shouting her name and wishing her a happy birthday. Elise kissed her and the two women hugged. 'Twenty?' said

Sharon. 'I can't believe it. I'm so bloody old now.'

'Oh, to be twenty,' said Elise.

'Don't be daft. You *are* still twenty.'

'Oh yeah. I thought I was my mother there.' Sharon laughed. 'Sort of thing she says every bloody day. When I was your age, blah, blah, blah.'

'Mums, eh?'

'It's a load of bullshit anyway. By the time she was twenty she was already bloody married.'

'At twenty? That's mad.'

'I know, tell me about it.'

A couple of the girls Elise did know crowded around her, kissing her and admiring her dress. Elise helped herself to another drink. *No Limits*, the old nineties dance hit, came on, and the girls danced and sang along, their arms around each other's waists, punching the air.

Elise was happy; the night was still young but this was proving to be a great night already. She had alcohol, music and her best friends with her; she looked great and was buzzing. What more could she ask for?

An hour later and feeling decidedly tipsy, Elise was returning from the ladies, humming along with *Him & I* by G-Eazy, blaring out across the pub, weaving her way through the masses when she bumped into a tall man. 'Oh, fuck, sorry.'

He turned and she almost staggered back on seeing just how handsome he was: blond, foppish hair, penetrating blue eyes, a heart-melting smile. 'No, my fault,' he said, with what her mother would call a *refined voice*. He was holding a pint, dressed in a sky-blue collared shirt, unbuttoned at the top, revealing a hint of fair-coloured chest hair. 'You in a rush?' he asked.

'Yeah, I'm with my friends,' she said, vaguely pointing in their direction.

'I shouldn't keep you then,' he said. 'Enjoy your evening.'

She made her way back to her friends rather regretting that he hadn't kept her. Why had she said she needed to get back to her friends? It's not as if they would miss her, she didn't even know most of them, and he was damn good looking. She could be such an idiot at times.

'You all right, El?' screeched Sharon, polishing off another glass of wine. 'Where have you been?'

'You did say it's a no-boy zone tonight, didn't you?'

'Bloody right. Unless they're super fit, then we're allowed to make exceptions. Why? Why are you asking?' She looked around the pub, scanning all the men. 'Who have you met?'

'I haven't. No one.'

'You've pulled already, haven't you? Fucking hell, El. You're sex on the legs, you are.'

'I've *not* pulled.'

'How's your William? Still in love?'

'Love? I like him but I don't think it's love.'

'You are right tease, Elise Tanner.'

'I don't want to talk about him. Right now, all I want is a drink. Another one, that is.'

Sharon topped up both their glasses. 'Here, a toast to you and me, best of friends, friends forever.'

The two women laughed, clinking their glasses.

'Oh, El,' said Sharon. 'I've gotta tell you about this shit that happened at work yesterday. Christ, it was mad, I'm telling you…'

Sharon proceeded to tell Elise her story while Elise drank her wine and smiled and nodded in the right places while trying, surreptitiously, to seek out the blond guy. Sharon, her hand on her chest, laughed raucously at her own tale. 'Honestly, El, you should've seen his face; I almost pissed myself…'

And then she saw him not too far away, standing with his pint still in his hand, listening to a friend, as she was. And he looked over and their eyes met, and Elise immediately averted her eyes, her heart beating, taking her by surprise.

Sharon carried on with her story, punctuated by several belly laughs. Drake's *God's Plan* was playing now, the music getting louder. Sharon's friends sang along with the chorus. And suddenly, he was there, standing next to her, that smile of his. 'Where are you going from here?' he asked, straight to the point.

'Where did you come from?' asked Sharon. 'And what's it to you anyway?'

The man totally ignored her, his eyes fixed on Elise, and her stomach flipped within her. 'We-we're going to The Keys.'

'Why not try The Signature?'

'Where?' barked Amara.

'Apparently, the light show needs to be seen to be believed.'

'That sounds good,' said Elise. 'Maybe, we should–'

'No fucking way,' said Sharon, getting a tad aggressive. 'We're going to The Keys. And, anyway, we don't want any boys sniffing around us so–'

He put his hands up. 'OK, I get it. Girls' night out and all that. I wouldn't want to intrude.' With a bow of his head, he backed away, returning to his friends.

'Bloody hell, Shaz, what did you do that for? You said no boys unless they're super fit, and he was super, super fit.'

'He *was* rather dishy,' said Amara.

29

'Listen,' said Sharon. 'Trust your old mate, Shaz. He's too posh for the likes of us.' She jabbed Elise in the chest. 'Never trust the posh boys. All old school and charming on the outside, total twats on the inside. And I should know, I've shagged enough of them.'

'I bow to your experience.'

'That's more like it. Forget him.' Turning to her friends, Sharon shouted, 'We've gotta go. Girls, girls.' She clapped her hands, getting everyone's attention. 'Finish your drinks and get your handbags, ladies, it's time to hit The Keys. Who wants to boogie all night long?'

The girls cheered loudly. The night was only just beginning. Sharon flung her coat over her shoulder, unsteady on her feet. 'Look, El, if you're that much into him, go give him your number.'

'I can't do that,' said Elise, draining her drink.

'No harm.'

'What about William?'

'Don't tell him. I won't if you won't.'

'No, I can't.'

'Suit yourself. Right, girls, are we ready?'

Elise coiled up her scarf and forced it into her coat pocket.

Together, they tottered towards the exit, a mass of young women about to paint the town red. The cold air outside hit them. 'Wow, Christ, it's freezing,' said Sharon.

'It's too bloody cold to walk,' said Amara. 'We should get an Uber, several Ubers.'

'Shit,' said Elise. 'I forgot my scarf. I can't forget that. It's too cold.' She rushed inside and immediately found him, talking to a group of friends. Without hesitating, she went right up to him. If he was surprised by Elise's sudden reappearance, he didn't show it. He stepped away from his friends.

'Get your phone out,' she ordered. He did as told. 'My number is…' He tapped it into his phone as she recited it. 'Got it?'

'Got it.'

'Give me a ring soon.'

He smiled that smile. One of his friends joined him, a thin man with dark hair and large glasses. 'So, who's this then?' the man asked.

'I'm sorry, I don't know your name.'

'Elise.'

'Elise. What a lovely name. This is my friend, Anthony. Anthony Browning.'

'How do you do, Elise?' said Anthony Browning, offering his hand. Elise didn't take to this man, something slightly creepy about him, and hoped he'd go away.

The blond man bowed his head and also shook her hand, 'Elise, nice to meet you.'

'I'd better go; my friends will be waiting for me.' She made to leave before stopping and turning to face him again. 'Sorry, you didn't tell me your name.'

'Me? I'm Dominic. Dominic Woods.'

Chapter 5: Benedict

Monday mid-morning, DI Paige and DS Gardiner decided to pay a visit to the staff looking after the naked man at St Cuthbert's Hospital. DCs Kelly and Prowse now seemed more confident in their work now that they knew how to pick up a cardboard box, even a heavy one.

Today, finally, it'd stopped raining but boy, it was cold, a nasty wind bringing the temperature down even further. The sun had made a feeble attempt to show before giving in.

Their first port of call on arriving at the hospital was the Fraser Booth ward that specialised in kidney and transplant care to see whether Maxine Hunt had returned to work. According to the ward sister, she had, returning to work that same morning.

Maxine saw them and immediately looked worried in a '*what now*' sort of way. Benedict and Jessica both smiled in a way they hoped would calm her but only managed to make her appear even more concerned. 'Don't worry, Maxine,' said Jessica. 'This is purely a social call. We wanted to see how you are.'

She let out a sigh of relief and smiled in return. 'I'm very well, thank you.'

Benedict hung back a little. Maxine had formed a bond with Jessica, not him. He heard Jessica whisper, 'You gave us quite a scare the other night, Maxine.'

Maxine shook her head. 'I've never been so frightened in my life.'

'It must've been terrifying for you.'

Maxine opened her mouth to speak but the words wouldn't come. Instead, the tears came. 'I'm s-sorry.'

'No, you don't. You listen here, Maxine Hunt; *you* don't have a thing to apologise about. You know that, don't you?'

She nodded; her cheeks wet.

'Come here.'

Benedict watched, his heart warming on seeing the two women embrace.

Another nurse appeared, the one Benedict remembered from before – Nigella.

'We're looking after her,' said Nigella. 'Aren't we, lovey?'

'Yes.'

'At least our so-called White Mouse Killer is off our streets now,' said Benedict. 'Isn't it a little too soon to return to work?' he asked, fearing it came across more harshly than he'd intended.

Maxine heard. 'No, I wanted to come back. I was getting bored at home, and everyone's been so... so...' She couldn't finish the sentence.

'Normality's good,' said Jessica.

'Yeah, that's right.'

'Look at my nails,' said Nigella, holding up her hands and showing off her bright purple nails adorned with little, finely painted rainbows.

'Wow,' said Jessica with a wink. 'Those must've cost you a fortune, Nigella.'

'By rights, yes, but I have a friend, you see,' she said, returning the wink.

'A very talented one, by the looks of it.'

Maxine blushed.

'How's your grandmother?' asked Jessica.

'She's very well, thank you. I saw her this morning.'

'Well, you make sure you send her our… our love.'

'I will. Thank you.'

From the Fraser Booth ward, Benedict and Jessica were directed two floors up to the Mary Keats in-patient's ward. There, they introduced themselves to Ward Sister O'Reilly, and asked how their patient was getting on. 'Physically, not too bad, as it happens, inspector,' she said in a gentle Dublin accent. She led them to the man's bed and drew the curtain around them in a fast, efficient manner.

'It won't surprise you that he suffered from severe hypothermia. The good news, he's passed the worst. But, not so good, his speech and memory are still impaired and he's still very drowsy, all classic symptoms of hypothermia and could remain so for a while yet. Don't ask me how long. But he's young, he's fit and strong, I don't envisage any long-term effects on his physical well-being.'

'We know he suffered a beating, sister,' asked Benedict. 'But any signs of a sexual assault?'

She shook her head vehemently. 'No, nothing like that, thank the Lord.'

'That's good. And what about the beating, how severe?'

'Well, no beating is pleasant, naturally, but, given the circumstances, I'd say he got off lightly. Nothing broken, just bruising. Nothing that will scar.'

'And mentally, how will he–'

'Ah now that, inspector, I cannot speculate on that because we don't know what exactly happened out there, do we? And we don't know how his subconscious will react to it. He might appear calm and normal within a day or two but it could easily manifest itself further down the line, as in weeks, months, even years ahead. Impossible to say, I'm afraid.'

The three of them stood and considered the unidentified man in the bed. He did look better, thought Benedict. The colour had returned to his face although that black eye still looked nasty. They were feeding him through a saline drip, and various other tubes and gadgets were monitoring him.

'Any idea who he is?' asked the sister.

'Not yet,' said Jessica, who summarised their efforts to find someone who might recognise his eagle tattoo. 'Need be, we'll take a dental plant and go that route. But that can take time. We're hoping we won't have to. Either someone will come forward or he'll wake up, and then he can just tell us himself.'

'Ah, don't be so sure. He might not remember or it could take a day or two for his memory to kick-in.'

'That bad?' said Benedict.

'Oh yes, inspector. This boy was this close to death,' she said, emphasising a small space between her finger and thumb. 'But don't you worry, we'll look after him, you can be sure of that.'

'And you'll let us know if–'

'Of course. You'll be the first to know, you have my word on that.'

They thanked the sister and made to leave. They'd only reached the swing doors at the end of the ward, when a woman came barging in, a frenzied look about her. 'Wow,' said Jessica. 'After you, lady.'

'Hang on a minute, Jessica,' said Benedict, gently pulling her to one side.

The woman, black with long black, curly hair, streaks dyed blonde, approached Sister O'Reilly. With much gesticulating, the woman explained herself. O'Reilly shot Benedict a look over the woman's shoulder. 'I think this could be it,' said Benedict. The woman rushed over to the mute man's bed, almost falling onto him, sobbing.

Sister O'Reilly beckoned the detectives back in. 'We have our identification,' she whispered.

'Good timing,' said Jessica.

'Why don't you wait in the office? I'll bring her through when she's ready. Could be a while though. Can you wait?'

'We have nothing else to do at the moment,' said Benedict.

For a moment, the sister almost believed him.

They accepted her offer of coffee, which she promptly delegated to a junior colleague.

Jessica began scrolling through her phone while Benedict picked up a copy of the free newspaper, the *Metro*, and turning it around, went straight for the sports' pages at the back. 'I see Arsenal lost yesterday.'

'I didn't know you followed the football, boss.'

'I don't in all honesty, but I have a football-mad son so he keeps me informed and I show an interest. You?'

'I don't have a son.'

'No.'

'My partner takes an interest. But she's a Spurs fan.'

'Right.' He kept his eyes focussed on the article, trying his darndest not to let his eyes betray his surprise – that his new assistant was gay. It never crossed his mind before. Not that it mattered, not in the slightest, it just took him a little by surprise – that's all. He glanced up at her and she winked at him before returning her attention to her phone.

Fifteen minutes passed, by which time they'd drunk their coffees, before Sister O'Reilly returned to the office, this time followed by the distraught woman, now looking somewhat less distraught.

'And these are the nice police officers I was telling you about.' Benedict and Jessica stood while the sister introduced them. 'And this is Mrs Hamilton.'

'Miss,' she corrected.

'Miss Hamilton. Now, I'll let you get acquainted. Call me if you need anything.'

They all thanked her. 'Miss Hamilton, please take a seat,' said Benedict. 'I can't imagine how you must be feeling right now.'

'Christ, yes. Relief and bloody anger, I'm telling you.' She'd been crying and still looked close to tears. Jessica passed her a tissue from a box on the office desk.

'I can imagine,' said Benedict. 'Is it alright if we ask you some questions? We promise not to keep you long.'

She sighed. 'Yeah, sure. Hit me.'

'What is your... partner's name?'

She told them... William Grant, or Will, aged twenty-seven, lived locally, a self-employed carpenter, stepfather to her three-year-old daughter, but recently separated and living apart. 'See, that's why I didn't call the police. Cos he's renting on his own, like. Got some horrible little bedsit near the high street. I didn't even know he was missing, you see?'

'Yes, I see. So, how did you find out?'

She shrugged. 'He said he'd take Daisy out today. We're taking turns this week, see, as it's half term and all that. So when he hadn't shown up by half ten, I rang him to ask him where in the hell he was, but his phone was off. Still is, in fact. I tried loads of times. And then a friend of mine shared your Facebook post about the tattoo and that's when I knew, and I came straight here.'

'It must've come as a shock,' said Jessica.

'What do you think? The man's a tosser but he's still stepdad to the kid, and I wouldn't wish this on him, even if at times I've almost taken a swing at the stupid bugger myself.' She smiled and her affection for 'the tosser' was still plain to see.

'Did Sister O'Reilly tell you what happened?'

'Yeah, but I didn't take it in.'

So, Benedict explained how William Grant had been found at eight fifteen that morning, tied to a tree in Greenfield Woods, gagged and naked. And, as she could see for herself, he'd been a victim of a beating but not, according to the sister, a severe one.

'You see, this puzzles me, Ms Hamilton–'

'Call me Kate.'

'Kate. Your partner was tied up to the tree and left naked. He was one hundred per cent at the mercy of his attacker or attackers; they had the opportunity to have beaten him to an inch of his life; they could easily have broken every bone in his body. But they didn't. Why?'

She shrugged again. 'Search me.'

'It was more a rhetorical question. So, either he, she, they were disturbed and they ran. If that was the case, then we need to find the person or persons who disturbed them. But is that likely? After all, they didn't leave behind a single item of Mr Grant's clothing, not even an errant sock, let alone his mobile or bank card or wallet. Or, and I think this is the more likely scenario, they only intended to frighten him.'

'Why would they do that?'

'I was rather hoping you might tell us, Kate.'

'I don't bloody know, do I?' She glanced at her watch. 'Look, is this going to take much longer? It's just that I've got me neighbour looking after Daisy and she's got to go out to work in thirty. I've got to get to work myself so I don't know what I'm going to do. If I don't work, I don't get paid. Zero hours contract, see?'

'Not much longer now, Kate. We're almost done here.'

'Did your husband, I mean, partner have any enemies, Kate?' asked Jessica. 'Did he owe people money, did he gamble, perhaps?'

'Will, gamble? Nah, not Will. He liked to keep hold of his money; that was always one of the problems. Tighter than a gnat's arse, that man.'

Benedict tried not to laugh at the woman's expression. 'Next scenario is a bit more delicate, Ms Hamilton, Kate; now that you and Mr Grant are separated, might he have fallen out with a woman, perhaps upset another woman's man? Sorry to have to ask.'

She laughed. 'Will's not a ladies' man. I mean, look at him; he's not that much of a catch, is he?'

'I'm sure he is, really,' said Jessica. 'We're just not seeing him in his best light at this moment.'

'Well, you can have any moment you want, and he's still no looker.' She paused and looked at the two of them. 'Oh, I know what you're thinking; I fell for him. Well, yeah, I did, as it happens. Because, you see, he's got more faults than San Andreas but, at the end of the day, he's got a good heart. And that's a rare thing in this day and age. Looks come and go and most fellas I've been with are just in it for themselves. But not...' Her hand rushed to her mouth, and she looked sideways. With the tears pooling in her eyes, she whispered, 'I can't believe I'm about to say this but I don't want him to go back to that horrible damp flat. When he's better, I'm taking him home with me; he belongs with us again now, me and Daisy. She needs her father, and me…'

'You'd like him back too?'

She nodded. 'Yeah. I do. It's taken him to almost die naked and tied to a sodding tree, but yeah, I want him back now.'

'Why would anyone do this to him, Kate?'

'I have no clue. Honest to God, I don't know, but please, find the bastard who did this, please, just… just find him.'

Chapter 6: Elise

Returning to work on Monday morning felt like a cold return to reality after the weekend Elise had had. She was still on cloud nine following her engagement party and hadn't yet got used to the ring on her finger. But still – the day had something to look forward to: come lunchtime, she and Phil were meeting their new landlord at the flat to pay him the deposit. It wasn't cheap, but that was London for you. It'd been such a struggle to find a semi decent flat, especially in this part of town. As soon as a new property went up on the market, the estate agent or the landlord / lady was inundated with phone calls. And Elise knew – she'd made that same phone call a hundred times or more. 'Hello, I'm phoning about your flat for rent–' 'Sorry, love, it's gone.' 'But you only put it up an hour ago.' 'What can I say? It's gone.' She'd been dead lucky to secure this place. They had to pay a hefty deposit and the first six weeks' rent in advance, costing them almost three thousand pounds between them, but that was standard now. What hope did they ever have of laying a deposit on a flat to buy when they were paying so much in rent; it'd be impossible.

Elise worked as a hairdresser, Phil as an assistant manager in a supermarket, neither were paid well. Financially, it made more sense to continue living at home and saving the money. But she and Phil were engaged now, she was twenty-five, Phil a year older. It was time to fly the nest. Her parents would miss her as she would miss them. Dad had only been out of prison a short while and liked having his only daughter close to hand, and her mother, Elise knew, would also miss her terribly. They'd grown so dependent on each other while Dad was away.

Elise's colleagues welcomed her with open arms, asking her about the party and admiring her ring. Her closest friends at work had been there, of course. But for the benefit of the others, she told them all the wondrous details and thanked everyone for their generous present. And that's when her heart dipped slightly. Whenever she thought of all the presents, she thought of that hideous painting, 'Country Dawn'. Phil loved it; said he couldn't wait to hang it in the new flat in pride of place. He said it reminded him of childhood holidays with his parents and sister, the English countryside at its best, bathed in sunlight, the gentle atmosphere, the days that stretched forever, always with the promise of an ice cream towards the end of it.

'It's a bit big, don't you think?' she asked. 'It'll dominate whatever room we put it in.'

'So what? It's beautiful. You know, I thought it might have been from Auntie Precious but she gave us that vase, didn't she?'

'She did. And she would've put her name on the tag.'

'But that's the thing, everyone would put their name. Maybe they just forgot. I mean, it must've cost a fortune. I'd want the credit if I bought someone something that expensive. Are you sure you don't have a mysterious benefactor somewhere, El?'

'If only.'

She'd wanted to ask her mother about it, whether she too had noticed the butterflies. Several times yesterday, she was on the verge of asking, but she couldn't bring herself to go there. The painting had brought *him* crashing back into her thoughts again, and she didn't want to subject her mother to the same dark thoughts. Her mother was the sort of woman who wore her heart on her sleeve. If she gave headroom to that man, it would have spoiled the day and her dad would have known. He'd asked and pestered until she gave in and told him and then the whole day would come crashing down around them. So, she hadn't mentioned it, but the thought never strayed too far away from her thoughts. At one point, she put the painting back behind the settee, saying it was in the way but her dad told her not to be so silly, and fetched it back out, leaving it leaning against the sideboard where no one could avoid it. Indeed, it was commented on several times during the day, far more than any other present.

Her mother had shown no sign of concern. She must've noticed the three butterflies, it was hard not to, but they'd obviously not registered the way they had with Elise.

She kept telling herself it was just a coincidence. Any painting of the English countryside during the summer might well feature butterflies, it didn't necessarily *mean* anything. But the doubt remained, firmly implanted in her brain.

Elise threw herself into work – cutting hair, dying, styling, reshaping, rejuvenating. She enjoyed her work, enjoyed the company of her colleagues and the banter they maintained all day. Unlike Phil, who found his job tedious, Elise enjoyed her work; it was *fun*.

Lunchtime came soon enough. She'd asked her boss for an extra half an hour off to have time to get to the flat and back. Her boss was fine with it.

As she left the salon, her mobile rang. She assumed it was going to be Phil, just checking she hadn't forgotten. But it wasn't Phil. It was an unknown number. Normally, she'd ignore unknown numbers but what if it was the new landlord? She'd better answer it. She was just passing a fruit and veg store, its displays spilling onto the pavement, lots of elderly women considering the brightly coloured displays when she heard his voice.

'Did you like the painting, Else?'

It took her a moment to register. 'I'm sorry? What painting? Who is this?'

'It's Dominic, of course.'

'Fuck,' she screamed, stopping in her tracks and earning several disproving looks from the elderly shoppers.

'I thought you might like it, Else. It's a beautiful piece of work, isn't it?'

'Why in the fuck are phoning me, Dominic?' She needed to end the call but, as if transfixed, found she couldn't.

'Else, Elise, don't sound so angry. You weren't always so angry with me; remember that. I heard you got engaged and I'm happy for you.'

'Like hell you are. How did you find out anyway?'

'Oh, come on, Else, think about it. It's all over your Facebook account: *Phil this, Phil that, what a lucky girl I am; I'm so in love. We're getting married in April; I'm going to be a spring bride.* Well, I just wanted to let you know, I couldn't be happier for you, Else. Can I expect an invite anytime soon?'

'An invite? You? I'd rather invite Vladimir Putin.'

He laughed at that. 'Oh, Else, you've not lost your sense of humour, I see. I used to love your humour. Listen, how about we meet up—'

'You've got to be out of your mind. I'd rather eat my own eyeballs.'

'Oh, come on, Else, we go back a long way, you and me. One drink – for old times' sake. Let's not be strangers any more. I'd love to hear all your news and I'd be fascinated in learning all about the wonderful Philip Edwards.'

The way he said his full name made her skin crawl. How did he know that? Had she put it on Facebook? She didn't think so.

'I've got to go. Please, never phone me again.'

'OK, hands up, I admit defeat. Still, I hope you like the painting and think of me whenever you see it. I bought it with you in mind, Else. And listen, you've got my number now, so if you ever change your mind, don't hesitate to ring me.'

'I'll tell you now, Dominic, that will never happen. Hell will freeze over first. Now—'

'Before you meet Phil at the flat, ask him about Tracey at work. Good luck with the flat. Bye now.'

'Wait, how did you—'

But he'd gone.

A number of the elderly women were still watching her, bemused, perhaps, by this sudden piece of soap opera playing out in front of them. She cursed and, slipping her phone back into her coat pocket, strode on, a fury burning her up from the inside.

So many questions crashed into her mind at once – how did Dominic know Phil's full name, and how in the hell did he know they were meeting at the flat? The bastard was spying on her; how else could she explain it? And, most importantly, who in the fuck was Tracey?

She was only five minutes late meeting Phil at the flat. He was already talking to the landlord, Mr Sheth, a Hindi man with a Bindi on his forehead, a pleasant enough gentleman. He welcomed her warmly and proceeded to tell the couple all the flat rules, of which there seemed to be several – no pets, no smoking, no vaping, no parties, no friends staying overnight without his prior consent, no redecorating, unless he sanctioned it, no subletting, no music after eleven p.m., no bleach down the toilet, etc, etc. But Elise found it difficult to concentrate, side-eyeing Phil, wondering if he was having an affair already. He was certainly good-looking and smooth talking, and she knew he'd be considered quite the catch, heck, she'd been there, indeed, she was still there. He was kind, gentle-natured and a good listener and such an empathic person; what sane woman wouldn't find him attractive? But none of that mattered; he was engaged to her now, her, no other woman, especially some star-struck insubordinate at work called Tracey. He caught her looking at him a few times and flashed a smile, each one a little less certain than the preceding one.

Then came the financial bit – the deposit and the rent in advance as agreed during their first visit, the day before the party. Phil paid his half via his banking app on his phone, and Elise paid hers. Next, Phil and Elise together with Mr Sheth signed the tenancy agreement. The deal was done; they shook hands. They could move in anytime they wanted, as long as they were in by nine at night. Mustn't disturb the neighbours. Mr Sheth handed them a set of flat keys each and hoped they'd be very happy in the flat. They thanked him and left.

Back outside on the street in front of the house, Phil leaned down to kiss her but she subtly edged away so he ended up kissing air. 'You alright?' he asked.

'Yeah. Why shouldn't I be?'

She started walking away.

'Hey,' called Phil. 'Hang on a minute, Elise. What's the matter with you?' He caught her up.

'Nothing,' she snapped. 'I need to get back to work. I'm late already,' she lied. Having got the extra half an hour off, she still had plenty of time. 'I'll see you later.'

She left Phil on the pavement looking puzzled. Having just paid for the flat, he probably expected a bit of a celebration, a cheer, a punch of the air, anything but a sulky fiancée storming off.

But she couldn't face talking to him, couldn't even look at him. She wanted to ask him there and then, get it over and done with, but she decided she needed time to process this, time to formulate a plan of action, because if it was true, if there was the slightest hint Phil was already playing away, there'd be hell to pay.

She couldn't believe she'd found out through Dominic, bloody Dominic. That man had been like a poison in her life. And now he was back, and within two minutes, he'd gone and spread his poison again.

Chapter 7: Dominic

Dominic had felt uneasy all day. Why, he kept wondering, did Anthony Browning want to meet him for a drink after work? He didn't like going into meetings unprepared. It made him uneasy, put him at a disadvantage. He liked to control things, to dominate meetings. Dominic Woods was not a passive sort of guy.

He looked up Anthony Browning's address on the company employees' database, then entered it onto his phone's Google Maps app. He then worked out how far it was from the Davenport pub to his home. A fifteen-minute walk if one took the short cut along Regents Canal. Well, that was something. He wasn't sure why but he felt better simply by being armed with this sort of information.

It was six fifteen, the end of another successful day. Time to wind over to the pub, see what Browning had to say for himself; what was it that was so darn important.

Despite being early, the Davenport was busy. It was a popular watering home for the local workers on their way home. Some old eighties tune by Frankie Goes to Hollywood played on the speakers, a poster advertised Tuesday's quiz night. Dominic found Browning at the bar. 'What can I get you, Dom?' he asked.

'A tomato juice, thanks.'

Browning looked surprised but Dominic had the feeling he'd need to stay sharp here; he couldn't allow his instinct to be dulled by alcohol. 'And a packet of cheese and onion,' he added, for good measure. 'I'll nab those stools.'

He settled at a high table with two stools, and checked his phone while Browning bought the round.

'Here we are, mate. One tomato juice and a packet of crisps. Busy in here, isn't it? I haven't stepped inside here for years.' He looked around. 'Nice pub though. It's got a good vibe, you know?'

'So, what is it that's so important we couldn't meet at work?' asked Dominic, going straight to the chase; he had absolutely no desire to make small talk here. He and Browning weren't friends; he couldn't give a shit about the man's wife or what he got up to at the weekend.

'Cheers,' said Browning. Holding up his glass.

Dominic clinked glasses. 'Cheers.'

'How was work today?'

'Alright, as it happens. Secured a couple new accounts, made sure others ran the distance, you know the score.'

'So, the thing is, Dom, I've been sort of spying on you.'

'Why? Did O'Brian ask you to?'

'No, he doesn't know anything about this. This is all off my own bat.'

'So why then? What business is it of yours what I do?'

'Oh, but I think it is when I believe you're running your own little Ponzi scheme.'

'Bollocks.' But, despite his bravado, Browning had it spot

49

on, the bastard. He needed to tread carefully here.

'So, using company time and on company premises, and using company contacts, you're building quite the empire of your own, Dominic.'

'And I say again, you're speaking bollocks.'

'Hear me out.' He wiped a line of froth from his moustache. 'You get your customers to invest in crypto fairly well guaranteeing them a good return on their investment without ever actually using the word guaranteed – because you know that'd be a red flag. And indeed, these initial investors do get their return, at whatever level *you* decide to pay out, nothing to do with the market because their money was never in the market to begin with. You pay them their return on the money your second set of investors put in. You pay the second set with the money the third set gave you, and so on and so on.'

Dominic sipped his drink, playing for time. He knew he didn't stand a chance here; if push came to shove, Browning could easily prove it. He'd put in place various security measures, covered his tracks with a smoke screen but O'Brian had the authority to make him open everything up, and then it'd be game over.

'It's game over,' said Browning, as if reading his thoughts. 'Admit it, Dom, I've rumbled you.'

'But everyone's happy. Everyone who's invested with me has had a healthy return. So where's the harm?'

'Where's the harm?' He removed his glasses and polished them. 'Because, my friend, by definition, your contacts, your new customers, will, at some point, dry up. And those at the end of the line will get sod all. Plus, the small inconvenient fact that you're lying to all your account holders and the fact that it's illegal. Or does the law not count in the world of

Dominic Woods?'

'OK, so what do you plan to do?'

He took a couple large gulps of his beer, keeping Dominic on tenterhooks. Nearby, a group of drinkers were singing *Happy Birthday*. 'Nothing.'

'Nothing?'

'I want forty-nine per cent.'

'F-forty… You're fucking joking.'

'I'll work for it, Dom. I'll find you new customers. I've got my own contacts list, you know that, as long as your arm.'

'You? Your contacts are nothing but retirees with five shillings to spare. My ten-year-old niece could sell better than you. Selling isn't your forte, remember? You don't have the gift for it.'

'It can't be that difficult. I've done some selling in the past.'

'Yeah, but it didn't last long, did it? O'Brian soon realised the error of his ways. Took you off fairly sharpish, if memory serves.'

Browning finished his drink, slamming his glass down on the table. 'You don't understand, Dominic. I'm not negotiating with you here; I'm making my demands. You don't have room to manoeuvre, you either agree to my terms, or tomorrow morning, O'Brian will be in receipt of a memo that will blow his mind, and blow career out of the water, mate. And you know what comes next – the police. They take a dim view of Ponzi schemes, and so do the courts. You don't have a leg to stand on, mate.' He pushed his glasses back up his nose. 'I'm going for a piss,' he said, sliding off his stool. 'I expect your answer by the time I get back.'

Dominic watched him weave his way through the crowds. He opened his pack of cheese and onion. He'd always known he was running a big risk, and that his empire, as Browning called it, was built on sand. But he'd closed his eyes to it, too buoyed by his success to worry about the implications. He'd secured six thousand pounds today, but that counted as a good day. Even on a bad day, he could count on a couple of grand. His average, therefore, was about three to four thousand a day. That was up to one hundred and twenty thousand a month, tax-free, that equated to almost one and a half million a year. That was on top of his routine salary and that was big enough. His plan was to do this for five years, then buy a property somewhere far away from London, Thailand perhaps.

Could Anthony Browning add to his business? No, he'd be a liability. Not only could he not sell, but potential customers would also smell a rat a mile off. He'd ruin everything. With Browning at his side, he'd be in jail within six months. No way he could allow this to happen; far too risky.

Browning returned from the toilets, a satisfied smirk on his face. 'Well, what's it to be?'

'OK,' said Dominic, finishing his crisps. 'Have it your way.'

Browning grinned. 'Excellent. Excellent. I knew you'd see sense.' He offered his hand. Did the twat expect him to shake on it? If it made him happy. He shook the man's clammy hand.

'But look, I'm going out tonight so I can't stop now.' He made a point of checking his phone. 'Stop by my office tomorrow morning while O'Brian's at his shareholders' meeting, and we'll discuss the practicalities.'

'Sure.'

Both of them stood and put their coats on.

'You're off home now?' asked Dominic.

'Yep. I'm watching that new Scandinavian drama on Amazon prime.'

'See you tomorrow then.'

'Will do, Dom. I look forward to it.' He was grinning like the fucking Cheshire cat now, the smug bastard. Dominic stormed off without another word. He turned left out of the pub, purposely bumping into a woman in a jaunty, pointed hat and dangly earrings. 'Sorry, love, my fault,' he said, bowing. She was with a man.

'No worries.'

He took the path leading south, to the left. But instead of walking on, he slipped behind the wall of the pub, and waited. Less than a minute later, Browning appeared at the pub door. He paused, lit a cigarette and, looking up at the night sky, blew out a plume of smoke. Then, turning right, he walked away, a cloud of smoke in his wake.

Thanks to his bit of research earlier on Google Maps, Dominic knew exactly where Browning was going, and he knew exactly where and how he was going to kill him.

Chapter 8: Elise, 2018
Five years earlier

Elise opened her eyes and swore. Her head was pounding, it was as if someone had buried an axe in it, the pain was intense. Her bedside digital alarm clock told her it was almost one in the afternoon. She groaned and tried to go back to sleep but without success.

Last night had been just the most brilliant night ever; she hadn't had such fun in ages. But it was the man she met in the Three Bells that dominated her thoughts. They'd only spoken briefly but she couldn't rid her mind of him. She was impressed by her own brazen behaviour, the way she marched up to him and demanded he take her number. She must've been drunk; there's no way she could have done that while sober. What was his name? Her fuddled brain took a while to remember. Dominic – that was it. Dominic Woods. The question now was – would he phone her? She certainly hoped so but, on a more practical level, she rather hoped he didn't. She had a boyfriend, after all. Having another man ring her could be… well, problematic. It was in his hands now. He'd phone her if he wanted to. And if he didn't… a pity but so be it.

Managing to avoid her parents, Elise crept to the bathroom and there found a packet of paracetamol. She took two, washed down by three glasses of water. She returned to bed and lay there, too much in pain to even look at her phone. She managed to doze off again.

She was awoken a while later by the sound of the doorbell downstairs. She heard her mother welcome William in. What was William doing here? That meant she'd have to go and see him, and frankly she had no desire to see or speak to anyone. It was almost two now, and her head did feel a little better.

There was a gentle knock on the door. Her mother stepped in, treading carefully over the carpet, bringing her a welcome mug of tea. 'A cup of tea for you, my love. How are you feeling?'

'Not too great. Thanks.'

'Oh dear. You really shouldn't drink so much. Staying out so late is not–'

'Mum, please, not now, eh? Save it for later, preferably never.' She drank her tea, feeling it doing her good.

'I'm just concerned for you, my love. Anyway, Dad's doing you breakfast.' She pointedly looked at her watch. 'If you can call it breakfast at this time. It'll be ready in a few minutes. And William's here. Shall I send him up?'

'No! God no. I must look a state. I'll come down.'

'If you're sure? Is there anything I can get you?'

'No, I'm fine. Tell William I'll be down in a minute.'

Her mother crept out. She could smell Dad's fry-up drifting up the stairs and, realising how starving she was, that was enough to get her out of bed. She flung on a pair of jogging pants and a sweatshirt emblazoned with an Adidas logo, and dragged a comb through her hair and then tied it up on top of her head with a hair band. She couldn't be bothered with make-up. William would have to take her as he saw her. She finished her tea and then brushed her teeth, not wanting to knock her boyfriend out with her morning, alcohol-infused breath.

Finally, she checked her phone. And there were dozens of messages and notifications, mainly on the WhatsApp group Sharon had set up specifically for their night out last night. But no texts or messages from Dominic Woods. She sighed, feeling more disappointed than she'd anticipated. Instead, there was a WhatsApp message from William, sent at two in the morning. 'Where in the fuck are you?' 'Twat,' she said aloud. Returning to Sharon's group, she skim read the many messages. They all said much the same – that it'd been a cracking night out, hadn't danced so much in years, hadn't drunk so much in years, how late everyone got in, how delicate they were feeling now, but it'd been worth it, so worth it, just a brilliant, fun night. Happy birthday, Shaz!

Elise knew as soon as she walked into the living room that William wasn't happy. He sat there, in the armchair, his arms folded high on his chest, and said, 'Morning,' in a pointed tone.

She wanted to say, Don't start, but instead just yelled through to her father in the kitchen to ask if breakfast was ready.

Her father came through with a mug of hot coffee and a plate piled high in all the essential components needed to make the perfect English breakfast. 'Oh, Dad, perfect. Thank you so much.'

'A pleasure, my love.'

'What brings you over, William?'

'Oh, you know, just wanted to ch… see how you were and all.'

He was about to say *check*, as in he was bloody checking up on her. 'Well, as you can see, I'm still standing – just about.'

'How was your evening, love?' asked Dad. 'Did you go anywhere nice?'

She glanced at William. 'Yes, tell us, Elise,' he said. 'How exactly was your evening?'

She hated him for talking like that so she decided to hit him with it; she was not going to tone it down, why should she? What right did he have to make her feel bad about a night out with her best friend? She made them wait while she tucked into her breakfast, relishing every mouthful. 'Actually, as you ask, it was a bloody brilliant night out.' She turned to her father. 'We went to the Three Bells and then to The Keys, you know, that nightclub on Camden High Street?' Then, turning back to William, she added, 'And there we danced the night away and got pissed as skunks.'

'Oh. Right.' William was quietly outraged, just as she'd predicted. So be it.

'Oh God, yeah. Talk about, *mothers, lock your sons up, the girls are on the town.* Ha! We had such a laugh. Sharon's such a hoot!'

'That's nice,' said her father in a gentle tone.

'Yeah, very nice,' said William in a markedly disgruntled tone. 'Feeling a bit rough now, I bet.'

'Yeah, I am in all honesty, but it'll pass and it was definitely worth the hangover, so…' She finished her breakfast and thanked her father again.

Later, William and Elise sat on the settee and watched some old film on TV that neither of them was interested in. Occasionally, Mum or Dad or both would pop their heads in, asking if either of them was in need of anything. Elise's phone pinged numerous times. 'Who's that?' William asked the first couple of times, sounding slightly put-out, and trying to read her phone over her shoulder. Failing, he returned his attention to the television.

'No one you know. Just someone on Sharon's WhatsApp group talking about last night.' She'd read the message and chortled loudly to herself. Elise wrote something back, adding to the conversation, laughing to herself as she typed. By the time she'd received her fourth or fifth message, William stopped asking or trying to see.

Then, the sixth message – a text from an unknown number. '*Nice meeting u last night. Fancy meeting up? 3 bells at 6 tmr?*' She had to stop herself from shouting out in joy or clenching her fist and punching the air. Sitting right next to William, she texted straight back: *Love to.*

Chapter 9: Benedict

Benedict entered the office and was greeted by DCs Kelly and Prowse. 'You all right, boys?' asked Benedict. 'Been carrying any heavy boxes around?'

'You can laugh, boss,' said Prowse. 'But it's very important that you get the right posture when lifting so that the weight is evenly–'

'Yes, yes, all right, DC Prowse.'

Benedict said a cheery hello to DS Gardiner who merely raised a hand in response. He logged onto his computer.

'Hey, Jamie,' said DC Prowse, 'why don't you speak with more of a Scottish accent?'

'Me? That's a bit random. I don't bloody know.'

'You do believe in Scottish independence?'

'Aye, I do, as it happens.'

'So what are you doing down here in England then? You're a long way from Scotland.'

'Well, I wanted to see for myself just how stupid the English are, and based on talking to you, mate, I reckon they're pretty stupid.'

'Did you hear that, DS Gardiner? That's racist that is. I have a good mind to report him.'

'Good idea, DC Prowse. You do that.'

DC Kelly laughed. 'You watch cricket. That just proves my point. What sort of game is that? We don't have cricket in Scotland.'

'I thought you had a team up there.'

'We do but no one pays them any attention.'

'Not many people pay attention to the English either, to be fair.'

'I rather enjoy watching the cricket,' said Benedict.

'There's a surprise,' said Jessica quietly.

'What did you say, DS Gardiner?'

'Nothing, boss.'

'Right, listen up, team,' said Benedict. 'Our visit to the hospital proved a good use of time.' He updated his team on the fact that the 'naked man' was now making a full recovery and that thanks to the posters, they now knew who he was, where he lived and more. 'But we've not spoken to William Grant. He's not well enough yet. But once he is, we'll know who left him for dead in the middle of a woodland. Oh, and also, Maxine Hunt sends everyone her love.'

This was met by a murmur of approval.

'Any news from here? Yes, DC Kelly?'

'Yes, boss. The council gave us the CCTV from that car park near where our man was found.'

'William Grant.'

'Yes, him. I've sent you and DS Gardiner a link. You'll see there's a fifteen-year-old white Ford transit van parked there for twenty-three minutes from five minutes past midnight. The problem is that because of the angle, the van obscures our view of who gets out. There are two of them but you can't use it to identify everyone. It's shit quality.'

'And how many return to the van twenty-three minutes later?' asked Jessica.

'That's it – just the one. Bulky coat so could be a man or a woman. But whoever it is, they're carrying one of those strong IKEA-like bags. Presumably containing the other bloke's clothes because *they* don't need to know about manual handling to lift it. It looks light as anything.'

'Please tell me the CCTV picks up the van's number plate, at least.'

'It does, boss, and we ran it through and... it's a stolen vehicle.'

'Oh right. Should have seen that one coming, I guess. Have you spoken to the owner?'

'I did, boss,' said DC Prowse. 'Spoke to her over the phone. She's very happy to have her old van back.'

'Well, that *is* nice to know, DC Prowse. Most reassuring but perhaps...'

'I was coming to it, sir. There's mud in the footwells, but on account she's a gardener and that there are normally two of them, that's nothing unusual. Everything is as it seems. Nothing was taken because apart from refuse sacks and stuff of no value, she empties it at night.'

'If she's using it for work, I'm surprised it's not better secured.'

'Like I said, it's old. She's planning on replacing it.'

'How far away was it when it was re-discovered?' asked Jessica.

'Just a couple of streets, ma'am.'

'Any CCTV of the van on the move?' asked Benedict.

PC Stevens put his hand up. 'Yes, sir, I've been checking. The earliest I can trace it is to Walford Street, three streets from where the owner lives. And from what I can tell, giving the distance, the timings, et cetera, it went straight from Walford Street to the park.'

'Any hint of what the driver looks like?'

'No, sir. There is one but he's wearing a baseball cap with the peak pulled down.'

DC Kelly put his hand up. 'The other thing while you were out, boss, is that Diana Pettigrew came down to see you.'

'Ah, I was about to go visit forensics–'

'She said not to bother, that I can tell you the headlines. The mud in the footwells Andrew mentioned is of no use to us. Too mixed up with the mud that was in there already. But she did say something of interest. There were several traces of William Grant's blood in the van. But we don't know whether he was beaten up in the van or prior.'

'This was no spontaneous act of violence. This was a carefully planned, one-man operation. The question is why? Was William Grant a random victim? No, it doesn't appear so. He was specifically targeted. Why? What had William Grant done, or not done, to warrant such a harsh punishment that almost killed him?'

Benedict thanked everyone for their time and went to make himself and Jessica a cup of tea. It'd been a constructive morning. Now, he looked forward to returning to St Cuthbert's and asking Mr Grant the questions that needed answering, and then he'd be able to put this particular case to bed.

Twenty minutes later, DCI Lincoln popped his head out from his office. 'Ben, Jess, a word, please.'

Benedict and Jessica exchanged looks. 'If this is about manual handling, I'm going to scream.'

They settled in the DCI's office.

62

'Right,' said Lincoln. 'Your day has just turned more interesting. Report's coming in of a body found in Regents Canal. White male, aged thirty-two. Found just a short while ago by a couple of dog walkers passing by. Uniformed officers are making their way over to talk to the man's wife as we speak. Here's the deceased's address…' He passed Jessica a Post-it note. 'The man's name is Browning. Anthony Browning. Go and check it out, please.'

'On our way, sir.'

Chapter 10: Dominic

The Flamingo Club was in full swing by the time Dominic Woods turned up at ten at night, a small queue of people waiting outside. The bouncers greeted him with a smile; they knew him by now. 'Is Nat in tonight?' he asked.

'Yeah, been in for a while.'

'Can you tell him to come down to see me when he's got a minute.'

'Sure, Mr Woods.'

Dominic knew that Nathaniel Turnbull had a job at The Flamingo monitoring the club's CCTV network, ensuring no one was kicking off and keeping an eye out for drugs. The club had sailed too close to the law recently, and Mr Etherington, the boss, wasn't taking any more chances.

The music, though loud, was bearable, some obscure dance track playing, only a few people dancing. He said hello to various people he vaguely knew, a few slaps on the back, a handshake or two. The light show flashed blue and green over the dance floor. Dominic liked it here, yes, it was rough and ready and some of the clientele definitely earned their money through dodgy means, but who was he to talk? People had to make their money through whatever means. White-collared crime was that much more lucrative.

He took his usual high table in the corner and settled himself on a stool. He caught the eye of a waiter and asked for a pint of lager, a pack of ready-salted peanuts and a small bowl of green olives. He waved at the DJ who gave him a thumbs up in return.

Dominic was feeling pleased with himself – he'd re-established contact with the love of his life, Elise Tanner. One phone call – that's all it took. He'd kept her number all these years and he was lucky she hadn't changed it. She didn't sound happy to hear from him, but he hadn't expected her to. Still, he'd laid the first seeds of doubt and he was pleased about that.

He hadn't seen her for years; spent too long in the US. He'd tried to resist, tried putting the memory of her behind him. He threw himself into work, he went out with numerous women, he'd especially liked Caroline Wozniak, but even she couldn't hold a candle to Elise. He often wondered what it was about her that he found so beguiling. She was attractive, for sure, with her big, expressive eyes and her blemish-free skin and her flowing locks. But it was so much more than that. She had an innocence about her, a purity in this cynical world that appealed to him. Life seemed so simple to her; she saw everything through a prism of optimism.

Finally, after five years, he knew he had to have Elise back in his life. He found her straightaway by searching for her name on Facebook and Instagram, and that's when he found him too: Philip Edwards. He viewed every post. Philip made his first appearance on Elise's feeds some six months back, and then he'd never left. Every post featured the handsome Phil to the point of it being nauseating. They went out to meals together, the cinema, to nightclubs, to theme parks, all of it documented in minute detail on her feed. He was a good-looking man, seemed a decent sort but if he was to get Elise back in his life, he'd have to do something about Philip Edwards.

He knew how Elise liked her men – traditional: the wage earner, a man who knew how to fix things, a man who was in control. Elise liked to feel safe. Dominic had a theory that this need to be protected stemmed from her father being sent away to prison for so long. She lacked a man in her life, the sort of man who'd look after her.

Was that the sort of man Philip Edwards was? Maybe, on the surface. He started following the man. He knew from Philip's own Facebook and Instagram accounts that, before Elise, he'd been dating a most attractive woman called Tracey, and, according to Tracey's own account, the two of them worked for the same supermarket. Perfect.

He knew where Philip lived, where he worked, what sort of car he drove, where he went to the gym. And slowly, a plan formed, a way to demoralise him, make him appear helpless. Make him less of a man in Elise's eyes. But he needed to employ someone to do the dirty work, someone desperate enough to risk it. And Dominic knew the man, and that was why, on a cold Tuesday night in February, he was sipping a lager on his own at The Flamingo.

He knew Nathaniel Turnbull had probably clocked him on his CCTV monitors by now. He was tempted to wave at a camera but decided it wouldn't look cool somehow. He'd come down when he had a minute. Even Mr Etherington allowed his staff toilet breaks.

Dominic also knew he wouldn't be alone for long and sure enough, within five minutes, his old companion Fiona turned up, or Fifi, as she insisted on being called. 'Dom, hey, long time no see. What brings you here?' She planted a wet kiss on his cheek.

'Hoping to see you, of course.'

'Nah, pull the other one. Oh, lovie, you here on your own? We can't be having that. Here, let me park me arse for a while.' A waiter passed, and Fifi grabbed him. 'A strawberry daiquiri when you have a mo, darling.'

'Always a strawberry daiquiri, Fifi.'

She laughed. 'Oh, you know me, sweetheart. Oh, look, you've got lipstick on your cheek. Actually, it suits you. Maybe we should leave it there, make all the girls jealous.'

'You're marking me now, Fifi?'

'Take me back to yours and I'll truly mark you, lover boy.' She reached over and, pulling him in by his tie, kissed him. 'So, Mr Handsome, tell me what's going down in your world of high finance. And what brings you back to this dive?'

'I'm here to see a man about a dog.'

'I'll be your dog, honey. Hey, me and the girls went to that new bar down the high street. Right posh, it is, that's the sort of place for a *gentleman* like you, not this old slapper's place. And I should know!'

Her strawberry daiquiri arrived. 'Ah, that's better,' she said, taking a long drink. She proceeded to tell him about the new bar, and a gentleman she met there whom she'd knocked up with for a while but he liked his sex *too* kinky, not that she minded a bit of kink, but even she had her boundaries, and this bloke had certainly breached it as far as Fifi was concerned.

'The mind boggles,' said Dominic.

'Oh, I can't begin to tell you. It's enough to make a girl blush, I'm telling you.'

Ten minutes later and Dominic was beginning to get a little tired of the gushing Fifi. Fifi was either comatose or on full power; there was no halfway point with Fifi. It was then that Nathaniel Turnbull finally made his appearance. 'You wanted to see me.' He stood there with his hands in his pocket. Nathaniel Turnbull never looked like the sort of man comfortable in his own skin.

'Ah, Nat.'

Fifi said hello. 'How's it going, Nat? Still stuck up in your cubby hole checking up on everyone?'

He didn't answer.

'What a job, eh? Suppose someone's got to do it.' Fifi, taking her cue, slid off her stool. 'I'll see you later, Dom. Maybe give me a shout as you leave,' she added with a wink. 'I'll be ready at your beck and call,' she added, running a finger down Dominic's tie.

'You can count on it,' he said, raising his glass.

She laughed and disappeared into the crowd.

'Nat, take a seat.'

'Best not, Mr Woods.'

'Suit yourself. I do believe I haven't paid you yet for doing my wall.' A couple weeks before, Nathaniel, a bricklayer by trade, had built Dominic a new garden wall. 'We need to put that right. How much was it again?' He pulled out his phone.

'One thousand pounds, Mr Woods.'

'Good value for good work. What's your account number and sort code?'

Nathaniel told him while Dominic tapped the numbers into his banking app. 'OK. Give it a moment... The wifi's a bit slow in here. Ah, there it is, all paid. I added a small tip for you, Nat.'

'Thank you, Mr Woods. Will that be all?'

'Actually, no. Come closer.' Nathaniel took a step closer. 'Would you like to earn some more?'

'More brick work?'

'Ah, no. I'll be honest with you, Nat, this is not legal by any stretch, so if you want to walk away now, that's fine. I respect that.'

'How illegal is illegal, Mr Woods?'

'I have various things in mind, a phase one, two and three. If the worst comes to the worst, we'd get away with a rap on the knuckles for the first two but the third… what I have in mind is quite risky.'

'How much are you paying, Mr Woods?'

'Ten grand for all three. But only if all three are completed to my specification.'

Nathaniel's eyebrows shot up. Dominic knew he was tempted. Nathaniel looked around at the various punters enjoying themselves, shouting, drinking and dancing. 'Risky, you say?'

'Yes. Obviously, I'd do as much as I can to mitigate the risk but there'd still be an element. You have first refusal, Nat.'

The man was torn, Dominic could see it. He almost felt sorry for him, to be that much in need of the money.

'I'm not sure, Mr Woods.'

'I can't wait all night, Nat. I need an answer. Either you're in or you're out. It's your choice.'

Nathaniel looked defeated. Dominic knew he'd lost him, that he'd pushed him too hard. 'I don't think I can do anything that risky. I'm sorry, Mr Woods.'

'Hey, no worries, Nat. No worries. Thanks anyway.'

'I'd better get back. Mr E will be getting antsy.'

'Actually, listen, I'll give you twenty-four hours. Give you time to think about it.'

'But what exactly would you need doing?'

Dominic looked left and right. People around him were too busy enjoying themselves to pay him any heed. 'I'll tell you but it goes no further.'

'You have my word on that, Mr Woods.'

Chapter 11: Benedict

'Is all of Regent's Canal under CCTV?' asked Jessica as she and Benedict walked quickly along the towpath.

'I don't think hardly any of it is.'

The time was approaching eight. The night was cold, a sharp wind blowing into their faces. The water of the canal looked sinister, reflecting in places the lights of overhead buildings. Along the way, a couple of canal boats moored-up, a man standing at the stern of one having a cigarette, a can of cider in his hand. He lifted his can by way of greeting as the detectives passed. The path underfoot was muddy.

They soon came across the crime scene, a uniformed officer standing guard next to a stretch of blue and white police tape. The detectives showed her their IDs and passed through. PC Stevens approached them. 'We've got the couple who found the body, sir.'

'Excellent. We'll be with you in just a moment.'

'Sir.'

They found DS Andrew Collins, fully attired in his white overalls. 'Hello, Andrew,' said Benedict. 'How's it going?'

'Ben. What we have here is one drowned white male. Divers have emptied his pockets. He is, according to his driving licence, Anthony Browning, aged thirty-two, lived just a few streets away from here.'

'He drowned.'

'No pathologist yet, so impossible to say at this stage. The fact he ended up in the water doesn't necessarily mean he drowned. The question is, did he fall or was he pushed? There're signs of a struggle next to the wall here. Two clear sets of footprints having a right song and dance. So, I reckon he was killed. Whether he was killed before he hit the water, I wouldn't like to say.'

The victim had been pulled out from the canal and laid on the grass verge. One of the officers had covered him with a small tarpaulin.

Benedict used his phone torch to look at the man's face on his driving licence. A good-looking man, a sweep of black hair.

'As far as we know, everything was still in his wallet, bank cards, cash, coins, the lot, so this wasn't a robbery. There's also a receipt. You can't see the details because of the water but you can see the logo – the Davenport pub.'

'Didn't we park up there, boss?' asked Jessica.

'We did. Popular watering hole with office workers. Tends to empty out after about eight o'clock. Then popular during the weekends with crowds drifting down from Camden market.'

'We'll have to ask the pub to check their CCTV then.'

'Someone's already on their way,' said Collins. 'It's a nice pub, been there many a time. They do a decent Sunday roast, Jessica. You and your partner might want to try it out one day.'

Jessica nodded a thanks.

'So, these scuff marks you mentioned. You definitely reckon they're a sign of a struggle.'

'Oh, for sure. There're dozens of stampings on the same patch of path, and some scraping too, implying that one of them was dragged, the heels scraping over the mud.'

'Male or female footwear?'

'Probably male. Both sets.'

'Let's speak to the couple.'

The couple stood close to each other, holding hands and looking worried. They introduced themselves as Mark and Mahak. 'So, just tell us what happened,' said Jessica.

'Yeah, what it was we were walking along the towpath this way–'

'We were going to the pub, the Davenport, you know,' said Mahak, interrupting.

'And we just saw this guy in the canal, face down, his arms out like this… as if he was flying, you know.'

'If it wasn't for the brass buttons on the back of his coat, on the belt, we might not have seen him. They were glittering, what with the reflections and all.'

'Any movement?'

'No. We reckoned he was already dead, didn't we, Mark?' said Mahak.

'Oh yeah, he was dead, all right. No bubbles or anything like that.'

'What did you do then?' asked Benedict.

'Called you guys, of course.'

'And we told you to hang around until someone turned up.'

'Which we did like the good citizens we are,' said Mahak. 'We're bloody freezing our balls off here now. We've been hanging around for ages.'

'We do appreciate it, gents,' said Jessica. 'Did you see anyone at any point, either as you approached here or just afterwards?'

'Not until three minutes after we called you. They thought us dead weird just hanging around here in the dark.'

'I reckon they thought we were about to mug them.'

They both found this amusing.

'Do you know who he is?' asked Mark.

'We're not at liberty to say at this stage but thanks, gentlemen, for your time. You've been most helpful.'

The two men, still holding hands, walked quickly in the direction of the Davenport pub, no doubt looking forward to fortifying themselves with a few drinks.

Having said their goodbyes to DS Collins and PC Stevens and thanked the whole team for their hard work on such a cold night, Benedict and Jessica walked back to the pub. By now, the pub was only two-thirds full, 'Waterloo Sunset' playing, a group of men playing pool in the corner, and a group discussing a book in another, each holding a copy of the book, something by Virginia Woolf. Benedict spied Mark and Mahak sitting at a table sharing a joke and laughing loudly, their pints in front of them.

They were shown through to the back by a member of the bar staff and there found two uniformed officers poring through the pub's CCTV tapes. 'Have you spotted them yet, boys?' asked Benedict.

'Yes, sir. There.' They both pointed at the screen. The man, Andrew Browning, dressed in suit and tie, was sharing a table with a similarly dressed man of about the same age, the same type. One could almost feel their arrogance emanating from the screen, thought Benedict. The CCTV camera had them by the profile so that whenever one turned his head slightly, they had a good, full facial shot of both men. Browning had a pint, his companion a smaller drink of some sort. They didn't seem particularly comfortable together. One didn't need to be a body language expert to know that these men were definitely not friends and that both were there, in each other's company, under sufferance.

'Have you clocked the timings yet?' asked Jessica.

'Yes, ma'am. We're watching it for a second time in case we missed anything the first-time round. The drowned man comes in first at six twenty-five. He's at the bar when his mate comes in five minutes later. Once they finish at the bar, they sit here the whole time except for about three minutes when the dead guy goes to the gents. Then, they leave soon after. The CCTV over the door covers it. The other guy leaves first, and you can see him leave. He turns left out of the pub. Then our guy leaves about ninety seconds later but he turns right out of the pub, heading towards the canal path.'

'What does our guy do during those ninety seconds?' asked Benedict.

'Just checks his phone. That's it. Then, he drains his glass and goes out.'

'To the right towards the towpath.'

'That's it, sir.'

Benedict handed one of the officers his card, asking him to email him the CCTV footage whenever he had it.

Next on their list of calls, Benedict and Jessica visited Mrs Jane Browning, the dead man's wife. She lived in a well-kept maisonette on the Kentish Town side of Camden. She was already being consoled by Michelle Garvey, the Family Liaison Officer. They declined her cup of tea; they knew they wouldn't be long. They offered their condolences and asked very little. Instead, they just listened as Mrs Browning extolled the virtues of her husband. He'd worked at Safe Hands Trading for five years or more. His boss, Mr O'Brian, rated him highly. He earned a good salary and always worked hard. He occasionally played squash with a friend and he liked cooking, especially Italian food. He had no vices she could think of, although he enjoyed the occasional glass of wine, and he was liked by everyone he met. No, there wasn't a single person Mrs Browning could think of that would wish her husband harm. His death was beyond her comprehension.

Afterwards, as they sat in the car not too far from the block of maisonettes, Benedict said, 'Right, tomorrow, I suggest we go speak to Mr O'Brian at Safe Hands Trading and see what he has to say about the unfortunate Anthony Browning. And hopefully, he might recognise Browning's companion in the pub.'

'Sounds like a plan, boss.'

Chapter 12: Elise, 2018
Five years earlier

Elise hurried home from the hairdressers where she'd worked on the high street, and, rushing up to her bedroom, tried on various different outfits before deciding on a flowing purple number with thin straps she'd bought online on Shein, one that showed off her bosom, finishing it off with a small dark green glittery cardigan. She inserted her favourite silver heart earrings and applied a fresh layer of make-up, piling on her lipstick that Sharon had so admired on Saturday night.

She needed to leave the house without either parent seeing her. But she failed, her mother catching her downstairs as she was grabbing her coat. 'You off out, Elise?'

'Yeah.'

'Don't you want dinner?'

'No, I'm good.'

'You look… lovely. Have I seen that dress before? Where are you going all dolled up?'

'Oh, you know, just meeting a few friends. Shaz and a

couple of others. No big deal. We're meeting at the Three Bells.' At least the last bit wasn't a lie.

'Aren't you rather overdressed for the pub?'

'Best overdressed than underdressed, that's my motto, Mum. See ya later.'

'Don't I get a kiss?'

'Yes, Mum.' Reluctantly, she kissed her mother. 'Gotta dash, my bus is due in a minute. Bye now.'

She caught a bus to the high street and, sitting down on the lower deck, checked her phone. No new messages.

It was almost six fifteen by the time Elise rocked-up at the Three Bells. She was a quarter of an hour late. It didn't matter; it was her prerogative as a woman. Being early on a Monday night, the pub, predictably, was a lot quieter than Saturday night, and she saw him straight away. He looked handsome, wearing a khaki jacket over a tight navy-blue shirt and a pair of stylish jeans. He stood on seeing her and smiled.

'I'm sorry I'm late,' she said, faking breathlessness. 'Got stuck at work.'

'Not to worry. You look fantastic.'

'This old thing? Oh, thank you. You look good too. Love the jacket.'

'What can I get you, Elisa?'

'Erm, actually, it's Elise.'

'Elise.' He slapped his forehead. 'Of course it is. I'm sorry.'

'No worries. It's no biggie. I often get called different things. What do people call you? Dominic or Dom?'

'Either. I don't mind. Anyway, back to the important things in life… what do you want from the bar?'

'Let's see, erm, a white wine spritzer, please.'

'Coming right up. Don't go anywhere now.'

He returned not with a spritzer but with two cocktails. 'I thought you look like a Mojito kind of girl,' he said, placing the drink on the table in front of her. 'So that's what I got you. But if you prefer the Margarita, we can swap.' He sat and pulled his chair closer to her.

'No, that's fine,' she said, thinking she'd much prefer the white wine spritzer. 'I love a Mojita.' She'd never had one before.

'Mojito,' he corrected her. 'With an 'o' at the end.'

She took a sip and found it revolting. 'Wow, that's lovely. Thank you.'

'A pleasure.' He sat so close to her she could feel his heat. Anyone else, William included, she'd be edging away by now, wanting her own space, but with him, Dominic, she could happily sit on his lap. She found it strangely intoxicating. She glanced at the skin between his shirt buttons, the hint of chest hair. His aftershave smelt divine, she wanted to kiss him there and then.

'What is it you do, Dominic?'

'Me? I work in finance, stocks and shares, that sort of thing.'

'Oh? That sounds very hifalutin.'

He laughed at her use of the word. 'I suppose it is rather. It's quite scary actually because I'm taking other people's money, sometimes a lot of it, like their whole life savings, and they trust me to do something with it, mainly to invest it in a way they get a good return on it. And you know, I'm only twenty-eight, yet they place their money and their trust entirely in my hands. It's a big responsibility.'

'My God,' she said, almost unable to breathe. 'That is just fantastic.'

'So, what is it you do?' he asked, leaning in even closer, his breath in her ear, that aftershave filling her nostrils, leaving her quite weak.

Willing herself to remain coherent, she said, 'Nothing exciting, nothing like you do. I'm just a hairdresser.'

'Hey, there's no "just" to it. Men or women?'

'Women.'

'Well, that's also a massive responsibility. You can't cock-up a woman's hair, can you? She sits there and she expects you to get it right and make her look beautiful. Honestly, I don't think I could cope with that much expectation. The stress of it would be too much for me.'

Was this man for real? She totally loved him for that, the way he took her humdrum job and bigged it up like that, making it sound like the most important job in the world. William would never say something like that; it'd never occur to him. He never asked about her working day, never took the slightest interest yet this man, on meeting her properly for the first time, actually felt rather proud of what she did.

'Can you cut my hair one day?' he asked with a smile.

'Yes! I loved to. Like I say, I usually only cut women's hair but...' She touched his blond locks, an excuse simply to touch him. What in the fuck was he doing to her? No one had ever made her feel this way before. 'But I could cut your hair if you'd like me to. It's quite long.'

'Exactly.'

They stared at each for a few moments and she wondered whether it was just her or whether he was feeling it too, this surge of electricity, this beating in her heart, the pulse between her legs.

'So, how was your night on Saturday?' he asked. 'The pub seemed very quiet after you and your friends left.'

'I'm sorry?' She needed to concentrate when all she wanted

to do was plant her mouth on his and run her fingers down his chest. She'd never been so aroused simply from talking to a man but by heck, she was now.

'I said…' He repeated the question.

She laughed, glad to have something to talk about, something to distract her. 'Yeah, we were a bit loud, weren't we? It's always like that when Sharon leads us out. I love her to bits but she's totally bonkers.' She told them about the nightclub, about how Sharon's friend was so desperate for the loo, she couldn't queue up for the ladies so instead gate-crashed the gents and there puked up in a cubicle.

'How revolting.'

She almost laughed but then realised he meant it. She thought it a funny story, and assumed he would too, but she saw now she'd misjudged it and he genuinely seemed appalled by it. 'Yes, I suppose it was, really.' She sipped her revolting Mojito, with an 'o', cursing herself. He was right – it was a revolting tale and a revolting thing to do, and she flushed with shame. 'What about you?' she asked quickly, wanting to divert attention. 'Did you end up at The Signature, like you said?'

'The others did, yes, but I didn't feel like it in the end. So I went home.'

'Oh? Were you poorly?'

'No, it's just that…' He took a sip of his Margarita.

'What?'

'I…' He looked around the pub as if expecting to see someone he knew. Turning his attention back to her, he said, 'I couldn't face staying out any longer; I had to go home.'

'But why?'

'Because I couldn't stop thinking about you, Elise.'

'Oh!' She hadn't in a million years expected that and had

no idea what to say. She felt herself blush; she couldn't look him in the eye. 'Really? That's… that's…'

'I'm sorry, I've embarrassed you now.'

'No, no, not at all,' she said quickly. 'I'm flattered, really, I am. But that's quite…'

'Yes?'

'That's quite something to say.'

'I know. And I wish I hadn't said it now. I feel rather stupid.' He finished his cocktail.

'No, please don't. It's a… a lovely thing to say.' She placed her hand on his knee over his. 'Thank you.' Lightening the mood, she said, 'Now, what can I get you? My shout.'

'No, no, I'll get it.'

'But you bought the last round.'

'And I'll buy the next, and the next. Seriously, all drinks on me. I wouldn't have it any other way.'

She could tell he meant it. She didn't like it, she liked to pay her own way, but she knew she'd be unable to make him back down here. So, instead, she meekly agreed but was assertive enough to say that, as much as she enjoyed the cocktail, it was going to her head so this time, please, a white wine spritzer.

He returned with two white wines, one each. Relieved, she thanked him. They clinked glasses and smiled at each other.

'So, tell me all about your friends,' he said.

'OK.' She had to tread carefully here. Her friends were, by and large, loud, boisterous and totally uncouth, Sharon especially. Because Sharon was right, Dominic really was a 'posh boy', and he wouldn't appreciate hearing about the antics of a bunch of spirited loud girls. She'd never met anyone like him; he was different from William and any man she'd ever spoken to. Dominic was 'Class' with a capital 'C', and she didn't want to alienate him, or upset him or appear stupid in any way, because she liked him.

She bloody liked him one hell of a lot.

Chapter 13: Nathaniel

Nathaniel Turnbull lay on his bed, unable to face another grim day ahead. The noise outside his bedsit was unbearable – they were digging up the road, and those pneumatic drills they were using were pounding in his head. So much noise and it was still only eight fifteen in the morning. Didn't they think people worked to late and needed their sleep. As usual, he hadn't got home until almost two a.m. last night following his shift at The Flamingo.

It was the same every morning, waking up with that same sense of dread resting in the pit of his stomach. The money Mr Woods deposited in his account last night was only ever going to be a temporary reprieve, a stay of execution.

Nathaniel lived in a horrible, second-floor bedsit not too far from the Flamingo, where, until late at night, women plied their trade beneath his window. Workmen in the morning, women of the night in the evening. He wouldn't even have this place if he didn't pay his rent soon. And then, Christ knows what he'd do. Things were desperate. It was something he tried not to think about but he knew just how precarious his situation was.

He knew he had no choice but to take up Dominic Woods' offer of work, however risky. That thousand pounds he'd paid him for rebuilding his brick wall would cover his debts and that was good, but he needed so much more going forward. He'd been heavily in arrears on his debt and he had to pay the last three instalments on his phone. That was all covered now, which was a huge relief. But what of the future?

He had promised himself that he'd put his life of crime behind him. Six years back, he got caught for burglary and car theft and ended up in prison for ten months, a horrific experience. Now, he was considering putting himself at risk again because what Woods was asking was indeed risky. He could do phase one and two, as Woods called it, but it was phase three that worried him. He even said he'd do the first two but not the third but Woods said no, it was all or nothing. Any fool, he said, could do the first two, he could do them both on the same day, but it took a man of courage to see through the last.

The money he earned from his work at The Flamingo just about covered his rent but left precious little for anything else. He recently asked the boss for a raise but Mr Etherington actually laughed in his face, saying no way and if he didn't like it, there'd be a hundred and one blokes happy to take his place.

The cost-of-living crisis was hitting hard; the cost of petrol had rocketed and he knew he'd soon have to sell his car, a sixteen-year-old Volkswagen Golf, as he couldn't afford to run it any more. His electricity and gas bills had gone through the roof, and food was so expensive now. He'd already reached that 'heat or eat' stage. It was still only February.

Hopefully, another month and the temperature would improve and that would help. If only he could get more bricklaying work. Problem was, supply outdid demand: too many brickies around and now, with the cost-of-living crisis, simply not enough demand. Splitting up with his girlfriend didn't help. Living together meant the benefit of economies of scale. Living as a couple was always cheaper than living by oneself.

Nathaniel dragged himself out of bed. Slipping on his paisley-patterned dressing gown and Homer Simpson slippers, he padded through to the tiny space that the landlord called a kitchen and flicked the kettle on and made himself a cup of tea. Sitting on his settee, he lit his first cigarette a day. That was something he needed to ditch – the price of fags these days. He breathed in his first hit of the day and momentarily felt better. He picked up his phone – a message from his ex, reminding him that it was their son's birthday in a week. That was all he needed right now. More expense.

He had to think this through. He only had the rest of the day to make up his mind. So, what if he took up Mr Woods' offer and what if it went pear-shaped? What would be the worst outcome? Surely, they'd see him as just the 'hit man', most of the responsibility would lie at Woods' feet. But would that be enough to avoid jail time? Possibly, possibly not. The risk was enormous, he knew that. But what choice did he have? That third phase worried him no end. Woods had already worked it out, said he knew the best place to do it, a quiet road, no CCTV cameras, no houses, hence very few pedestrians and next to no traffic. But you only needed one sharp-eyed witness and it'd be curtains. Woods' plan still left so much to chance.

But ten thousand pounds? Hell, that'd keep him going for months. That would be like winning the lottery. The thought of declining Mr Woods' offer and kissing that sort of money goodbye was too unbearable for words. He needed that money. OK, he'd do it; he'd bloody do it.

He rang Dominic Woods' number.

*

Half past seven in the evening. Nathaniel had to get to work by half eight; Mr Etherington didn't appreciate 'tardiness'. He drove to a block of flats in Camden's Kilburn district, and parking up, looked for a ten-year-old, blue-coloured Saab 900 hatchback, a big car with huge headlamps. Earlier, he Googled it, so he knew what he was looking for. He saved an image to his photos.

He wore a pair of black jeans and a hoodie. There were so many cars parked up here, and being dark, this was no easy task. This was meant to be the 'easy' task, phase one, but he still felt like shit, his heart thumping two to the dozen. He was assured that Edwards would be back from work by now, his car parked up. And if it wasn't, Woods told him he'd have to come back after work but the thought of doing this at half two in the morning made his blood run cold. It was difficult enough as it was. He hid behind a transit van while a couple of elderly women passed, casting long shadows. They didn't notice him.

Finally, he found a blue Saab. He checked its registration plate with the number he'd scribbled down. Yes, this was it. Quickly, he took out his house key from his jeans' pocket and, checking the coast was clear, scraped it down the passenger side of the car. God, it made so much noise, surely the world and his wife would hear this. And keying a car properly takes longer than people think, especially if you want to make a good job of it. But, finally, twenty seconds later, the job was done – a nice deep line from under the bonnet, along both doors, and to the back. Brilliant. Phase One completed. Hands in pocket, hood pulled up, Nathaniel strode away, not looking back.

Half an hour later, he was safely at work.

*

Nathaniel's second task, which he had to do the following day, was that much harder. He consoled himself with the thought that he was now one third of the way to that ten grand. He woke early, awake even before the workmen started their shift, digging up the road outside his bedsit.

He had his morning cup of tea and cigarette and got showered and dressed. He would've had breakfast but felt too on edge to eat.

He wore gloves and a high-visibility tabard. In his experience, no one ever questioned someone wearing hi-vis. People assumed you were doing whatever you were doing in some sort of official capacity and that you knew what you were doing.

It was raining out. He drove the mile to his local B&Q store. There, he bought two one-gallon cans of pillar box red emulsion paint. He had to pay for them himself but, just in case, he kept the receipt. He stacked the two cans into a rucksack – they weren't light, a combined weight of almost a thousand grams. One gallon would, according to the instructions, cover a small room like a bathroom, so two gallons, Nathaniel reckoned, would be plenty to do the job. He'd already packed a screwdriver in order to prise open the lids and the tools of the trade to break into a flat. He only hoped it was an old-fashioned door, easy to break into, like the ones he used to target back in the day.

He drove over to the address supplied by Dominic Woods and walked up the stairs to the second floor of the small block of flats. He needed flat thirty-four. But, turning the corner from the stairway onto the corridor outside the flats, he saw activity. A young black guy was at the door, a set of keys in his hand. Was he going in or going out?

Nathaniel quickly went back to the stairway and skipped up half a level, so he could see without being seen. Sure enough, the man walked quickly along the corridor and down the stairs. Going to the balcony, Nathaniel watched him walking across the street to a blue Saab 900. My word, he thought, it's him. He watched the man get in his car and drive off. Had he noticed the scratch down the passenger side of his car yet? Was he moving in already? If so, he could be back at any time. He had no time to lose.

He walked back down the stairway, along the landing and to number thirty-four. Yes, for once he was in luck; it was an old door, bed and butter stuff for a man of his experience. Checking that no one was around and comforted by his hi-vis tabard, he quickly set to work. It didn't take long, and he was in.

Philip Edwards, for he now knew it was him, had deposited three boxes and two suitcases worth of stuff in the corner of the living room, but he hadn't unpacked anything yet. Presumably, he'd be back soon. It was a decent looking flat, far nicer than his rotten bedsit. But he wasn't here to admire the decor.

Nathaniel opened both cans of emulsion red paint then, taking the first one, threw it against the living room wall. It went everywhere – on the wall, the ceiling, the carpet, over the settee and the table. He didn't enjoy doing this, it seemed such a sacrilege somehow, this wanton act of vandalism, this violation of someone's home. But he was, he reminded himself, simply the hit man, doing someone else's dirty work. He threw the second can of paint all over the bedroom, splattering the window, the bed and carpet. What a mess, what a horror. He felt thoroughly ashamed of himself, sick to the stomach. Still, needs must.

He placed both cans in separate plastic shopping bags and returned them to his rucksack. Quickly, he walked back down the stairway and to his car, relieved to have escaped.

Two jobs done, one to go.

Chapter 14: Elise

Elise returned from a long day from work in a foul mood. Ignoring her mother, who was in the kitchen making dinner, she went straight to her room and flopped down on the bed and hugged a pillow. Despite the promise the day had held, it had turned out to be a fairly shit day. Now that they'd secured the flat, she really needed to start packing up her stuff. She didn't have much, and much of what she did have, she was leaving here. Phil was coming over to drive her stuff over to the flat tomorrow morning. No point hanging around; no point renting a flat and not moving into it. The thought of moving in with Phil had excited her no end until Dominic rang her. Now, the thought of moving into that tiny flat filled her with dread. Its bedroom was barely a third the size of this room. That was why she was having to leave so much behind.

She thought she'd rid herself of Dominic years ago; felt safe that he was out of her life for once and for all. She should've known that he'd be there lurking, waiting for the opportunity to make his awful presence felt in her life again.

Taking her phone, she scrolled through her past Facebook posts. Sure enough, the last six months or so had been dominated by her life with Phil. She'd posted several photos of him and of them together – the day they went to Alton Towers, a meal out at a Thai restaurant, at a funfair last autumn, inside the Van Gogh immersive experience in Whitechapel, going on a Jack the Ripper walking tour around the backstreets of Shoreditch, just a young couple, happy and in love, doing stuff that young couples do. And of course, every time she tagged Phil's name, one could click on that tag and be taken to Phil's own Facebook account.

Now, she went down that particular rabbit hole, going back to the time before she'd met him, trying to find any mention of a Tracey. And yes, there it was – dated last June, two months before she'd met him. Her stomach somersaulted with dread. And then another post featuring the two of them together, and another, and another, loads of them going back a year or more. God, she was beautiful, far more *conventionally* attractive than Elise, she thought. A Black girl, tall, long braids, layers dyed blonde, always immaculately turned out. She stared into the woman's eyes. Was she in love with Phil? Yes, Elise reckoned she was, one could see it, the way she looked at Phil, her hand resting on his chest in that possessive way girls do when they want to show the world, this man is mine. If Facebook was correct, they'd been an item a whole year. A lot longer than she'd been with him. She wondered why they'd split up, if indeed, they had truly parted ways. Dominic had sown that seed of doubt all right. *Ask him about Tracey at work.* The bastard, the two-timing bastard.

She heard her father downstairs, coming back from work. He'd got himself a job working as a delivery driver for Evri. Long hours and low paid but as a man with a criminal record now to his name, he was grateful to have that. Still, a far cry from the corporate job he had in planning before the day he mowed down that cyclist and almost killed the poor sod.

Her phone rang. It was him, the two-timing bastard. At least it wasn't Dominic; she couldn't have faced that. Phil asked if he could pop by after dinner. She wanted to say no but couldn't think of an excuse so reluctantly, she agreed. He picked up on her tone but she brushed him off, saying she'd see him later.

Her Alexa speaker pinged – an announcement from Mum saying dinner was ready. Elise wasn't the slightest bit hungry and so did not want to talk but if she stayed in her bedroom, that would only make things worse, so she pulled herself up, dragged a brush through her hair, and joined her parents downstairs for dinner.

Dinner, a chilli con carne, was actually very nice. Her mother had always been a good cook, a trait that Elise sadly had not picked up. Her parents fired her lots of questions about the flat and she answered with as much enthusiasm as she could muster but it all seemed rather sullied now. She couldn't get Tracey out of her head. After dinner, Dad did the clearing up and loaded the dishwasher while she and Mum flopped in front of the television to watch their favourite early evening soap. That bloody painting was still leaning against the sideboard. 'Phil's coming round in a bit.'

'That's nice.'

Half an hour later, Phil duly appeared, looking dapper as always, a shine in his hair, a ready smile on his lips. Always the charmer. She waited while he exchanged pleasantries with her parents, then took him upstairs to her bedroom. The first thing he noticed was that Elise hadn't packed a thing yet, everything was where it usually was. 'We are moving in tomorrow, Elise, in case you'd forgotten. I'm all packed. In fact, I've already been to the flat with my first load. Looks more like home already.'

'Yeah, I know. It won't take long; it's just my clothes and a few basics. We won't have room for half this rubbish anyway.'

'If you're sure. I can give you a hand now, if you want.'

'No, it's OK.'

Together, they lay on the bed, Elise twisting her engagement ring around her finger. He continued talking about the flat, excited to move in tomorrow. Not getting anything in return, he laid to his side, his hand propping up his head. 'Is there anything wrong, Else?'

'No?'

'Have I said something?'

'Why do you ask?'

'I don't know. You just seem a bit off with me, and today, at the flat, you seemed a bit...'

'A bit what, Phil?'

'Well, weird. Up in the flat when Mr Sheth was talking about everything, you looked a little...'

'Weird?'

'You're not changing your mind, are you, Else? Because we've paid and everything now. We can't—'

'Who's Tracey?' There, she'd said it; it was out in the open.

'What? Who's Tracey?'

'I don't know. Tracey. Are you shagging some girl called Tracey?'

'Whoa!' He sat up. 'Where in the fuck did that come from?'

'Well? Are you?'

'Fuck, no, Hell, Else, what's got into you?'

'Who is she then?'

94

His eyes darted to the window. 'Tracey?'

'Yes. Tracey. Who is she? I want to know. And I'm not moving in with you until you tell me. The truth, Phil.'

'Tracey. She's... she's s-someone I work with.'

'And are you? Shagging her?'

'No, Christ no. I mean...'

'Oh? You mean what exactly? You either are or you're not. It's not a complicated question, Phil.'

'She was...' He looked down at his shoes, anywhere but her. 'She was my girlfriend before you, is all.'

'And now?'

'Now, hell no, it's finished between us, I swear, Elise. I swear to God. We finished it before I met you. Ages before. Well, a couple of weeks.'

'A couple of weeks? Is that all? Did you finish it or her?'

He didn't answer, just quickly checked his phone.

'Answer me.'

'She did.'

'Oh right, that's interesting. Two weeks before meeting me. So, I was what? The rebound.'

'No, nothing like that.'

'Pretty girl.'

'How do you know?'

'For fuck's sake, Phil, she's all over you in your old Facebook posts.'

'Oh that.'

'Yes, that. Dozens of the two of you together, really loved up you are.'

'I can't help the past, Elise. It's history now.'

'Not if she's working with you.'

'We hardly speak. Professional matters only. She's got a new boyfriend.'

'How would you know if you only speak about professional matters?' she said the last two words in air quotes.

'I just know, OK? Who told you anyway?'

'None of your business. You know, I can't believe I'm hearing this. I had this strange romantic notion that you were waiting for me all these years but oh no, up to a fortnight before I turned up you were fucking some girl you still work with, someone you still see every bloody day at work.'

He reached out for her hands but she quickly withdrew her own, not wanting to be touched by him. 'No, you have to trust me on this, Else. It's truly finished between us now. You're my girlfriend now–'

'Your fiancée, actually, in case you'd forgotten.'

'Yes, I know that. And in two months, you'll be my wife, and that's all that matters to me, Else. Please believe me. There's nothing going on between Trace and me, not any more, I swear on my mother's life.'

'What did your mother think of her?'

'Mum? Does it matter? She liked her, I guess. But that's not important, is it?'

'Your mother doesn't like me; I'll tell you that for sure.'

'Of course, she likes you.'

'I promise you, she doesn't. I don't know what it is. It's as if she thinks I'm not good enough for you. Did she think Tracey was good enough for her precious son?'

'Yes, No. I don't know.'

'She thinks I'm a floozy just because of the size of my chest, I know. She stares at them, makes no secret of it.'

'Shut up, Elise, you're just talking shit now.'

'I think you should go. If you think I'm just talking shit, there's no point in you being here, is there?'

'No, Else, please. Don't chuck me out, not like this.'

'Just go, Phil, just bloody go.'

Chapter 15: Benedict

Diana Pettigrew wasn't sure whether Anthony Browning was already dead when he hit the water. His killer strangled him, that she did know by the extensive bruising around the neck, which also tallied with what DS Collins said about the evidence of a struggle on the towpath. But whether Browning was actually dead when his killer threw him in the water, it was, she said, hard to tell. Pettigrew said that even if a person is dead when they enter the water, the lungs will eventually fill up anyway. If Browning wasn't already dead, then he'd been severely weakened at the point of entering the canal and keeping him down by simply pushing down on his head would have been relatively easy for a killer possessing a degree of strength.

Within an hour of seeing Pettigrew, Benedict finally received a breakthrough, of sorts, on the naked man tied to a tree case. A man came forward claiming he'd seen two men, one manhandling the other into a white van, a white Ford transit van. It was just past midnight that night, bitterly cold, when the man, who was on his way home from the pub, saw the two men and the van in the distance. It was so cold, he didn't think much of it at first; he just wanted to get home as quickly as possible into a warm house. But as he approached, he heard the distinct sound of the van doors closing at the back. One of the men came round from the back of the van and the two men almost bumped into each other. Our witness said, 'good evening' and the other simply nodded in return. And that was it, but yes, he did clock his face quite clearly. He hadn't given the occasion another thought until late the previous evening when he came across one of the police's 'Have you witnessed' appeals dotted around the area. Even then, he didn't think about it. It was only on waking this morning that he made the connection.

The station employed an artist, Dave Turner, on an ad hoc basis on account his services were rarely needed nowadays. But yes, he was available and could come to the station straight away. The witness was happy to wait. The artist arrived almost rubbing his hands in glee; this was a man who enjoyed his work, even if there wasn't much of it these days, thanks to the sinister prevalence of CCTV cameras monitoring our every movement. Add to that, photofitting could be done digitally now but Benedict still preferred the human touch.

An hour later, the artist and witness had finished, satisfied with their collective effort. Dave Turner presented his work to Benedict as a child might present his artwork to the teacher, eager to please, hoping to receive praise, while the witness hopped with excitement behind him. The image showed a middle-aged white man with a five o'clock shadow, gaunt features, deep-set eyes, hair that was once black but now tinged throughout by grey, bushy eyebrows, rather large ears. It was definitely an individual, thought Benedict, as opposed to some generic 'dubious bloke'.

'And as far as you're concerned,' said Benedict, addressing the witness, 'this is a definite likeness to the man you saw that morning with the white Ford transit van.'

'Yes, definitely. Your man here knows his way round with a pencil.'

Dave positively beamed with pride.

'He certainly does.'

'I do court drawings too,' said Dave, eagerly. 'You know, those ones you always see in the papers and on TV?'

'Oh yeah, they're very good too, mate. You have a real talent there.'

'Well, thank you but it helps when the witness is as observant and articulate as you are.'

'Look,' said Benedict, 'as much as I hate to break this up but I need to get on. Is there anything else you need to add at this stage?'

'Who?' said the witness. 'Me? Nah, that was it.'

'In that case, I can only thank you. You've been most helpful.'

Dave cleared his throat.

'You both have. Thank you. Thank you both very much.'

Once he'd managed to usher the two men out, Benedict turned to Jessica, and said, 'I think we've got a blossoming friendship there. Right, I reckon it's time we spoke to William Grant again, see whether this photofit jogs any memories.' He rang St Cuthbert's hospital but was told Mr Grant had been released the day before and was convalescing at home. He got Grant's mobile number and address from the ward sister and thanked her. Next, he rang William Grant. Grant didn't sound keen on seeing the police but, after some persuasion, agreed.

William Grant lived in a shabby bedsit on a street not too far behind Camden High Street. It was approaching lunchtime when Benedict and Jessica found his address. Grant offered them a Pot Noodle each to which, although tempted, they both declined. The room, painted uniformly brown, contained old furniture that, by even the lowest of standards, left a lot to be desired. Mr Grant apologised for his accommodation, explaining he was 'in-between proper homes at the moment.' Benedict wondered whether his girlfriend, Kate Hamilton, had made good on her promise to herself to take William back in.

A goldfish swam around a small, rounded bowl on top of the sideboard, not too far from the tiny television set. Grant's face still showed signs of the battering he'd received but he had had a wash and brushed his hair and was looking halfway to decent.

'How are you feeling, Mr Grant?' asked Jessica.

'Oh, getting there, thanks.'

'Quite an ordeal you went through.'

'Yeah, I know. Worse things happen at sea.'

'I'd say suffering from hypothermia while tied naked to a tree would take some beating. I mean, that was no accident you suffered there but a planned, vicious attack in which you were left for dead. If it wasn't for Betty–'

'Betty?'

'The dog that found you, the Jack Russell.'

'I don't normally like dogs.'

Jessica stifled a laugh. 'Well, I think you have plenty of reasons to be grateful to this particular canine. She saved your bacon. God knows how long you could've been stuck there, tied to that tree.'

'I try not to think about it, to be honest.'

101

'What's your goldfish called?'

'Goldie.'

'Hmm. Did you know the man who did this to you, Mr Grant?' asked Benedict.

'No.' He fiddled with a loose threat hanging off the sleeve of his jersey.

'So, as far as you're concerned, this was a total random attack, and you happened to be the victim simply because you were in the wrong place at the wrong time. It could've happened to the next man. It just happened to be you.'

'No, I reckon my attacker got the wrong bloke. He got me instead.'

'What do you mean?'

'What I mean is it should've been someone specific but he attacked the wrong guy. That's what I reckon.'

'You can't know that for sure.'

'How else would you explain it?'

'It was certainly planned, Mr Grant,' said Jessica. 'The van was stolen and left abandoned after the attack. He specifically chose a deserted spot in the dead of night. It's too baffling for words.'

'Telling me.'

'A witness has come forward,' said Benedict. He described what the witness had claimed to have seen that morning. 'Here's a photofit of the man we believe attacked you. Could you have a look at it, please.' He handed William the artist's drawing.

'There's no point. You see, I never got to see the man. You see, he put a hood over me head, like one of those hessian sacks, you know?'

'Did he indeed? Nonetheless, have a look, please, Mr Grant.'

William took out a pair of glasses from his inside pocket. Benedict saw his eyes widen. 'No, sorry. I don't recognise this man.'

The man was lying. 'You sure? It's important we catch this man; he's obviously a very dangerous individual.'

'Like I said, I never got to see him,' he repeated, more firmly this time.

Benedict left the drawing on the low table between them. 'Tell us exactly what you were doing on the night of the attack, please.'

'Erm, let me see.' He removed his glasses, returning them to his inside pocket. 'So, yes, Thursday night. I watched some documentary on ITV Hub, something about undercover cameras in a care home, that sort of thing, then I went out to the pub, on my own, like, for a quick drink and a catch up on the news in the paper. I do that occasionally since I moved into this place. This was the Red Lion, you know it?'

'We do.'

'Got talking to a couple of old guys who'd been playing dominoes. You can check all this out, you know–'

'You're not a suspect, Mr Grant,' said Jessica.

'Yeah, of course. So, then I left and–'

'What time was this, Mr Grant?'

'Some time after closing time, so just after half eleven, I guess.'

'And then?'

'Yeah, I felt hungry by then. So, I went to the chippie and ate in. I had a saveloy and chips. Very tasty too. By now, I guess it must've been about midnight, just gone, perhaps. I started walking home, a little tipsy, mind you, and next thing I knew – *whoomph*! Everything went black and I couldn't breathe. I started panicking, I can tell you.'

103

'How distressing for you, Mr Grant,' said Jessica, shaking her head.

'It was.'

'What happened then?'

'I heard this door opening, like the back of a van, and I was forced in. I tried to fight him but I guess he was bigger than me and, like I said, I had that hessian hood on my head. He hit me a couple of times. He tied me to a bar somewhere in the van and gagged me. Then, he started driving.'

'Did he say anything?'

'No. Not a word. I can't remember how long we drove for but not long. Then, he parked up and came back to me and he started taking my clothes off. I bloody feared the worse then, I can tell you. I thought what in the fuck is this guy going to do to me. Once he's got me down to my underwear, he untied me and dragged me out of the back of the van. I knew straight off we were in the woods by the sound of the trees and that. He tied my hands again, behind my back and started dragging me up this hill. I was freezing, I can tell you. And I still had that hood on. We got to the top of that hill, and he made me sit at the base of that tree. Then he yanked my arms back so much I thought my shoulders were going to dislocate. He tied my hands behind the tree, really tightly. He then removed my underwear and that's when I thought I was a goner.'

Mr Grant paused. 'Sorry, this is more difficult than I thought.'

'It's fine,' said Jessica. 'Take your time. We appreciate it must've been a terrifying experience for you.'

He found a handkerchief from his trouser pocket and blew his nose. 'So then, there I was, bollock naked. Then, from behind, he removed my hood and then just walked away without another word. I wanted to call after him, beg him not to leave me there, freezing, but I still had that gag on. It was frightening being up in the middle of the night, shivering like mad and thinking I'm going to die here. I guess I passed out and the next thing I knew, some dog was barking at me.'

'You were very lucky, Mr Grant.'

'I know. I know.'

'So, the whole time, he never spoke to you once.'

'Yes. That's right. Not a word.'

They sat in silence for a while. Benedict could hear the faint wail of a siren. Eventually, he asked, 'Have you heard from Ms Hamilton since?'

He looked at his watch. 'She's due in ten minutes actually. I'd better have a shave and all that.'

'We should leave you then.'

'Yes. Thanks, by the way.'

'Thanks?'

'For getting me to talk about it. It helped. A lot. So thanks for that.'

'A pleasure, Mr Grant. Look after yourself now.'

Returning to the station, Benedict tasked DC Kelly to photocopy two hundred copies of the photofit and distribute them to uniform to get them plastered up all around the local area. 'Someone's got to recognise this man.' he said. 'Whoever he is, he needs to be held to account for what he put that poor man through.'

Chapter 16: Elise, 2018
Five years earlier

Elise's alarm sounded at 7 a.m. She stretched and remembered – last night she'd had sex with Dominic. The memory brought a smile to her face. She'd never had sex on a first date before but it felt so right and so natural that she hadn't hesitated. They'd spent the whole of the previous evening in the Three Bells talking non-stop and getting to know each other. Dominic was so easy to talk to; he knew how to listen and paid attention as if everything she said was the most fascinating thing he'd heard. Before Elise knew it, they'd been chatting for over three hours. He paid for every drink, as he said he would, and Elise simply accepted that this was how it was going to be. He spoke about his work in trading. Elise had to ask Dominic to clarify what trading encompassed and it was the only time in the evening that her mind wandered a little; it was such a far cry from the world of hairdressing.

And then it was time to go home. 'I'll order you a taxi to take you home,' Dominic had said.

'I'd rather you ordered us a taxi to take us back to yours,' said Elise, shocking herself by her assertiveness.

Dominic looked at her as if considering this, as if he should even grant permission. Finally, he said with that wide smile of his, 'Why not?'

But Dominic didn't order a taxi; instead, they walked home arm in arm, a full moon illuminating the way. Elise thought this was possibly the most romantic thing she'd ever done; she could have walked for miles. She laughed at the thought of doing this with William.

'So, who's your friend then?' she asked as they strolled back to his house. 'The one I met the other night.'

'That's Anthony. We've known each other since sixth form and now we work together but I wouldn't say he's a friend, as such. More of a hanger-on. Wherever I go, Anthony is sure to follow. He's a pain in the backside, frankly.'

'Do you have many friends?'

He thought about this for a while before answering, 'No, not really. I'm happy on my own.'

'Oh,' she said, feeling inexplicably disappointed by his answer.

He picked up on it: 'No, I mean male friends,' he said quickly. 'I always have room in my life for a beauty such as you, Elise.' She smiled at that.

So they returned to his house, and my, thought Elise, what a house. The hallway had a grandfather clock, of all things. Elise had never even seen a grandfather clock before. It had a chandelier, a gold-framed hexagon-shaped mirror, and a marble-topped hallway table with curvy legs. A Grade II listed building apparently, dating from the 1790s, so Dominic informed her matter-of-factly.

He took her through to the living room and there Elise

met Dominic's mother who was watching TV. Dominic introduced them, and Elise wanted to the ground to swallow her up – it was obvious why she was here, this young woman with too much make-up. Mrs Woods' eyes spent far too long gazing at her breasts and it was all Elise could do not to cover them with her hands. She felt immediately judged by her. She wondered whether Dominic made a habit of bringing random women home with him. Naturally, she hoped not. Dominic's father, apparently, had already 'retired' to bed. That, at least, was a relief, thought Elise. Mrs Woods asked her where she lived and it was obvious from her response that she had no idea where Elise was referring to.

Dominic, luckily, saved the day by dragging her away and up the stairs. 'I'm sorry about that,' he said, once he'd closed the bedroom door. 'She can be rather…' He searched for the word. 'Protective.'

'Same with me,' she exclaimed. 'Protective is the word. My mum's even worse. If I go out, it's all where are you going, who you're going with, what time will you be back. Gets on my tits after a while.'

His bedroom was, she thought, typically single male – dark grey walls, a grey bedspread, a desk in the corner with a computer and desk lamp, no books except one on wealth creation, everything minimalist and Unitarian. 'I should've offered you a drink,' he said. 'I'm sorry.'

'I don't need a drink,' she said in her most seductive voice. She stepped up to him and kissed him.

Afterwards, they lay in bed, grinning. She cuddled up to him, a part of her wondering why such a well-to-do man as Dominic should be so drawn to her. 'You really are something, Elise,' he said, drawing her closer to him. 'You are so beautiful.'

'You don't mean that.'

'Don't tell me what I mean or don't mean. I'm telling you, you are beautiful.'

She smiled but something in the way he'd said it, the compliment either side of the reprimand, made her uneasy. She brushed the thought away. They talked of mundane things, pleasant things. Her phone buzzed – a WhatsApp message from her mother asking, almost demanding, to know where she was. She answered with just two words: *I'm fine*. Then, as an afterthought, added a kiss. Half an hour later, seeing the time, Elise declared she had to go.

'Go?' asked Dominic. 'What do you mean?'

'As in, I've got to go home, Dominic. I can't stay.'

'Why on earth not?'

'Because...' Did she need to have a reason? 'Because I've got work tomorrow and–'

'You can go to work from here, can't you?'

She laughed although she wasn't finding this remotely funny. 'I can hardly go in dressed in what I was wearing. No, Dominic, I need to go home and–'

'OK, you made your point, go home then, fuck off.'

She sat bolt upright. 'Don't talk to me like that.'

'Just go. I don't care.'

'I'm going,' said Elise, jumping out of bed, naked. She gathered up her clothes from the floor, and quickly got dressed. 'I'll see myself out, shall I?'

'As you wish.'

She didn't kiss him or even say goodbye but although she felt like it, she didn't slam the door. Instead, she crept downstairs hoping not to bump into his mother again. But all the lights were off downstairs, everything quiet. She took her phone from her handbag, its light illuminating the space, and ordered an Uber. Seven minutes it said. She swore but booked it, nevertheless. It was too cold to wait outside; she'd have to wait here in the silence, a silence punctuated only by the slow tick-tock of the grandfather clock.

Six minutes later, she heard someone's footsteps coming down the stairs. Were they his? Yes, Dominic appeared in a purple dressing gown. 'I'm sorry, Elise. I can be such an idiot at times. Of course, you need to go home. I was being selfish. I can run you home, if you want.'

She appreciated his apology and smiled, wanting him to know he was forgiven. 'It's fine; really, I've already booked an Uber. It'll be here in a minute.'

'If you're sure.' He hugged her and she kissed his cheek. 'Thank you for tonight. You're the best thing to happen to me for a long time. Can I see you again?'

'I'd like that.'

'I'll give you a ring.'

'I can give you a ring.'

'No. It's just… I get busy, what with work and things. Let me call you.'

'OK. Sure.' The lights of a car swept the hallway. 'That's my Uber.'

They kissed, their arms around each other. 'I'd better go,' she whispered. 'Thank you for tonight. It's been lovely.'

'Hasn't it? Look after yourself, Elise. See you soon.'

'I look forward to it.'

Chapter 17: Elise

Today was the day Elise was due to move into the flat with her fiancé, and what had been a source of excitement, a sense of turning a new leaf, had become loaded with dread. She'd packed three boxes and two suitcases worth of stuff. Phil had phoned, saying he'd pick her and her stuff up in his car. Dad lugged her things to the hallway, and from there, a few minutes before Phil was due, placed them on the driveway, ready for Phil to put in his car.

Phil arrived on time at her parents' house in his Saab 900 but without his usual ready smile. 'You're not going to believe this,' he said, coming into the house, looking flustered. 'But some skank of a kid's keyed my car.'

'Oh, you're joking,' said Dad.

'Right down the side, the whole length of it.'

Mum, Dad and Elise followed Phil to his car parked outside the house across the driveway. Sure enough, on the passenger's side, an ugly line that stretched the whole length of the car. 'Wow,' said Dad, shaking his head in dismay. 'They meant business, whoever it was. That's severe. When did this happen?'

'I don't know. Being on that side, it could have been days ago. That's going to cost me an arm and a leg to get fixed. Look at it, the little…'

'Where did this happen?' asked Mum.

'Outside my parents' place.'

'Any other cars done?' asked Dad. 'Or just yours, Phil?'

'Just mine, I think. I looked. I mean, what's the point in doing that? It's not even if it's anything special. It's just a bloody Saab, for God's sake. I don't get it.'

'I'm sorry this has happened to you, Phil,' said Elise.

'Yeah, thanks. Anyway, shall we get your stuff in the car?'

Between them, Phil and Dad put all of Elise's things into his Saab. They were ready. Elise hugged her father and then, with tears forming, hugged her mother.

'What's with all the emotion, darling?' Mum asked. 'Anyone would think you were moving to the moon, not five minutes down the road.'

This was a bit rich coming from her mother, thought Elise; it was usually her mother who went over-the-top on the emotional front. 'I know,' she said. 'I know. It's just that…'

'I know, darling. Things get on top of you. You worry too much. Things are better now, aren't they? You have your whole life stretching ahead of you; you've got a lovely young man, a job you enjoy, a mum and dad who love you, and the past is behind us now. All that business – all gone now.'

'I know all that.' She held onto her mother while her dad and Phil stood a respectful distance away talking football, as often they did when they didn't know what else to say to each other. 'It's just that things get on top of me every now and then. The memories, you know, of what happened. Sometimes they come back and get hold of me, and I can't shake them off.'

'You have to think of the future now, love.'

'I've only known Phil for six months and yet we're already engaged and moving in together. What if I've made this terrible mistake?'

'Has he done anything or said anything to make you think that?'

The image of Tracey flashed through her mind. 'No, not at all, it's just... sometimes I worry I've asked for too much too soon and I get frightened it's going to bite me in the backside.'

'Oh, Elise, my love, you're being paranoid. Everything will be fine. Think of what you've been through. You survived that, didn't you? If you can survive that and come out the other side still smiling, as you have, you can survive anything. Trust me, I know. I was there with you, wasn't I?'

'I know, Mum.'

'Go on, go to Phil now, get in that car. Your future starts now.'

'Yes, Mum. I know. I love you.'

'I love you too, my darling. I love you so much.' Her mother kissed her forehead, then gently pushed her away.

Wiping her eyes, she hugged her father a second time, got into Phil's car and buckled up. 'My future starts now,' she said to herself before Phil got in the car.

'I still can't believe why someone should key my car like that,' said Phil, putting his seatbelt on. 'Little bastards.'

Elise waved at her parents as Phil eased away.

They didn't speak during the drive, the silence hanging awkwardly between them. Phil, she could tell, was still fuming about the scratch while Elise had a deep, nasty feeling she knew who'd done this. But surely, an act of petty

113

vandalism was beneath him; he wouldn't stoop so low. But then, this was Dominic Woods she was thinking about. That man would do anything to get under her skin, to unbalance her. Would he again? Now? Surely not. But one could never tell with Dominic; that man was capable of anything if he thought it furthered his foul plans.

Twelve minutes later, Phil parked up on the street where their new flat was. 'This is it,' he said, unnecessarily. 'Let's get your stuff up, then I suggest we get a takeaway in tonight. What do you fancy, Else? Indian? Chinese? Your shout.'

'Not that hungry, to be honest.'

'Oh, for Pete's sake, Else, have you not got over this Tracey business yet.'

'This Tracey business?'

'Yeah, OK, she *was* my girlfriend, I've already told you that. But I can't be held responsible if you're jealous of a girlfriend I had before we'd even met.'

'Yeah, I understand that, Phil. But she still works with you, doesn't she?'

'So what, we—'

'If I find out you two are sleeping together, God, Phil, it's over between us. I mean it, Phil. No second chances. It's finished.'

'Alright, calm down, Else. For God's sake. I'm not sleeping with her. She's got herself a new fella, we're sound, all right? Sound. Come on, let's go up.'

Phil carried her heaviest box, Elise her lightest suitcase. As he opened the front door to the house, he turned to her and said, 'I bought a bottle of something sparkling. It's cooling in the fridge.'

'Nice.'

They climbed the stairs to their new first floor flat. Phil put

114

the box down to open the flat door. 'Right. Maybe I should carry you over the threshold.'

'I think you only do that on our wedding night.'

'Yes, you probably… Shit, it looks like… Someone's been at the lock. Has someone broken in?' With his fingertip, he pushed open the door. Elise's heart went to her mouth. Phil glanced back at her, the look of fear on his face. He stepped in, switching on a light. 'Hello?' he called out nervously. 'Is anyone here?'

Elise stepped in behind him, her hand on her beating chest. The flat seemed eerily quiet.

'It seems alright,' said Phil. He stepped into the living room. 'Oh, fuck!' he screamed.

'What?' shouted Elise, pushing past him. 'What is it? Oh my God.'

The main room had been desecrated with bright red paint, huge dollops of it thrown against the walls, across the carpets, over all the furniture, so much of it, thick, so thick, still glistening, still smelling of fresh paint, the colour of it, so vivid, so vile, so much of it everywhere, just everywhere.

Elise sank to her knees and sobbed.

Chapter 18: Benedict

'Mr O'Brian, thank you for your time.' Benedict and Jessica settled in the Irishman's office. The office resembled a small art gallery, the walls adorned with landscape paintings. On his desk, several framed photographs. Craning his neck, Benedict could see various smiley family portraits. 'Can you tell us a little about Safe Hands Trading?'

The company, said O'Brian, was his. He started it from the ground up when he realised that cryptocurrency was the place to be. He'd worked as a City trader for many years previously and built up his experience and knowledge to the point he felt confident in branching out on his own. The company he'd worked for considered Bitcoin and the others as a flash in the pan or too variable or unstable to consider as any part of an integral part of their strategy. More fool them, said O'Brian with a hint of a smirk. He hired one assistant and rented a dingy office in Willesden. Success came easily and quickly, exceeding his already ambitious plans. Thus, he moved into his current premises five years ago, and employed more staff, and that is where Safe Hands Trading currently found themselves.

'And what about Anthony Browning?' asked Jessica. 'How

long had he worked for you?'

'I knew you'd asked, so I've got the dates here.' he said, putting on his glasses. 'He began in October three years ago.'

'An important member of the team.'

'All my staff are important members of the team, otherwise they wouldn't be here. I don't employ anyone for their pretty looks.'

'He was good at his job then?' asked Jessica. 'No issues that caused you concern?'

'Of course. I mean, if, for whatever reason, I had to cull my staff, then, yes, OK, I'd say Anthony might not have survived. Also, I had reason to speak to him in the past over his conduct regarding the female members of staff. He could push the boundaries of what we might consider acceptable.'

'Can you expand on that?'

'If I come into work wearing a new suit, I don't expect anyone to comment on it, you know? It's not necessary. We're not a fashion company. It's important we look smart, obviously, but Anthony used to comment on the women's outfits that perhaps made them feel a tad uncomfortable. So, I told him to stop, and he never did it again.'

'Did anyone complain about his behaviour?'

'No.'

'Did he have enemies, people he'd worked with in the past? Dissatisfied customers? That sort of thing?'

'No. At least, not to the extent anyone would want to drown him in Regent's Canal.'

Neither detective corrected him by saying that actually, Browning had been strangled before being pushed into the canal.

'What about his personal life? We know he was married.'

'I take no interest in my employees' personal lives, so I

wouldn't know.'

Jessica produced a screenshot of Browning and his companion and slid it across the table to O'Brian. 'This was taken in the hour before Anthony's death last night, taken in the Davenport pub. Do you recognise the man he's talking to?'

'Oh, yes. He works just down the corridor. That's Dominic Woods. My top trader, bar none. He'd be the last person I'd cull. Much of the success here at Safe Hands is down to this man. Can't fault him. He'd be happy to talk to you.'

Benedict and Jessica thanked O'Brian for his time, and as instructed, walked down the corridor to the door that had Dominic Woods' name upon it.

They found Dominic Woods on his mobile. He waved at them to take a seat. There was only one, so Benedict stood to Jessica's side. In contrast to his boss's office, Mr Woods' office was bare of any adornments, no photos on the desk, no personalised touches. It was as if the man was just passing through.

'Listen, Mr Chan, ultimately, it's your choice. I can't force you to stay put but at the very least, I would suggest you pause and think carefully about this. To cash in now, I believe, would be a mistake, one that, over time, you may rue. Yes, there's a slip at the moment but, as you know, that's the nature of the beast. While I can't guarantee anything, I'm confident that if you keep your money where it is, this time in two months, you'll be thanking me… Yes, Mr Chan, that's right… Yes… No problem… OK, give me a ring at the beginning of next week… Sure… Thanks… OK, speak to you soon. Bye bye now.'

Mr Woods finished his call with Mr Chan. 'That,' he said, 'is a conversation I have every day at some point. These people, they put their money in and then immediately get nervous and want to pull it all out again. I understand, this is not a business for those not prepared to play the long game. But it's infuriating having to explain in words of one syllable that they're not going to see a massive return in five minutes. Anyway, sorry about that, I get carried away sometimes. You're the police officers Mr O'Brian told me to expect.'

'We are, sir,' said Benedict who then introduced himself and Jessica.

'I tell you, it's been a shock. It's hard to fathom that this time yesterday, Anthony was here, another routine day. And now he's gone. Makes you realise just how precarious life can be.'

'Did you get on, the two of you?' asked Jessica.

'Yeah, all right. I mean, I'm not going to pretend we were the best of mates or anything, but, yes, as work colleagues, we rubbed along OK.'

'Was he good at his job?'

'Yeah. But then we all are; we have to be. O'Brian's no one's fool. He knows when someone's not up to the task. He runs a tight ship. You're only as strong as your weakest link, as they say, so he keeps us on our toes, as indeed, he should. It's his company, after all.'

'You wouldn't know anyone who'd wish to do Mr Browning harm?'

'God no. I didn't know him that well. Like I said, it's not like we were best of mates or anything but he was a decent sort. I just can't get my head around that he's no longer with us.'

'You went to the pub with him last night,' said Jessica. 'Was that something you often did, the two of you?'

'No. That was a first.'

'So, why was that?'

'He just asked yesterday morning out of the blue. Took me by surprise, to be honest. At first, I was going to say no, because our relationship is… was purely work-related but then I thought, why not?'

'What did you talk about?'

'Work. Honestly, that was it. He didn't mention his wife or the football or where he'd been on holiday, nothing like that, we just talked about work.'

'So, why did Mr Browning want to go to the pub with you just to discuss work matters?'

'I wondered the same. The only difference was, we were a bit more…' He searched for the word. 'A bit more catty about some of our customers, used words that we might not have used in the office.'

'An opportunity to de-stress, perhaps?' suggested Jessica.

'Yeah, exactly that.'

'Was he stressed?'

'Not particularly. I mean, this job can be demanding and Mr O'Brian is a hard taskmaster, but no, Anthony wasn't suffering from any more stress than normal.'

'We know you left the Davenport at seven ten, Mr Woods, and Mr Browning a minute or so later. Where did you go?'

'I went home. Which meant I was going the opposite way from Anthony. I bumped into this woman at the door. I remember her because she had this large hat on.'

'We saw her on the pub's CCTV,' said Benedict. 'And Mr Browning didn't contact you again?'

'No. That was the last I saw of him.'

'Apart from the killer, I believe that was the last anyone saw of him.'

Chapter 19: Elise

Phil fell to his haunches and wrapped his arms around Elise. Elise could not stop crying, covering her eyes with her hands, unable to look at the horror all around them. All that red paint, thrown everywhere with apparent abandon. It seemed so bizarre, so surreal, as if it wasn't really happening, that it was just some horrendous trick of the mind. Whenever she removed her hands from her eyes, she sobbed again, huge great sobs. All four walls had been splattered with this bright red paint, splashes of paint had reached the ceiling, it was on the settee, the armchair, the sideboard, on the lampshade, everywhere on the carpet and, to the side, the wooden floors.

Elise screamed into Phil's chest. 'Why? Why would anyone do this to us, Phil?'

Phil too, she noticed, was crying. 'I don't know, I don't bloody know.'

Whoever did this had left footprints here and there. The paint was still wet, this had been done within the last couple of hours. It still stunk of fresh paint, overpowering.

'We're going to have to phone Mr Sheth and let him know.

He's not going to be happy.'

Phil rang the landlord and Elise could hear the man shouting at the other end of the line.

Phil rang off. 'He's on his way over. Shit, Elise, why would anyone do this? I mean, it's not as if they took anything, it's just... vandalism for the sake of it.'

'It's cruel, that's what it is.'

Eight minutes later, the landlord arrived at the flat. He came in and stopped in his tracks, his face turning white. 'Oh my God,' he muttered, his voice shaking. 'Oh my God. What is all this?' He turned to face Phil, his face like a ghost.

'We just found it like this, Mr Sheth.'

He opened his mouth to talk but nothing came out. The man was in shock. He cast his eyes around, seeing the huge splashes of red, breathing in the smell.

'Some of your things are here,' said Mr Sheth, his voice shaking. 'Are they yours or hers?' he barked, addressing Phil.

'Mine. I dropped them off earlier.'

'So, you didn't double lock the door. That was a good lock.'

'I thought I had.'

'You didn't double lock.' He was shouting now. 'That's why they can break in. This is your fault, *your* fault,' he said, jabbing Phil in the chest.

'We just found it like this, Mr Sheth.'

'Oh my God, what can I do? You idiot,' he shouted, clamping his hands against the sides of his head. 'Look at it. It's ruined. All of it – ruined. Everything needs replacing. All you have to do is double lock the door, is not difficult. How stupid can you be? How can–'

'Stop shouting!' cried Elise, clinging onto Phil, her cheeks soaked with tears. 'Just stop shouting at us.'

'Why can't I shout? Would you not shout when you have two imbeciles. You pay for this.' He waved his arms about. 'The new wallpaper, the carpet, the cleaning, all my furniture, the labour, everything, everything, you pay for all of it,' he screamed.

'You've got our deposit, Mr Sheth,' said Phil meekly.

'Deposit? Ha! You think your deposit is enough? Nowhere near enough.'

'But we didn't do this, we—'

'You sign the tenancy agreement, no? That means while you live here, you are responsible for this flat. You!'

'But we hadn't even moved in yet,' screamed Elise, crying again.

'You are responsible from the moment you sign that agreement, that is the law. You understand the law, no? How long will this take? All that time with no rent. I have my bills to pay too, you know. I need this money. I have a big family, we need this… oh my God, I can't believe this has happened.'

He'd stopped shouting now and instead looked close to tears. Turning to face Phil, his voice rose again. 'I call the police, I have to call the police. Get out, go on, get out, out! Take your bloody things and get out of my flat. You disgust me. And stop your bloody crying, girl. It's me that should be crying, not you, this is my property. I have your number, Mr Phil. I want my money for this. I use your deposit and then I'll need more. I'll phone you. Now, get out. I can't bear to look at your faces. Get out! Get out!'

It didn't seem possible but Phil and Elise were loading Phil's car with the very things that, twenty minutes before, they'd lugged up the stairs and into their new home. A home that was theirs no more. It didn't seem possible. Back inside

Phil's car, they sat, their seatbelts on, not talking. Elise gazed into the distance but unable to see anything through the haze of tears.

Eventually, Phil muttered, 'I can't believe anyone would do such a thing. I keep asking why – why would someone do that? What sort of sicko could be so possessed?'

Elise didn't answer but she knew, she knew exactly what sicko had done this. She played with her engagement ring.

'It's going to cost us thousands. We'll never find anywhere to live now, we're fucked.'

'Yeah, all right, Phil. Stop talking.'

'Oh, so sorry, Elise. Sorry if I'm in shock.' Phil looked down at the car's footwell. 'Oh shit, it's in the car. And your side. We've got paint on our shoes and now it's in the bloody car. Damn it.' He thumped the steering wheel. 'Shit. I can't believe this is happening. First, some bastard keys my car and now... now *this*. I feel sick, I actually want to be sick.'

'Take me home, please, Phil.'

'What? Yes, sure.'

Twelve minutes later, Elise was back at home. Phil helped take her things from the boot and back seat of the car and deposited them outside her parents' front door. Elise removed her shoes, leaving them outside and rang the bell. Her mother answered, the face creasing with concern. 'What's happened?'

'Oh, Mummy.' Elise fell into her mother's arms and sobbed again, her whole body shaking. Mum led Elise indoors, Phil, also removing his shoes, following with the first of Elise's suitcases.

Elise's father appeared from the kitchen wiping his hands on a tea towel. He stopped on seeing Phil, then his daughter curled up on the settee being comforted by her mother.

'What's wrong?'

'Quite a lot as it happens,' said Phil. Phil related the story, running his hand through his hair.

'Red paint, you say?'

'Everywhere. It's as if they'd arrived with several cans of the stuff, and just randomly threw it all over the place. It was disgusting, and now we have to pay for it.'

'Your deposit?'

'You should see it. It's going to cost a lot more than that, a lot more.'

'Could we not offer to do the work ourselves?'

'I don't think Mr Sheth will allow us back in the flat after all this.'

'Christ almighty. What a mess.' He looked at his daughter. 'I'm sorry, Elise.'

Elise untangled herself from her mother's arms. 'I'm going to my room.' She stood. 'I've got such a headache.' Turning to Phil, she said, 'I'll see you soon, Phil.'

'Yeah, sure.'

He didn't look sure what to do with himself. It was obvious, thought Elise, that he wanted a reassuring hug but she didn't have it in her to provide one. Instead, Elise turned her back on him and headed up the stairs.

Chapter 20: Benedict

For the first time in what felt like weeks, there was a hint of sun when Benedict woke up. Sonia was already up and about. He could hear her in the ensuite, having a shower and humming to herself. She came out wearing a towel around her, her hair tied up. The children were still on their half term break and though they'd never admit it, Benedict had the distinct feeling they were getting bored. They had the house to themselves which, he guessed, must have felt like great fun to begin with but the novelty was fast wearing off. Especially, as he kept leaving them notes with things to do – empty the dishwasher, please, vacuum the stairs, clean the toilets, sweep the kitchen floor, etc. He never said who should do these little jobs, he let them argue that between themselves. He knew they probably argued over who was to do what longer than the task actually took. The thought rather amused him.

'What's amusing you?' asked Sonia as she dressed.

'Oh, I was just thinking that after this week, the kids might have a greater appreciation of what we do for them.'

'You think so? Just because they had to flick the hoover

around for five minutes. I don't think so, Ben. How's it going with work?'

'An ongoing murder investigation and some poor sap left to die in the middle of the night tied naked to a tree in the woods, you know, everyday stuff.'

She laughed. 'Oh, for such a glamorous job. No, don't tell me, someone's gotta do it.'

He yawned and stretched.

'Shouldn't you be getting up.'

'Just five minutes more, just five minutes more.'

*

Benedict arrived at the office near half past nine. Everyone was in and looking busy. He got himself a coffee and while waiting for the kettle to boil, wolfed down a banana. He'd much prefer his usual almond croissant but sometimes a person had to try harder. So a banana it was.

Settling at his desk, he turned on his computer and logged in.

DC Prowse called over. 'Boss, now that you've got your coffee, I've got some news for you.'

'Good news?' he asked, swivelling around in his chair.

'Sure is. That photofit has thrown up a name.'

'Really? Already? That's great.'

'Yes, someone rang through earlier this morning. You weren't here yet.'

Benedict chose to ignore his subordinate's little dig. 'Did this *someone* leave a name or explain how they recognised our man?'

'No, he didn't want to leave his name and he didn't explain.'

'Pity.'

'I'll email you over the details.'

'DC Prowse, I am sitting here, I'm no more than ten feet away from you, can't you just tell me the details, man?'

Prowse laughed. 'His name is Hans Tanner, aged fifty-four. Got his address here. He lives with his wife, Nicola Tanner. The thing is, Mr Tanner has only just been released from prison. He served three years out of a five-year sentence. He'd hit a child on a bicycle while driving drunk. Pleaded guilty. First offence.'

'Did you hear that, Jessica?'

'I've already got my coat on, boss.'

'Let me finish my coffee first. DC Prowse, can you ring this Hans fella and tell him we want to speak to him today.'

*

'William Grant recognised the man in the photofit,' said Benedict, as he drove down Camden High Street.

'I know. It was obvious, wasn't it?' said Jessica.

'Question is, why would he lie?'

'We need to find out.'

'One can't help but wonder about the long-term effects this attack will have on William Grant.'

'I thought he was coping very well, all things considered,' said Jessica. 'But he may have to have some therapy at some point, help him come to terms with it.'

'Him helping us catch the swine who did this to him would certainly help. Let's see what this Hans Tanner has to say for himself.'

Hans and Nicola Tanner lived in a semi-detached, red brick house on a pleasant road called Harriet Avenue, not too far from Regent's Park. Benedict noticed a pair of women's shoes next to the front door. On closer inspection, they seemed to be splattered with red paint. Mr Tanner's wife, Nicola, opened the door to them and invited them in. Mr Tanner stood on seeing them. He was short, but solidly built, had large hands and hairy arms. He looked the sort who, despite being in his mid-fifties, could look after himself. But, wondered Benedict, would he be able to manhandle a man into the back of a van and up a hill. Frankly yes, he did.

Nicola Tanner joined her husband on the settee.

Benedict admired the large painting propped up against the sideboard. "Country Dawn',' he said. 'It's lovely. By Justin Travers. Can't say I've heard of him.'

'It's an engagement present to our daughter and her boyfriend, well, fiancé now.'

'Nice,' said Benedict. 'There's a certain Constable feel to it, don't you think?'

'I'm sorry?'

'John Constable, as in the painter, nineteenth century, did the *Hay Wain*. Beautiful work, and this reminds me a little of it. It's a wonderful picture you have here, very evocative of an English summer at its best. Your daughter has friends with taste.'

'Yes. I suppose.'

Sitting down, Benedict thanked Mr Tanner for his time and explained why he and Jessica wanted to speak to him. 'On Thursday evening cum early hours of Friday, a man was subjected to a horrific assault.' Benedict described the attack.

'And why are you telling me this?' asked Mr Tanner. 'I mean, I sympathise with the bloke but what's it got to do with me?' The man spoke with a trace of an accent – German maybe? His name was, after all, Hans.

'A witness saw the two men, the attacker and the victim, next to a van near midnight that night. He was able to describe the attacker in some detail. From that, we produced a photofit that you may have seen posted up around the area. And from that, someone came forward just a couple of hours ago and named *you*, Mr Tanner.'

'Me?' he said loudly, jabbing himself in the chest. 'That's mad. Whoever told you this was lying.'

'Hans wouldn't do such a thing,' said his wife, speaking quickly. 'No way. It's too horrible for words.'

'Here's the photocopy of the photofit, Mr Tanner,' said Jessica, passing them both the sheet of paper.

The couple considered it. 'Looks nothing like you, Hans.'

Hans Tanner passed it back. 'She's right, it looks nothing like me.'

Benedict looked again at the photofit and back up at the man sitting opposite him. It was, in all honesty, difficult to tell. Photofits were often like this, too subjective; what one person might think is a dead cert, the next will argue the opposite. There was a similarity, for sure, but was it enough? Would it convince a jury? He feared not.

'Where were you on Thursday night?' asked Jessica.

'At that time? Midnight? I was in bed with my missus, of course. Where else would I be? And no, apart from my wife, I have no one to collaborate on this, but that's hardly surprising, is it? I tend not to receive visitors in my pyjamas.'

'Before bedtime, though, did you go out?'

'No. I don't often go out. I prefer to stay indoors these days.'

'With me,' added his wife.

He smiled at her. 'With you, love.'

Benedict could hear someone padding around upstairs. Hans Tanner heard it too, glancing up at the ceiling.

'Mr Tanner,' said Benedict, adopting a deeper tone. 'You

don't have much of an alibi here.'

'He has me,' said Mrs Tanner.

'I'm sorry but that doesn't constitute what we'd call a cast-iron alibi.'

'I'm telling you the truth,' said Mr Tanner. 'What else can I say?'

'OK, moving on for now. You've recently been released from prison, Mr Tanner, is that right?'

'You know it is. Or you wouldn't be asking. Yes, four months ago. I made a mistake, I admitted it at the time, I admit it now. But I did my time without complaint and I've paid back my debt to society.'

'No, Hans,' said his wife. 'You're still paying. You can't get a job now, not a proper job.'

'She's right, actually. I used to have a job working in planning. I made good money. Now, I work as a delivery driver.'

'Luckily,' said Mrs Tanner, 'this house is paid for otherwise…' She didn't finish the sentence.

'You knocked down a child on a bicycle while driving under the influence,' said Jessica.

'Why are you asking me this when it's obvious you know all you need to know, and what's it got to do with Thursday night anyway?'

'We just like to get a full picture on anyone we talk to, sir.'

'Well, you're wasting your time. Now, if you don't mind, I've got to get to work.' Slapping his knees with his hands, Hans Tanner stood.

Benedict heard someone coming down the stairs. A moment later, a young woman with long dark hair, pale face, tired looking. 'Oh, sorry,' she said. 'I d-didn't know.'

Hans introduced the detectives. 'This is my daughter,

Elise.'

Benedict stood. 'I hear congratulations are in order, Elise.'

'I'm sorry?' She looked genuinely confused.

'Your engagement.'

'Oh, that! Yes, of course. T-thank you.'

'I was admiring your wonderful gift,' he said, motioning to the painting.

'What? The painting, yes. It's… it's lovely.'

She didn't appear overly enthusiastic about the painting. He thought it best not to draw attention to it any further.

Chapter 21: Elise, 2018
Five years earlier

Elise returned from work, tired after a busy day but more from the intense night the night before. Dominic had dominated her thoughts all day to the point of distraction. She checked her phone continuously, hoping for a missed call or a text from him but nothing came. Her boss, Mary Angelopoulos, the owner of the salon, asked many times if she was OK, the first couple of times sympathetically, but increasingly less so as the day progressed to the point she demanded that Elise concentrate on the job. Elise blamed it on a cold coming on. Why hadn't he been in contact? Several times, she almost called him but she remembered how adamant he'd been about her *not* contacting him, and she shied away, too fearful to make the call.

Sitting in the Uber last night, she received another WhatsApp message from her mother, wanting to know what time she was coming home. Elise swallowed down the annoyance; she was twenty years old, for God's sake, she didn't want to have to account for herself any more. She responded by telling her mother to go to bed. By the time the Uber had dropped her off at home, it had gone midnight. Luckily her mother had gone to bed, her father too. Come the morning, she'd managed to get out of the house before her mother, never an early riser, got up.

But now, coming home after work, she had to face her. She found her mother in the kitchen, stirring a large pan on the hob. 'Spaghetti Bolognese tonight. Is that OK?'

'Lovely. Thank you.'

'You were very late last night, lovey,' her mother said in that passive-aggressive way she often adopted, calling her 'lovey', as if, somehow, that softened the implied criticism.

'Yes, I was,' said Elise, pleased with her answer.

'Where were you then?'

'Out.'

Her mother stopped stirring. 'Elise, please. What were you doing? Where were you?'

'It doesn't matter, does it, Mum? I'm not sixteen any more, you don't need to keep checking on me.'

'I do while you live under my roof.'

'I'll move out then.'

'Huh! On your salary, lovey. I don't think so.'

Her mother was right, of course. She knew she didn't stand a chance of affording London rents.

'So, where were you then?'

'I'm not telling you, Mum. It's none of your business. I'm sorry but it isn't. I'm going to get changed.'

She fled to the sanctuary of her bedroom and flopped down on her bed. She lay there thinking of him, thinking of his exquisite body, the way he made love to her. Such a contrast to the lumbering efforts of William. Poor William. Her phone buzzed on her bedside cabinet and, scrambling over, she couldn't wait to see what it was. Surely now, it'd be Dominic. It wasn't. It was just a text from William. She groaned loudly. 'I'll pop by in a minute,' it said.

She wanted to text him back, to say, no, don't come over, not tonight, but he'd only quiz her as to why and she couldn't face it. She didn't respond. She changed out of her work clothes and removed her make-up. Normally, she'd have applied fresh make-up, to make herself look presentable for her boyfriend but tonight she had no desire to. Why hadn't Dominic been in contact yet? The wait was agonising. She knew she'd two-timed William and should be feeling bad about it but, in truth, she didn't care. She'd never really fancied William. He was her boyfriend because she'd wanted a boyfriend, nothing more. She'd hoped she'd become fond of him but that never materialised and she'd already been resenting him and now that Dominic was on the scene, she couldn't wait to be shot of him. But how? That was something she'd never been particularly good at.

Coming downstairs, her father had returned from work. They ate together; eating as a family was something her mother always insisted on. No TV dinners in this household, thank you very much. Her mother limited herself to asking Elise about her day, Elise answered in monosyllables.

Sure enough, William arrived just as Elise was clearing the plates. He exchanged pleasantries with her father. Elise sat on the settee and turned on the TV, flipping channels until she found something that might hold her attention for a while. William, uninvited, plonked himself next to her. 'Fancy going out to the Three Bells for a quick pint?' he asked.

'No.'

'Fair enough. Let me down gently, why not?'

'I want to watch this.'

'What, some random documentary on badly behaved kids. You're joking, right?'

'Looks good.'

'Listen, do you mind if I stay the night? We could have an early night.' He nudged her in the ribs.

She did mind; she minded very much but before she had a chance to answer, her mother came bustling in asking William how he was.

While they were talking, Elise's phone vibrated in her pocket. She risked looking – her heart somersaulted: it was a text from Dominic. *Hi beautiful. How r u? Been thinking of you all day. Cdn't concentrate.*

'Yesss!' she mouthed.

'Good news?' asked William.

'Hmm? Oh yea,' she said, quickly stuffing her mobile back into her pocket. 'A friend of mine. Some lad she likes has just asked her out.'

'Cool.' He coughed. 'So, how about it?'

'What?'

'Early night.'

'I'm very tired.'

'All the more reason–'

'Yes, OK.' She should have said no but, too distracted by Dominic's text, she couldn't think of how to.

Her mother returned to the living room, sitting down with a sigh. William offered to make her a coffee. She accepted, asking for decaffeinated. William, happy to oblige, pulled himself off the settee.

Elise took the opportunity to text Dominic back. *Hi handsome. Me too. Got told off for daydreaming.*

The answer came back immediately: *Who were u daydreaming of?'*

You obvs.

Good answer! A few seconds later, another text: *I so want to be inside you again.*

Oh my god, she mouthed.

'Anything wrong, lovie?'

'No. It's nothing.'

William returned, bearing her mother's mug of coffee. 'Decaf, Nicola, as you like it.'

'Oh, William, thank you. You are a darling.'

Elise grimaced. Her phone vibrated again. This time, she couldn't risk looking at it. Instead, she made the excuse of wanting the toilet and ran upstairs. Sitting down on the toilet, she viewed the message: *Fancy dinner tmr nite? My treat.*

Yes please.

Great! I'll find us somewhere good.

Cant wait!

Flushing the toilet, she returned downstairs, trying to wipe the smile off her face.

'We've changed channel,' said William. 'Is that OK?'

'Sure. Whatever.'

'You all right, El?'

'Yeah, sure. Never better.'

She tried to concentrate on a TV reality show featuring dogs while wondering what to wear on a dinner date with Dominic and, more awkwardly, how to finish with William. She also worried about Dominic texting again while simultaneously desperate for him to do so. Twenty minutes later as the dog show came to an end, she did receive another text. Unable to prevent herself, she whipped her phone out. 'My friend again,' she said. *Booked us a table at DiMaggios. Meet me at Camden tube at 7. Dont be late! Your gonna love it!*

Whoa, she'd heard of DiMaggio's, heard that it was

mightily posh and mightily expensive, a sort of place she'd never venture into. She replied quickly: *Fab! Cant wait to see u again.*

'She got a name, your friend?' asked William.

'It's not important.'

'Let me see.' He reached over, reaching for her mobile.

'No, get off, will you?'

'Elise!' said her mother. 'Be nice.'

'Exactly,' said William. 'Come on, let's see.'

'I'm going to bed.'

'Now? It's only... jeez, El, what's up?'

'Nothing. I'm just not feeling so good. I'll see you later.'

She trotted upstairs, knowing her mother would be cross she hadn't kissed her goodnight. She closed her bedroom door and sighed with relief. She texted Dominic. *Going to bed early. You tired me out last night!* That'd make him smile, she thought, throwing her mobile onto the bed. She was indeed deadbeat after her long night and a tedious day and the thought of an early night did appeal. Another text arrived: *Can u stay the night this time?* She thought about this for a moment and decided damn it, she didn't care what her mother thought. If she wanted to stay at Dominic's house for the night, she bloody well would. *Sure can*, she texted back. Dominic responded with a series of happy looking emojis.

She'd washed, cleaned her teeth and, having removed her top, was about to unclip her bra when there was a knock on the door. Assuming it to be her aggrieved mother, she said come in.

But it was William. 'William, I'm getting changed,' she said, her arms crossed over her breasts.

'Don't mind me.' He removed his jumper, throwing it on Elise's wicker chair in the corner.

'I'm going to bed.'

'I know, you said see you *later*.' He walked right up to her. 'So I thought…' With adroit movements, he pulled her in, put his lips against hers, and cupped her breast.

'William, get off me, will you?' She pushed him back.

'For fuck's sake, El, I thought we was going to have an early night.'

'No, *I'm* having an early night, not us.' She snatched her pyjama top and, quickly as possible, put it on. 'William, I want you to go.'

'All right, all right, I take the bloody hint.'

'No, what I mean is…' She took a deep breath. Her phone vibrated again. This time, William saw it light up on her bed. He made her grab for it but, Elise being closer, she got there first.

'Who keeps texting you?' he shouted.

'I told you, it's—'

'Bullshit, El. Who is it really?'

'You know, William, it's none of your sodding business.'

'If you don't tell me—'

'What? What will you do, William?'

He spun away. 'Nothing.'

'I want you to go, William. And…' This was it. 'And the thing is, I don't want you to come back.'

'What do you mean?' he asked, his voice faltering.

'I'm sorry; I don't want to go out with you any more.'

He stared at her, uncomprehending. 'You don't want to go out with me any more? But… I don't understand, I thought, you and me, El, I thought we were OK together.'

'I'm sorry.'

'You've got another fella, haven't?' he asked, his voice rising.

'No. It doesn't matter either way. I just don't want to see you any more.'

'What have I done wrong? I mean, I'm sorry if I was a bit heavy with you just now, I—'

'William, it's got nothing to do with that. I just—'

'What?'

'Please don't make me say it again. I just want you to go.'

'And that's it? Bye bye, William, it's been nice knowing you but now fuck off.'

'If that's how you want to see it, there's nothing I can do about that.'

He gazed around the room, as if knowing he'd never see it again. Turning to her with fury in his eyes, he said, 'You bitch. You *have* met someone else, haven't you, you slag?'

'Get out of my room. You don't come in here and talk to me like that. Get out now, go on, fuck off.'

'Oh, don't worry, I'm going.' He snatched up his jumper from her chair. He looked at her one final time. 'I hope you'll be very happy together, bitch.' He slammed the door behind him.

Elise fell on her bed, close to tears, such was her exhaustion. She heard William's heavy footsteps on the stairs. He said something to her mother and, seconds later, she heard the front door closing.

She looked at her phone. *Good night beautiful.*

She smiled. *Good night gorgeous.*

Chapter 22: Nathaniel

Today was the day, the day Nathaniel was prepared to sell his soul for ten thousand pounds. He woke up hideously early and immediately ran to the toilet and vomited. He staggered into his small living room, his legs weak, his stomach achingly empty. He'd hardly slept, kept awake most of the night running through all the scenarios where this could go horribly wrong and he'd end up in a police station. The more he thought about it, the more he realised Dominic Woods hadn't really planned this at all and left too much to chance. His plan, such as it was, had more leaks in it than a sieve, the potential for disaster was immense. He'd spent ten months in prison, and the experience scarred him; he never wanted to go through that again.

He'd spoken to Dominic the night before. Dom was happy with his work thus far but as far as being paid, it was meaningless unless he completed this, the most difficult and risky task. Nathaniel had his tea but today, given his nerves, he smoked three cigarettes and promptly felt sick again.

His mobile rang, making him jump. It was his ex-girlfriend

asking if Nathaniel could take her son out of school for a doctors' appointment. No, he said, he couldn't, not today. The expected tirade came – why did he have to be so effing useless all the time, what did he have on today that was so important. Nathaniel found it difficult to absorb her scorn, he felt particularly vulnerable today and his ex shouting at him was not helping. He wanted to plead with her, not today; I can't take this today. But that, he knew, would only make matters worse. He simply wanted to go back to bed and curl up in a ball. The boy wasn't even his stepson. He was a product of his ex's previous boyfriend, and the two of them had never got on that well, Nathaniel had never truly bonded with the boy.

He so wanted to tell his ex his woes, to share the burden. He wanted to go see her now, and hug her and rest his head against her bosom, and to hear her say nice, soothing things that would make everything seem better. But he knew he'd get zero sympathy from that quarter.

He got himself a bowl of cereal and stared at it. He had no appetite. He forced himself to eat but still ended up throwing half of it away. He had another cigarette.

Dominic rang again, making sure he was OK. 'I reckon now would be a good time to go sit outside his flat. He leaves for work in about half an hour. He catches the thirty-one bus towards town. Get yourself over there.'

'Yes, Mr Woods. I'll leave now.'

Nathaniel drove the two miles from his bedsit to where Philip Edwards lived with his parents. He parked along the street a few doors down and waited. And waited. So, where was he? Why wasn't he going to work? Maybe he was off today. After an hour, he rang Dominic but was told Mr Woods was in a meeting, try again in thirty minutes. This waiting was killing him. He kept wanting to be sick, his stomach churned again. Why was he putting himself through this? He lit another cigarette. He feared someone would see him just sitting for so long and get suspicious and call the police. The thirty minutes passed and he tried Dominic again. This time, Dominic answered. 'Let me try and find out what's happened to him. Perhaps he changed shifts and you missed him. Give me five.'

'Thank you, Mr Woods.'

He waited, biting on his thumbnail. Dominic phoned back almost fifteen minutes later. 'I rang his supermarket. He's called in sick.'

'Has he? What do I do now?'

'Come back tomorrow, what else?'

Really? OK. Thanks, Mr Woods.'

The thought of going through all this again tomorrow was too much to bear. His heart couldn't cope with this, the stress was too much. God, why was this so difficult? At least he could go home now and sleep for the rest of the day until he had to go to work at the club.

He turned his car engine on and, indicating, was about to pull out when he saw *him*. Yes, it was him all right, Philip Edwards, dressed casually, not so sick after all. He was walking quickly, looking at his phone.

Nathaniel eased the car out. Luckily, no one was behind him because he was driving at walking pace. Edwards glanced behind him, about to cross the road. NOW, NOW, NOW! Nathaniel slammed on the accelerator. The car roared into life and sprang forward. He gripped the steering wheel, his foot down hard. Edwards saw him and jumped backwards just as Nathaniel's car veered towards him. Breaking, Nathaniel jerked his steering wheel hard left, just avoiding a parked car, then back to the right, he steadied himself. He could see Edwards through his wing mirror screaming at him. Speeding up again, Nathaniel took the next right at speed, then the second left. Here, at last, he slowed down. He feared he was about to have a heart attack. He stopped the car and clutched his chest. 'Oh my God,' he muttered several times. 'Oh my God.' He'd failed; he'd bloody failed. It took any age for his heartbeat to slow down, to stop shaking. He'd failed and either he'd have to try again or watch ten thousand pounds slip through his fingers. He reversed the car, and slowly returned towards Warboys Avenue. He parked just before the junction and waited. This time, he only had to wait a minute before a thirty-one bus rumbled past. He had to assume Philip Edwards was on that bus. Indicating right, Nathaniel turned into Warboys Avenue and followed.

As expected, the bus moved slowly. Nathaniel stayed behind it, much to the frustration of the car behind who, understandably, expected him to overtake. The car flashed its headlights at him. Eventually, the car overtook both Nathaniel and the bus, only for another vehicle, a van this time, to take its place. Every time the bus stopped at a bus stop, Nathaniel edged his car to the left and hung back a little to get a better view of who was getting off.

Fifteen minutes later, the bus took a turn onto Selwyn Avenue, a one-way street, a short, steep nondescript road that led up to a set of traffic lights before the high street. Being a quiet road, the traffic lights here were invariably red. Here, finally, Philip Edwards alighted from the bus. Nathaniel stopped on a double yellow line, earning a beep from another car behind. Edwards had his ear pods in and either didn't hear or took no notice. He walked up the street briskly, looking at his phone. Gripping the steering wheel until his knuckles turned white, Nathaniel eased his car forwards. Again, Edwards crossed the road, barely a discernible glance behind.

Again, Nathaniel slammed his foot on the accelerator. The car lurched forward. This time, Edwards, on hearing the car, froze on the spot, indecision stripping his ability to move. Nathaniel's car slammed into him. The deafening thud assaulted his ears. Edwards flew over the bonnet and beyond. Where, Nathaniel didn't stop to see. Somewhere, a woman screamed. Glancing in his rear-view mirror, he could see Edwards' crumpled figure in the middle of the road, a woman, perhaps the one who screamed, rushing towards him. The traffic lights ahead were predictably red. Still, he eased his car out, breaking the light, indicating left, earning himself another beep from an oncoming transit van, and onto the high street.

He drove slowly for five minutes, his vision blurred by tears, before taking a left onto a quiet, leafy street. Here, he stopped, opened his car door and, leaning out, spilled his guts.

Chapter 23: Elise

Elise's father wandered into the kitchen in his blue Evri jacket. 'Right,' he said. 'I'll be off. Listen, Elise, money's tight at the moment, this job doesn't exactly pay loads. But your mother and I were talking last night. We'll try and help you pay for the repair job at the flat.'

'Oh, Dad, you are the best; thank you so much.'

'I don't see why you need to pay at all,' said Mum. 'It's not your flat, after all. It wasn't your fault, was it?'

'She'd signed the tenancy agreement, love, so yeah, technically speaking.'

'We should've told the police while they were here.'

'Mr Sheth said he'd be phoning the police. Not that it'll do any good.'

Hans kissed his daughter. 'Have you spoken to Phil since last night?'

'No, not yet. Maybe, he's getting his car fixed. I should phone him but I keep putting it off. Anyway, he can always phone me, can't he?'

She saw him exchange a glance with her mother. She knew

what they were thinking – that somehow the shine had rubbed off this engagement.

'Work were OK about you having another day off?' her father asked.

'Yeah. I wished I'd gone in, to be honest. It would've taken my mind off things. I'll go back tomorrow.'

'Good girl.' He kissed his wife. 'I'll see you both later.'

Elise fell onto the settee. She felt exhausted. Maybe, the shine *had* rubbed off her relationship with Phil. That name still kept ringing in her head – Tracey. Did she believe him when he said it was all over between them, that she had got herself a new boyfriend. Yes, she did believe him, so why this heaviness in her gut whenever she thought of her, when those Facebook images of the two of them together came to mind, as frequently as they did now. The desecration of the flat had also sullied things, she realised that now. It wasn't as if Phil had done anything wrong; he'd been in much shock as her, but she'd been so disgusted and so upset by what had happened, she wanted to put as much distance between it and now as possible, and, somehow, that included Phil.

Her mother sat beside her. Elise could tell she was concerned for her but she didn't want to talk.

'What's happening, love? Is it just the flat?'

She glanced at the painting. Bloody thing. Every time she saw it, she hated it more and more. 'It's fine, really. I'm just tired, that's all. I'll be fine soon.'

'Do you want to talk about things?'

She shook her head.

Her mother patted her knee and stood. 'OK. You know where I am if you need to talk. I need to get ready for work too now. Mid-morning shift today. Will you be OK by yourself?'

Elise nodded. 'I'll be fine.'

'Because I can always—'

'I said I'll be fine, didn't I?'

'Yes. Sorry, love.'

Elise winced at her use of the word 'love'.

It was rare for Elise to have the house to herself. All three of them were usually out at work at roughly the same time. She remained on the settee, her legs wrapped beneath her, and stared at the painting. She wondered how much it cost. Knowing Dominic, probably thousands but he wouldn't have thought about the price, wouldn't even have noticed. He might have noticed had it been too cheap, but otherwise no.

Life seemed so unfair. How was it that a manipulative, evil bastard like Dominic should waltz through life without a care, never having to worry about money, while a decent, hardworking soul, like Phil, was stuck in a supermarket job he hated, shrimping and working hard for the little he got. Between them, they'd worked so hard for that deposit and the advance rent, and to see it gone in a flash was simply soul-destroying. Was it to do with race? Dominic being white, Phil black. But no, it went much deeper than that. Dominic was ruthless; he didn't care how many corpses he walked over to get what he wanted, while Phil, the archetypal Mr Nice Guy, cared too much, was *too* considerate of other people's feelings. If she'd ended up marrying Dominic, not that it would have happened in a thousand years, but if she had – she'd be a very rich woman by now, rich and utterly miserable. Instead, she was engaged to be married to Phil, and, consequently, she was poverty-stricken and utterly miserable.

Her mobile rang. It was Phil. That was a relief. Since Dominic had been in contact, her heart skipped every time her phone rang for fear it might be him again. But, to her surprise, and relief, he hadn't phoned since.

'Hi,' said Phil. 'Fancy meeting for a coffee?' He sounded as tired as she was.

'Aren't you at work?'

'No. I called in sick.'

'So did I.'

'I feel sick.'

'So do I.'

'How about that café Berties, you know? On the high street.'

'Yeah. Shall we meet in twenty?' No, she needed to clean herself up first, put some make-up on, do her hair, change her bra. She *needed* to look nice for him to distract him from thinking about Tracey. 'Actually, make it an hour and a half.'

'That long?'

'I've just got a couple of things to do first.'

'All right. See you then.'

*

It was a good twenty-minute walk to Berties. Once upon a time, she might have caught an Uber, but those days, she realised with a heavy heart, were gone. No money to spare for such luxuries. She had to walk. But it felt good to be out, taking in the cold air. At least, it'd stopped raining at last. The world seemed full of kids out on their bikes and their skateboards, playing football on the streets, running around, so many of them, making so much noise. Then she remembered – it was half term. Lucky them. At one point, she stopped in her tracks and jerked her head around. A shiver ran down her, someone stepping over her grace. Was she being followed? No one there. She was being

149

paranoid. She moved on, but cautiously now, her ears on stalks, listening, checking, aware.

She arrived at Berties five minutes late, and breathed in the sweet, caffeine aromas. Mid-morning, it was busy, mainly mums with their kids, enjoying a half term treat. Lovely and warm inside, almost too warm. At least she looked good; she'd made damn sure of that. She wanted Phil to clock her and for his eyebrows to rise and say 'oh wow, you look great' the minute he saw her, as he always used to, perhaps not so often now. But, looking around, he hadn't arrived yet. A member of staff approached, George, according to his name badge.

'Hello, hello, lovely,' he said in a shrill voice. 'Take a seat. I'll come over shortly, pet.'

She thanked him and took a seat next to the window so she'd see Phil as he arrived. George approached the first time and she waved him away, saying she'd order when her boyfriend turned up, then wondered why she'd said *boyfriend*, not fiancé. The second time, she felt obliged to order now, so she asked for a ham and cheese Panini and a black latte.

'Coming right up!'

She checked her phone – a message from Phil apologising for being late but he'd gotten a call from his sister. But he was on his way now. She smiled, happy to realise that she *was* looking forward to seeing him, remembering that feeling she always had – that life *was* better when Phil was in it. She texted back with a thumbs up and a red heart, and settled back in her seat to watch the world go by.

She heard a siren fast approaching. An ambulance. She watched it transfixed as it made its way towards the café, weaving its way through the traffic, jumping a red traffic light, cars slowing down to allow it to overtake, pedestrians jumping out of its way. It came towards the café then swung abruptly onto the side road, the one nearest the café. Having disappeared from view, its siren ceased, as if it'd been turned off, as if the ambulance had got to where it needed to be.

Elise rose from her chair. Calmly, she collected her handbag and coat and slipped her mobile into her coat pocket. She pushed her chair in, and looking straight ahead, made for the exit and headed out of the café.

She didn't hear George shouting at her, about her Panini and coffee being ready, that she couldn't just walk out, that she needed to pay for them. She stepped outside, the sudden cold air causing her eyes to water. She walked at a steady pace in a daze, unaware of anything around her, as if floating. The world had turned silent, her own heavy breath and her shoes pounding on the pavement the only things she could hear. She wasn't even sure where she was going, what she was doing or why. It was as if she was being propelled by some hidden force within, something pushing her own, telling her where to go, urging her onwards. She turned right onto the side street. She saw the ambulance some seventy yards ahead, a small crowd of people already gathered as the paramedics hoisted a stretcher from the ground, the weight of the person on the stretcher telling on them. Elise's heart speeded up a hundred times over. She began to jog as the adrenalin began coursing through her veins. The tears came suddenly, taking her by surprise, blurring her vision. She could see only the ground directly in front of her now. The yellow ambulance, the paramedics were simply a blur as they carried their patient inside. She called his name, twice, thrice, four times, over and over, screaming it, screaming it. The sound of his name sounded as if it was coming from afar, but no, it was coming from within her, her very core, her very being. The gathered crowd looked up at her as she approached, parting ways to allow her through. The two paramedics re-emerged from the back of the ambulance, one closing the back doors behind him. She screamed at them, taking them both by surprise by the strength of her outburst. 'Is he dead? Is he dead? Tell me, is he dead?'

Chapter 24: Elise, 2018
Five years earlier

The seven a.m. alarm woke Elise up. Immediately, she remembered that she'd finally finished with William and the relief washed over her. He'd called her a bitch and that hurt but it was a price worth paying simply to be shot of him. Why had she gone out with him for so long? It didn't matter now. She had Dominic, and tonight, he was taking her to DiMaggio's. She googled the restaurant on her phone and scanned the numerous Google reviews – all excellent or good, not a bad word amongst them. Fantastic! She still hadn't decided what to wear. Maybe, she should buy something new but she wouldn't have time, not with work today.

She jumped out of bed, energised, and, opening her wardrobe, flipped through her clothes. She didn't have long to decide but better now than under pressure after work. Nothing too revealing, she needed something elegant. She plumped for her most expensive dress, a dark blue, butterfly-sleeved dress with a shiny sash for a belt, another online purchase from Shein. Perfect. Then, she picked up her smartest pair of pyjamas, a set of clothes for work tomorrow and, naturally, her toothbrush. She folded it all neatly into a small shoulder bag.

Sitting on a stool at the kitchen island, Elise tucked into her breakfast: honey on toast. Her mother wandered in, still in her dressing gown. Flicking on the kettle, she asked whether Elise wanted a tea. 'William left in a hurry last night. Was everything OK? Nothing wrong, is there, lovie?'

Elise knew she'd have to tell her at some point but now, twenty minutes before she had to leave for work, was not the time. 'No, nothing's wrong.'

'So, why did he—'

'Mum, I've got to get ready for work. I can't talk about this now.'

'Why are you always brushing me off these days? I am your mother; you can talk to me.'

'Later, all right? We'll talk later but right now...' She glanced at the kitchen clock. 'God, I've got to rush.'

In contrast to the previous day, Elise's day at work went well, such was her buoyant mood. The day flew by, she worked hard and, for once, enjoyed chatting to all the different customers. Even Mary, her boss, noticed, complimenting her. Finishing work, she rushed home.

For once, the house was empty. She showered, changed and doused herself in liberal amounts of her favourite perfume, and slipped on her only pair of high-heeled shoes. But she needed jewellery to finish it off. She plumped for her silver heart necklace and her butterfly ring, both looked classy without being overly ostentatious. She stood in front of her wardrobe mirror, swirling left and right, and thought, yes, she looked good; in fact, she looked bloody fantastic.

She trotted downstairs and chose a warm coat – it was terribly cold out. Now, she considered her outfit in the hallway mirror. 'Not too shabby,' as Shaz would say. Her mother came through from the kitchen wearing her apron. 'Oh, Mum, you made me jump. I thought you weren't in.'

'Are you going out again?'

'Yep. I won't be needing dinner. Sorry, I should have told you.'

'Yes, you could have told me. Not to worry. So, where are you going? You eating out?'

'Yep.'

'With William?'

'Nope. With friends.'

'Anywhere nice?' She opened the fridge, removing a pack of pork chops.

'Yeah, absolutely. We're going to DiMaggio's.'

'DiMaggio's? Not heard of that.'

'It's meant to be nice. The Google reviews are great.'

'Lovely. Well, you look… actually, you look super nice.'

'Thanks, Mum.'

'You're wearing your ring, I see, the one Granny gave you.'

'Ahuh.' She picked out a scarf. 'Oh, by the way,' she added as casually as possible. 'I'm sleeping over at Sharon's tonight.'

'Are you? What for? She only lives a taxi ride away.'

'Girls' night, Mum.' She hoped that she didn't need to explain any further. Her mother, predictably, did not look happy about this.

'Don't fret, Mum. I'm a big girl now. You forget.'

'Yes. Sorry, love. I just worry so.'

'I know. I'd better go, I'm already late.'

She made to leave.

'Don't I get a kiss?'

'Yes, Mum.'

It was just a kiss, so why did she find it so difficult?

Elise caught a bus to the underground station and from there the tube to Camden tube station. Despite her warm coat, she shivered. By the time she reached the DiMaggio's, Elise was ten minutes late. It didn't matter; it was a woman's prerogative. She paused outside and peered in. It had white tablecloths, chandeliers, parquet flooring, glass cabinets stocked with wine and, oddly, a fully-grown tree in the middle of the restaurant. Yes, this wasn't her usual sort of place; far from it, she was more of a Nando's sort of girl. Still, she was here now, might as well enjoy it.

Taking a deep breath, she walked in and despite feeling a little in awe of her plush surroundings, the maître d's welcoming smile helped ease her a little. He escorted her to her table to find Dominic already seated. He rose upon seeing her but Elise knew straight away that something was wrong. The maître d pulled out a chair for her. She thanked him and sat. The first words Dominic said were, 'You're late.' It wasn't so much what he said but the venom with which he said it.

'I'm sorry,' she said, her heart beating furiously. 'I got held up at work.' The lie slipped out easily. So much for it being a woman's prerogative.

'I don't appreciate being kept waiting. There's no excuse, it's just bad manners.' His face looked like thunder. 'I was giving you another five minutes and if you hadn't turned up, I'd have walked out.'

'I said I'm sorry. Really I am, Dominic.'

'Doesn't matter; you're here now. That's the main thing.' He smiled and his whole demeanour changed in a second. 'You look fantastic, by the way.'

156

'Thank you.'

His eyes scanned her top. She willed herself to keep her hands on her lap. 'You look fucking amazing, actually.'

'You don't look too bad yourself.' He was wearing a light green collared shirt under his beige jacket, but even Elise could see these weren't items he'd picked up in a Marks & Spencer sale, these were expensive brands, top quality.

'The food here is amazing; you're going to love it.'

Elise ran her eyes down the menu but it wasn't the names of the dishes that stuck out but the eye-watering prices. 'Yes, it all looks lovely.' She considered the options. 'I like the idea of the Beef Wellington.'

'No, you have to have the sea bass.'

'I'd rather– '

'Trust me, Elise. You have to have the fish.'

He was doing it again, deciding what she wanted. 'I'd rather decide for myself, Dominic.'

He opened his mouth but didn't say anything, instead picked up the wine menu, rattling it open. She sensed his annoyance, his attempt to remain calm. Did it really matter that much, she wondered. Without looking at her, he said, 'Are you purposefully trying to undermine me, Elise?'

'No, it's… OK, I'll have the fish.'

Now he smiled. 'You won't regret it, and I know the perfect wine to complement it.'

Her phone buzzed – a text from her mother. She ignored it.

The restaurant was busy for a Wednesday evening, mainly older people, people with money and that confidence that money gives a person.

'Who are you looking at?' asked Dominic, eyeing the people at the adjoining tables.

157

'Me? No one, Dominic, I was… I don't know, admiring the place. The decor, it's lovely, isn't it?'

He narrowed his eyes at her as if not convinced.

Did he think she was ogling a man, she wondered. Wanting to change the subject before it escalated, whatever *it* was, she asked, 'Have you been here before?'

'Yes. A few times in fact. It's one of my favourites.'

'It's lovely. You have good taste, sir.'

He laughed. She'd done it, averting whatever it was that was bothering him. Was he always so damn sensitive?

A waitress came and took their order, Dominic ordering for her.

'You really are the most beautiful woman I've met, you know,' said Dominic, once the waitress had gone. 'I want you to know that.'

'Oh, Dominic, stop it; you're making me blush.'

'OK, let me change the subject – I like your necklace but I'm intrigued by your ring. What is that?'

'It's a butterfly. My grandmother gave it to me after I graduated from college.'

'It's lovely.'

'I have a thing about butterflies: red admirals, swallowtails, painted ladies, holly blues, I know them all.'

He laughed. 'I never knew.'

'We've only just met, Dominic. There's a lot you don't know about me.'

'I know the important things,' he said with a salacious wink. 'So why butterflies then? Aren't they just bugs with pretty wings?'

'Ha ha! I don't know why. I've always had a thing about them. My mum bought me a picture of one as a Christmas present when I was small and I guess I've liked them ever since.'

'So butterflies are your thing?'

'Butterflies, chocolate éclairs and honey. But not necessarily in that order.'

'Right. I'll have to remember that.'

Chapter 25: Elise

Elise hadn't stopped crying. Phil had just come out of surgery and was lying comatose in his hospital bed. His left arm was in a cast, his neck in a brace, padding across his stomach and various tubes hooked-up to various monitors, keeping an eye on his progress. His parents had just gone to the restaurant, if only to stretch their legs. Phil's father almost had to carry his distraught wife away from her son's bed. Her own parents were with her. The doctor had told her the full extent of Phil's injuries: a broken leg and arm, five broken ribs, two broken collarbones and a fractured neck, but, far more concerning, was the collapsed lung and a bleed on the brain. They still needed confirmation of how bad and extensive the latter.

Two detective constables had come by, their names being Kelly and Prowse, Elise couldn't remember their first names, both no older than her, young Londoners, the former white with a trace of a Scottish accent, the latter black with an educated London accent. Elise had to tell them she hadn't witnessed the accident. She'd been sitting in Berties' café waiting for Phil when she heard and saw the ambulance and some instinct telling her that her fiancé had been hurt drew her to the scene of the accident.

'We do have one witness,' said the white detective, DC Kelly. 'She's currently helping us with our enquiries, mainly trying to identify what type of car it was. It's a quiet road, no shops, just the back of a few storage units and a garage. A bus had just passed by and we'll be checking its CCTV cameras. No one has come forward to admit their responsibility. Although that doesn't mean to say they won't. We've known people to drive off, only to wake up full of remorse and then come forward. We'll be checking your boyfriend's clothes in case we can trace any fragments from the car. I'm sorry, Miss Tanner.'

'I didn't pay them.'

'Who?' asked Prowse.

'The café. I ordered a Panini and coffee but when I saw the ambulance, I just walked out without paying.'

'How much was it?'

'I don't know. Seven, eight pounds.'

'Don't worry,' said Prowse. 'We'll sort it for you.'

'Would you do that?'

'Sure. No problem. We'll do it today.'

'I'll pay you back.'

'Don't worry about it,' said Kelly. 'We'll put it on expenses,' he added with a wink.

Elise burst into tears again. Their kindness struck something inside of her and it set her off again.

After the two detectives had left, Elise fell asleep sitting upright in her chair; she hadn't meant to but the tiredness overcame her. She woke up to find a nurse taking Phil's blood pressure. The nurse said something but Elise didn't take it in. She began to cry again. Her mother hugged her and her father rested his hand on her shoulder.

After a while, Dad went off to buy a round of tea from the machine in the corridor.

'Something's happening here, Elise,' said Mum. 'This time last week, everything was normal. But since you had your party, you've had...' She counted them off on her fingers. 'The vandalism to Phil's car, your flat being ruined and now this. Are you telling me, love, that this is all just a terrible coincidence?'

'Yes, of course it is.'

'I don't believe it.'

'Mum, I don't need this right now.'

'He's back, isn't he?'

'Who's back?'

'You know full well who I mean. It's... I can't even say that man's name. It was him who sent you that painting, 'Country Dawn' or whatever it's called. Of course, it had the butterflies on it. That's why it had no name on it. Of course! It makes sense now.'

'No, Mum, just stop it. You're seeing things that aren't there. What... are you doing?'

'I'm phoning the police.'

Elise tried to grab her mother's phone. 'No, Mum, you can't. Don't do this to me, please, Mum, I'm begging you.'

Her mother relented, putting her phone away. 'You know, if your father catches wind of this, he'll kill him. I mean, literally. He'll kill him.'

'I know, Mum. I know.'

Phil's parents returned from the restaurant and sat down either side of their son's bed, forcing Elise to move her chair away a little. Elise's mother asked them what they had to eat.

162

They hadn't eaten. Phil's mother, Phyllis, stroked her son's arm.

Hans returned bearing three plastic cups of tea. 'Sorry, Phyllis, Michael, did you want one?' They didn't. 'Here, love, I got you this. Help you keep your strength up.' He handed Elise a Twix chocolate bar.

Phyllis began crying again. 'My poor boy, my poor love,' she said in a strong Caribbean accent. 'We'll look after you, son. Whatever happens, we'll be there for you, day and night, every day.' She wiped away her tears. 'Do you remember when you broke your arm falling off your bike? I looked after you then, didn't I? Oh, how you cried. You were more worried about that girl. So typical of you, always more worried about other people than yourself. And when your granny fell ill. You were only fourteen, but you stayed next to her every minute you could. I had to drag you away to get you to school, you so didn't want to leave her side. And she knew, didn't she? When she woke up and got better, she said, do you remember? She said she felt your presence and it helped her get better.

'Oh, why didn't you stick with Tracey?'

Elise smarted on hearing that name. She glanced at her mother who shot her a concerned look back.

'We loved Tracey. You were so right for each other, so in love. I still don't understand why you... you split up from her. She loved you with all her heart; she told me once. None of this would have happened with Tracey–'

'No,' said Elise. 'You can't say this. This is unfair.'

'We loved Tracey too. She was like a daughter to us.'

'Enough now, Phyllis,' said Michael, Phil's father.

She turned to him, the anguish in her eyes. 'It's true though, Mike. You think it yourself, don't pretend you don't.'

'You're upsetting yourself and you're upsetting everyone else.'

She returned her attention to Phil. 'I don't care about that; I don't care about everyone else. I only care for Philip. It's true what I say, anyway. He loved that girl, she loved him. They belonged together, not with... with...' She looked at Elise with pure disgust. 'Not with *her*.'

'He does love me,' said Elise, trying to stop the tears.

'Not like he loved Tracey,' she shouted. 'That was *real* love. They were engaged. Did you know that? Engaged.'

Elise shook her head; she had no idea.

'Phyllis,' said Michael, rushing to her side of Phil's bed. 'Stop this now. You have to stop.' He tried to take his wife's hand but she brushed him aside.

'They wanted to get married, they *should* have got married, then none of this would've happened.'

'So, why didn't they fucking get married then?' shouted Elise through her tears.

'Elise!' shrieked her mother.

'Don't you *dare* curse in front of me and my poor son.'

'He's *my* fiancé.'

'You turned his head against what was proper and right. You – with your eyelashes and your big bosom and your ways.'

'Ways?' shouted Mum. 'My daughter doesn't have *ways*; you can't talk to her like that. Listen to your husband.'

'I'm sorry,' said a nurse, a ward sister, suddenly appearing. 'Is there anything wrong here?' She looked at each of them but was met with a stony silence. 'I cannot have shouting on this ward and I cannot have you upsetting the patients. Please don't make me ask you to leave. Although, as it is...' She checked her watch pinned to her tunic. 'Visiting time is

164

just about done, so if you wouldn't mind reconvening in the car park where you can shout at each other to your heart's content.'

They did as told, each standing up and collecting their coats and bags. They each kissed Phil before leaving. Phyllis and Michael left, Michael struggling to keep up with his wife.

'Well, that went well,' said Elise's father.

'Shut up, Hans.'

'I can't believe she'd talked to me like that, Mum.'

'I know, love. I know.'

Her mother hugged her and Elise allowed the tears to flow afresh.

*

Half an hour later, the Tanners had returned home. Elise was exhausted and went upstairs to her room. She lay on her bed and hugged a pillow, replaying all the terrible things Phil's mother had said about her, and how the sun radiated from Tracey's arse. She knew then that even if Phil did survive, she could never marry him, not with all that hatred of her, the resentment.

To think it all started with that wretched painting downstairs. Everything had been fine up to that point; the point Dominic Woods unleashed his poison.

Without giving herself time to change her mind, she reached for her phone and dialled Dominic's number. He answered straight away.

'Else, I've been expecting your call.'

'OK, you win. When and where do you want to meet?'

Chapter 26: Nathaniel

Midnight. Nathaniel Turnbull sat in the cramped back office of the Flamingo club watching the punters via the club's internal CCTV system. He'd been told to keep an eye on any drug activity, which, given his previous habit of using and dealing himself, he found nicely ironic. Still, it was a job, albeit a poorly paid one, but it kept him off the streets, and the work, though dull, was easy. It wasn't even as if he had to deal with any confrontations; he merely had to radio through and tip-off the security guys on the door, and no one messed with those thugs in suits. Mr Etherington, the Flamingo owner, knew he was skating on thin ice and that the council were simply looking for an excuse to close the club down.

Mr Etherington came into the office. 'You alright, Nat?'

'Sure, Mr Etherington.'

'Anything going down?'

'Nope. All quiet out there.'

'Good. That's the way we like it. Make sure it stays that way.'

'Yes, Mr Etherington.'

Nathaniel squinted at the screen, watching a couple of likely customers standing at the bar. Were they getting confrontational? They certainly seemed agitated. He couldn't afford for there to be a fight on his watch. This last weekday hour between midnight and one was the tricky hour. This was the hour all the punters got kicked out of whatever pubs they'd been in and rocked up here to continue drinking. Indeed, as a younger man, this is exactly what Nathaniel used to do with his mates. The beer here was much more expensive but by this time, they were usually too drunk to care.

The two blokes at the bar seemed to have calmed down, their body language decidedly more relaxed now.

It was then on camera three, he thought he recognised a familiar figure. He zoomed in, and yes, sure enough, it was him – Dominic Woods, and he was with that over-the-top woman again, Fifi. That man had the gift of the gab and that woman could talk for England! Woods ordered two large cocktails at the bar and was now seated with Fifi under the flashing lights, Fifi all legs and fake fur and big earrings. They were certainly laughing a lot. Nathaniel went out into the corridor and could see the manager wasn't in his office. Now would be a good time to 'bump' into Mr Woods and remind him that he had a bill to settle.

Nathaniel snaked his way through the punters, skirting around the dance floor towards the seated area. Dominic Woods didn't see him until he stood over him and his companion. 'Oh, Christ,' said Woods. 'You made me jump. Cheer up, Nat, might never happen.'

Fifi laughed. Dominic Woods was certainly a good-looking man with his wide grin and white teeth and his tanned complexion and his sweep of blond hair. He had public schoolboy written all over him. He could have been no more than thirty. How does someone so young get to be so successful? The privilege of a white man's education and upbringing, that's how. Even as a boy, Dominic Woods would've been sure of his place in the world. Something an insecure young black kid like Nathaniel had never experienced.

'Can I have a word, Mr Woods?'

'Fifi, darling,' said Woods. 'Why don't you go and powder your nose or something?'

'OK, OK, I can take a hint. See ya later, Nat.'

Nathaniel waited for her to go before asking, 'Were you happy with my work, Mr Woods?'

'Yeah, absolutely. Thanks, Nat. I rang St Cuthbert's hospital this morning, pretending to be a concerned relative. Mr Edwards is in a bad way. You did a good job there.' He took a sip of his drink. 'Can you come round to mine before work tomorrow evening, say about eight?'

'Can't you pay me now?'

'No. I need to make a transfer first and do a little jiggery-pokery to cover my tracks. But I always pay my debts, you know that, so don't you worry.'

'OK, tomorrow's fine then. I'll be there.'

Nathaniel slunked back to his office. Mr Etherington was back in his office. Nathaniel crept into his CCTV room, hoping the boss hadn't noticed his absence. Half an hour now until closing time. He spent the time watching Woods and Fifi, the resentment bubbling and growing within him. But it didn't matter – tomorrow he'd get his money and then he'd never think about the slimeball ever again.

*

168

Nathaniel had arrived ten minutes early at Dominic Woods' house on Faversham Avenue. He knocked but no one was in. So, now, he paced up and down the street and waited. He'd parked in a different street and walked, too embarrassed to park his battered Volkswagen Golf on a street like this.

Dominic Woods lived by himself in a large, detached four-bedroom house on the affluent side of Camden Town. It was fronted by a lovely brick wall (even if Nathaniel said so himself) and a cast-iron remote-controlled gate. Nathaniel did wonder how Woods could afford such a grand place by himself. It didn't seem right, somehow, having all this space to himself when so many struggled to find anywhere to live at all. Mr Woods had been happy with his work but there was still something deeply humiliating about the whole thing – the impoverished black man coming to the big white man's house to beg for his money.

Whenever someone passed by, which, in truth, was rare, Nathaniel walked on. Somehow, he didn't think it looked good, a man like him hanging around outside this house. People would assume he was staking it out. Then, ensuring the coast was clear, he'd return and maintain his vigil.

Finally, at five minutes past eight o'clock, Nathaniel's patience was rewarded. Dominic Woods' silver car came into view, a sleek Audi A3. He paused while the electronic gates opened to his command. Nathaniel stepped out of the shadows, wanting to make his presence felt without spooking the man. He waved and smiled, as if he was greeting a long-lost friend. Woods scowled at him from within the Audi. Nathaniel slipped onto Woods drive before the gates closed on him.

'You're here for your money?' asked Woods, locking the

car behind him.

'Yes, Mr Woods.'

He unlocked his front door, deactivated his alarm and went through.

Nathaniel, conscious he hadn't been invited in, followed nonetheless.

He'd been inside the house several times while working here but it still surprised him just how lovely it was: the grandfather clock, the chandelier, a gold-framed hexagon-shaped mirror, the marble-topped hallway table with curvy legs. A Grade II listed building apparently, dating from the 1790s, so Mr Woods informed him before. Mr Woods hung his coat up and went through to his kitchen. Nathaniel, not sure what to do and feeling a bit broadsided by the lack of acknowledgement, took the liberty of following. The kitchen was equally impressive with two Welsh dressers, one painted off-white, the other Shaker blue, and a large, granite-topped kitchen table. Nathaniel's eye was drawn to the large, metallic pig with large ears on the centre of the table.

Mr Woods went to a cabinet and there, started fixing himself a drink, a gin and tonic. 'Ten thousand, yes?'

'That's right, Mr Woods.'

'I haven't got cash though.'

'Bank transfer is fine. In fact, I'd prefer it.'

'You? You don't want cash? Come on, your likes always want "cash in hand",' he said in a terrible Cockney accent. 'Don't want the taxman getting his greedy paws on it, do we?'

'I pay my way.'

'Yeah, right, like the little tart I was with last night. You're not telling me that seedy little job you've got at the Flamingo doesn't pay you in cash?' Placing his tumbler on the table, he took his phone out. 'Right, let's get this over and done with. Give me your bank details. Actually, I've got them from last time, haven't I?'

'Yes, Mr Woods.'

Two minutes later, the job was done – £10,00 deposited into Nathaniel's bank account.

'Thank you, Mr Woods. Are there any more jobs you want doing?'

'Not for now. I'll give you first shout if anything comes up though.'

'Thank you, Mr Woods.'

Nathaniel left, stepping back into the cold, misty night. He had ten thousand pounds in his account, add that to the thousand and one hundred from before, he was suddenly well off and debt free. He should have been punching the air, dancing a jig down the street. Instead, he thought of Philip Edwards lying in hospital not too far away from here, and wanted to be sick.

Chapter 27: Elise

It was approaching nine o'clock in the evening. The night was bitter, dry and so cold. Elise blew into her gloved hands and stood back on the other side of Faversham Avenue looking at Dominic Woods' house. She checked her jacket pocket, beneath her coat, for her mother's sharp kitchen knife. Before leaving home, she'd sharpened it. The blade wasn't long but it'd do the job.

She never thought for a single moment she'd ever find herself back here again. Yet, here she was, about to enter the lion's den. She remembered the first time she'd been here. Was that really her? The memory felt like it belonged to a different woman entirely, not her. It wasn't even that long ago, five years. She was a different person then, younger, more confident, excited to get on with life. Now, still only twenty-five, she felt so damn old. Meeting Phil six months ago had changed everything for the better but she realised now that she'd moved too fast. Men, she realised now, didn't like to be rushed but boy, she'd rushed Phil. And looking back on it, she'd done all the running. It was she who'd asked him out on that first date, chose the restaurant, the pub and the nightclub. Phil never had a say. *We're going here first, then there second; I've got it all planned out and you have no choice but to do as I say.* She hadn't even thought about it at the time. She decided and never gave a thought about what he wanted. And it was she who initiated sex that first time – the night of their first date, no less. Weren't 'classy women' meant to hold off, at least get to know their new man first? But no, after that night club, they dossed down at a friend's house, and, lacking two spare rooms, they slept in the same bed and she seduced him there and then. The man didn't have a say – again. Looking back on it, was he that keen? Yes, once he got into it but she'd sensed a definite reluctance to begin, something she'd never thought about before.

And who proposed? Who demanded to meet his parents at the first opportunity, who suggested they move in together? Elise, every step of the way. He could've said no, or let's slow up a little, let's think about this. But she never gave him a chance. She had her agenda, maybe not laid out in her head, but an agenda, nonetheless. And Phil was required to play along.

And now look where they were – Phil in hospital fighting for his life. Assuming he survived, and the doctors assured her the prospect was good, what sort of life-changing injuries would he carry? They said he'd have difficulty walking, he'd have to take things gently perhaps for the rest of his life, that he'd never be as fit again. Why did it feel as if it was all her fault?

And all because she wanted a 'normal' life and to have a 'normal' relationship with a 'normal' boy, a kind-hearted boy, a sexy, good-looking boy, a man that made her heart race on seeing him. Did it race still? The realisation hit hard – it was the relationship that made her heart race, not the man himself. She didn't love Phil in the way, all those years back, she'd loved Dominic. She wasn't to know that her love for Dominic and his love for her was poisonous, destructive and soul-destroying; she wasn't to know. By the time she'd truly realised it, he'd almost destroyed her. Phil had been part of her rehabilitation, a way to rebuild her life into what she considered normal and healthy, the sort of relationships her friends had, the sort you showed off on Instagram. Look, here's my man, here's my beautiful life.

A man passed by, walking his dog, smoking a cigarette. He said, 'good evening'. She responded in kind.

It was ten past nine now, time to take revenge on the man who had almost destroyed her. She ran her gloved fingers over the knife, put her phone on mute and walked up to his drive and up to his door. She didn't even ring the bell when he answered. 'Oh my God, you're here, sweetpie. Come in, come in.'

She walked into the familiar house, her heartbeat going into overdrive. The place screamed money and class. Everything so tasteful, expensive, and spotlessly clean. It hadn't changed much from when Dominic lived here with his parents. She wondered how they were, dreadful people, his sycophantic mother especially. The grandfather clock, the chandelier, a gold-framed mirror, the marble-topped hallway table with curvy legs – everything as it was. She removed her gloves, stuffing them into her coat pocket. She felt conscious of every move she made, as if watching herself from afar.

'Come through,' said Dominic, leading her through to the drawing room, as it was called.

Ah, the carpet was new – a bright green carpet now, and the curtains too, heavy, dark green drapes, but still the same bookshelves lined with old books no one would ever look at, a solid, oak table decorated with a vase of winter flowers.

'You live alone now?' she asked, as he took her coat and scarf. Dominic was as good looking as ever, indeed, now that he'd lost that Hugh Grant, boy-ish charm, he looked even better. He was, she guessed, what a Pride and Prejudice character might describe as a 'rake'. He'd filled out too. He wasn't a 'gym bunny' as Phil was, he didn't have Phil's muscles, but he was toned, he looked after himself.

'Of course,' he said, like it was a foregone conclusion. 'I've been waiting for you, sweetpie.'

'Stop calling me that, please.'

'Ha ha! Still as feisty as ever.'

She chose to let that misogynist word slide. They stood several feet apart. If she was going to hurt him, she'd need to get close to him at some point.

'What can I get you? How about a glass of champagne? Several glasses of champagne! This calls for a celebration!'

'No, thanks. I won't be staying for long.'

'Oh, come now.'

'I want to know why.'

'Why? Take a seat, why don't you. Take the weight off.'

'I prefer to stand, thanks. So, answer me – why?'

'You're going to have to give me a bit more of a steer here, sweetpie.'

'OK, if that's how you want to play it. You knew I'd got engaged to Phil. You *knew* I was happy, so what made you so bloody arrogant that you felt the need to sabotage everything?'

He put his hands in his pocket and rocked up and down on his toes. 'I was trying to save you, Elise. Still trying to save you.'

'*Save* me?'

'From yourself. You know I know you like nobody else. I know you better than yourself, Elise. You're not happy, you're only Instagram happy, but you don't need me to tell you that's not real happiness. You're just pretending at being happy.'

'Oh right. So you took it upon yourself to *save* me from myself – for the sake of my happiness.'

'In a word – yes.'

'Oh, how noble. I knew it was you that sent that painting. Took me about five seconds–'

'That's good. Shows how attuned we are to each other still.'

'Attuned? So attuned, you thought, I know, let's vandalise Phil's car – that'll make Elise happy. Even better, let's destroy her new home. Do you know how much that's going to cost me?'

'Nothing. I've spoken to Mr Sheth, and we estimated how much it was going to cost him, so I sent him the money with twenty per cent on top – just in case. He won't be charging you.'

'Oh? Right. Thanks.' She gathered herself quickly, telling herself she mustn't fall for his tricks, and that's all it was – a trick. 'Better still, was it perhaps better not to vandalise the flat in the first place? Actually, you didn't do it yourself, did you? No, of course not, far too seedy. So you paid for that too. Astonishing.'

'You know me, sweetpie, I like to surprise people. It's so lovely to see you again, Elise. You sure you wouldn't like a glass of bubbly?'

'No!'

'Well, I do. Let's go through to the kitchen.'

Elise followed him through. 'Why did you hire some… hit man to almost kill Phil?'

'Yeah, I'm sorry about that. He misinterpreted the remit. I told him to scare the man, give him a fright, not bloody kill him.'

'Why, Dominic? Why?'

He sighed and cast his eyes down. 'Because he doesn't deserve you.'

'And you do?'

He looked up at her. 'You know I do.'

'I love Phil, Dominic.'

'You don't. You think you do but you don't. You'll never love anyone as much as you loved me. OK, hands up, I made mistakes before. I was young, I was stupid, immature.'

'Dominic, if you think your behaviour is a way of attracting me back, you're still just as stupid. You do one more thing and I swear, I'll go to the police.'

'Don't be so silly, Elise.'

'I'm going to leave now, Dominic, and you're not going to stop me.'

He stepped back, his hands up in the air. 'No, I'm not going to stop you, but you'll think about what I said, I know you will, and you'll come back when you are ready.'

'So, I'm going to go now.'

'I'll call you a taxi, an Uber, whatever–'

'No, it's fine. Thank you. I'd rather walk for a while.'

'Clear your head.'

'If you like.'

'OK, if you insist. Let me get your coat.' He held the coat open for her, like the old-fashioned gentleman he always pretended to be.

She put her arms through the sleeves, thanking him. She

slipped her hand into her pocket, feeling for the knife, her fingers closing over the handle.

His head tilted to one side, a half-smile on his lips, Dominic put his arms out, asking for a hug.

Why not, thought Elise. This was her moment. She'd hug him; it'd be the last thing he ever did…

Chapter 28: Elise, 2018
Five years earlier

Elise and Dominic had agreed to meet at the Three Bells pub. They weren't meeting until half past eight. Nonetheless, Elise left home in plenty of time, not daring to be late – not after the last time. She realised now that her boyfriend had a temper on him. She knew she hadn't experienced the full blast of it but there'd already been several hints that had made her uneasy. But, on the plus side, he knew how to spoil a woman. The meal at DiMaggio's had been nothing short of spectacular. Dominic had been right – the sea bass, and the accompanying wine, was to die for. For dessert, she had a vanilla cheesecake, something she'd had many times before but never as mouth-wateringly smooth as this. She couldn't talk, it was so delicious. Dominic bought two glasses of a Hungarian dessert wine, syrupy with the texture of velvet. She loved it. Dominic paid the bill without even looking at it, simply passing the waitress his bank card. He ordered an Uber to take them back to his house.

This time they managed to avoid his parents. They slipped

upstairs and made love, and it was exquisitely passionate and exciting! She'd never experienced sex quite like it!

Delicious food, wonderful wine, delightful company and fantastic sex – it'd been a nigh-on perfect evening.

She caught a bus to The Three Bells and bumped into Dominic outside the pub. Delighted, she embraced him and kissed him hard.

'Elise, we're on the street here in full view.'

She slapped him on the chest. 'Stop being such a fuddy-duddy. Live dangerously, Dom.'

'You're probably right. Shall we go in?' He held the door open for her. The pub was half full, *Rockstar* by Post Malone was playing in the background. Three elderly gentlemen at the table nearest to the door were playing cards.

'Let me buy the drinks tonight,' said Elise, as they approached the bar. 'You bought me dinner, it's the least–'

'No, it's fine. Drinks are on me.'

'But, Dominic, I'd like to–'

He put his hand up. 'No, no. Don't you worry about it now.' He ordered her a white wine spritzer and himself a gin and tonic. They sat not too far from the card-players.

'It's my friend's birthday on Saturday week,' said Elise. 'We're meeting here like last time for Shazzer's birthday.'

'The night we first met each other.'

They clinked glasses. 'Indeed. A moment of destiny. You were with your friends, what was the name of the one who spoke to me?'

'Anthony Browning.'

'How is Anthony Browning?'

'Erm…' He pondered this for a moment. 'A right pain in the arse, to be frank. Anyway, I don't want to speak about him. Tell me about your friend's birthday.

'There's going to be a whole bunch of us. After meeting here for a drink or five, we're heading to Nando's but I was thinking maybe I should persuade them to go to DiMaggio's instead.'

'Oh, really? Not sure if they'd take a whole gaggle of pissed-up women.'

'Ha. Only joking. We wouldn't want to lower the tone. Anyway, at those prices, gee.'

'Does your birthday friend have a name?'

'Amara. You'd like her, Dominic, all men like her. She's stunning; a right fit Asian babe.'

'I'm happy for you, Elise.'

'Of course you are.' She reached over the table and squeezed his hand.

'Saturday week, you say?'

'Yeah. You can come too, if you like. In fact, yes, go on, do come, Dominic. I'd love to show you off.'

He thought about this a while. 'Nando's? Not really my style.'

'Oh, hark at you. *Not my style*,' she said, impersonating him.

'Fuck it, why not? If you're sure. Last time, with your friend Shannon–'

'Shazzer. Well, Sharon. We just call her that.'

'That was just girls.'

'Partners are allowed to this one. So you'll come?'

'Sure, if you'd like me to.'

'Oh yeah, totes. Oh, Dominic, that'll be brilliant. I'm looking forward to it even more now. Thank you.'

'Oh, I almost forgot,' said Dominic. 'I bought you a little present.'

'Really.'

'Here.' He passed her a slim box, a piece of jewellery, she

guessed, a necklace by the shape of the box. Opening it, it was indeed a necklace. It took her breath away. It was silver with an intricate butterfly. 'Oh my God, Dominic. This is… it's so beautiful. I love it. Thank you. Thank you so much.'

He smiled. 'A pleasure, Elise.'

'Can I put it on now?'

'Of course.'

She clipped the necklace on. 'What do you think?'

'It looks lovely on you. Perfect.'

She squeezed his hand. 'I'll keep it forever.'

Elise and Dominic chatted merrily away for the next hour. He was so easy to talk to, the time simply slipped away. Although three spritzers might have helped. The pub filled up a little, *Girls Like You* by Maroon 5 was playing and everything seemed right in Elise's world. It was proving to be another lovely evening – until the point it wasn't.

Elise jumped on hearing her name. 'Oh, William, God, hello.' Her heart froze as William and Dominic clocked each other, their expressions stormy. 'How are… Who are you with?'

'Couple of me mates,' he said, his eyes still on Dominic who stared back at him with venom in his eyes. 'Didn't expect to bump into you though.'

'Sorry, this is my… this is Dominic. Dominic, this is William.'

'All right?' said William.

'So, who are you then?' asked Dominic, his voice hard as stone.

The question took William by surprise. 'Me?'

'Well, I'm not talking to that tosser over there.' His fingers holding his glass had turned white.

Elise spoke. 'William is a friend, just a friend, Dom.'

'Yeah,' said William. '*Just* a friend, that's right, that's what I am. Nice to meet you.'

'How do you know Elise?'

'William's an old family friend,' said Elise, aware of how shaky her voice sounded. 'Aren't you, William?'

'If you like. Well, I can see you're busy, so I'll... I'll head back.'

'Yeah, fuck off,' said Dominic.

'What did you say, mate?'

'No, no,' said Elise. 'It's all fine here.'

'Don't call me mate.'

'Jesus, you have an attitude problem, don't you?'

Elise stood. 'I'm sorry, William.' She led him away.

'What in the actual fuck, El?' he asked, peering over her shoulder at Dominic.

'I'm sorry, William, he's had a... a difficult day. His grandmother died.'

'Is he the *friend* who you were texting that night?'

'That doesn't matter now.'

'Is he your *boyfriend*?' he asked, spitting out the last word.

Elise felt herself deflate; she couldn't bring herself to lie again. 'Yes, William, he is.'

She saw the shocked expression on his face. 'You dumped me for that twat? Jesus! Well, good luck with that, El.' He turned to leave but then added, 'Look at him. He looks like he could kill a man. What are you thinking of?'

'He's not always like this.'

'Well, I hope he makes you very happy.'

Elise returned to Dominic, a stone in her stomach. 'Sorry about that,' she said meekly, sitting down.

'You've slept with him, haven't you?'

'Not any more, Dominic. I mean, yes, he was my boyfriend

183

for a while, a short while but—'

'Fucking hell, I thought you had standards, but Christ, you slept with that lard arse? How fucking disgusting.'

'It was a long time ago, Dominic. I was younger then, I—'

'Shut the fuck up; I don't want to hear it; I don't want to hear your bleating voice.'

'Dominic, please, don't let it spoil...' He stood and grabbed his coat from the back of his chair. 'Where are you going?'

'You don't seriously think I'm going to stay here while your fat ex-lover is only a few feet away? Unlike some around here, I have my self-respect. I can't even bear to look at you right now.'

He stormed off, his coat flung over his shoulder. The pub door swung shut behind him.

Elise bit her lip, trying not to cry. A sad song she didn't know played over the speakers and she sat there by herself, half a spritzer left, feeling like the loneliest woman in the world. The three card players gazed at her with pity, and she knew William would be watching her. There was no point staying. She downed the rest of her drink and then made her way to the ladies.

Returning from the toilets, William stepped in front of her to the point she almost walked straight into him. 'Leaving already, Elise?'

'Leave me alone, William.'

He grabbed her arm. 'You've got to listen to me.' He ran his fingers through his hair. 'Look, I accept you finished with me but that doesn't mean I don't care for you still. I'll always care for you. And that man there, he's bad news, El.'

'No, I said, didn't I? His grandmother—'

'Don't give me that shit. He's bad through and through. I

saw him leave. I thought he was going to hit you, El. Seriously, you have to look after yourself.'

'I can look after yourself.' Elise dug her fingernail into the ball of her finger, desperate not to cry.

'You think so? I hope you're right, Elise, because I'm telling you now, that man's dangerous and if you're not careful – you will be in danger.'

Chapter 29: Benedict

Benedict and Jessica drove speedily over to Faversham Avenue on the northern side of the borough. Benedict wished he'd brought his gloves; it was freezing now.

'So, they're saying Dominic Woods has been murdered now,' said Jessica. 'Is that right?'

'It appears so.'

They found a uniformed policewoman at the gate of Dominic Woods' residence, her nose bright red with the cold, who waved them through.

'Nice place,' said Jessica. 'Worth a pretty bob or two.'

Benedict parked the car up on the gravelled drive next to a nice-looking Audi A3. 'Worth killing for, wouldn't you think?'

'Wouldn't hesitate. I mean, look at it.'

'Georgian, I believe.'

'They knew how to build houses in those days. How old is Georgian?'

'1800, give or take. This would've all been countryside back then of course. You can imagine Gateshead Hall being like this.'

'Where?'

'Jane Eyre's childhood home.'

'I've read *Jane Eyre.*'

'There you are then.'

The PCSO at the front door pointed them in the direction of the kitchen which had already become a hive of activity, with various people in protective clothing. Benedict and Jessica put on their slip-on shoe coverings and stuck to the narrow passageway denoted by a run of small, red cones. Someone was taking several photographs from every conceivable angle. Benedict heard his name being called. 'DS Collins, hello. Are you Crime Scene Manager again?'

'For my sins. Nice house, isn't it?'

'Yes, we were just saying.'

Andrew Collins led them around the table. 'Here's our man…'

The deceased was lying face down between the kitchen island and the Belfast sink, congealing blood on the back of his head, a fine spray of blood dotting the bottom cupboards.

'Nasty,' said Jessica. 'It must be connected to the death of his colleague.'

'Anthony Browning, yes,' said Benedict. 'Mr O'Brian now has two members of staff he needs replacing.'

Jessica shot him a look.

'Sorry, that sounded disrespectful.'

Dick Evans, the pathologist, made an entrance. 'Ah, Ben, Jessica, knew you'd be here sooner than later. We meet at the best parties.'

'How's it going, Dick?'

'Yes, fine.'

'So, as you know' said DS Collins. 'This unfortunate soul is

Dominic Woods, aged thirty-three. Killed with one mighty blow to the back of the head.'

'So, there's been no sign of a break-in?'

'No,' said Collins. 'I reckon they must have known each other.'

'I wonder if he was opening the bottle of champagne for himself and the killer.'

'There are two glasses on the island. I think as far as Mr Woods was concerned, this was a social call.'

'Well, he misread that one,' said Jessica.'

'Yes, indeed,' said Evans, staring at Benedict's shoulder, a disconcerting habit of his. 'And that…' he added, pointing to a metal pig lying on the floor, the other side of the island, 'is what I believe is the murder weapon.'

'A pig?'

'It appears so. The angle suggests he was hit by a left-handed person. Poor bloke. He turns his back on his guest and then wallop.'

'Will the killer have blood on their clothes?'

'For sure.'

Addressing Jessica, Evans asked, 'So, how are you settling in London, DS Gardiner?'

'Very well, thank you. My partner's just joined me so… all's well.'

'Partner, eh?' Turning to Collins, Evans muttered, 'Lucky chap.'

'Anyway,' said Benedict loudly.

'Yes?'

'Erm… Actually, I can't think of anything else.'

'Did he live alone?' asked Jessica.

'Yes, exactly. Did he live alone?'

'Yes,' said Collins. 'According to the cleaner, he's never

been married but had lots of girlfriends, often at the same time.'

'Oh?'

'He had this whole house to himself?' asked Jessica. 'No new partner or whatever?'

'Nope. But, also according to the cleaner, who's still in the living room if you want to speak to her, he lived here man and boy. Was brought up in this house and his parents only moved out about three or four years ago. Got themselves a much smaller place in Southgate.'

'Talk about silver spoon in your mouth,' said Jessica.

'Yes, but we mustn't let that prejudice us,' said Benedict.

'Also,' said Collins. 'Might be of no importance, but we found a pair of Woods' shoes. Actually, he has several, all very well made, expensive stuff. But there's one pair where the soles are caked in mud.'

'Mud?'

'We're going to analyse it, see whether it's from the towpath where Anthony Browning was killed.'

'Excellent, now that would make things interesting. He'd turned left out of the pub, straight to the car park. No mud there.'

'Exactly.'

'Right, Jessica, let's go speak to this cleaner.'

They found the cleaner in the living room, clasping a handkerchief, speaking to a uniformed officer. Benedict decided not to interrupt. Instead, waiting in the dining room, the officer sought him out.

'She came into work this morning soon after nine like she does the two times a week she cleans here, by which time Mr Woods has usually gone to work. She has her own key. She saw Mr Woods' car was still in the drive but nothing unusual about that. He usually walks to work. She said she always starts in the kitchen. So, she came through and that's when she found him, lying on the floor with the back of his head caved in, that funny pig next to him. She screamed, cried and called 999 in that order. She didn't see another person until we turned up, and that was about half an hour ago. That was about as much as I could get really.'

'Yes, most interesting.'

'No other cars in the driveway?' asked Jessica.

'No, just the Audi.'

'Does she have a car?'

'The cleaner? No, she only lives a bus ride away. Oh, and before I forget, I nabbed a photo I found of him at some party. Thought it might be useful, sir.'

'Yes, good man, thank you.'

'Right, DS Gardiner. I think we're done here. Shall we go see the parents?'

Chapter 30: Benedict

Benedict and Jessica were about to head off to Southgate to see Dominic Woods' parents. As Benedict put his coat on, he asked DC Kelly for any updates on Phillip Edwards' hit and run.

'We might have a name already, boss. The one witness, the woman, said there was a thirty-one bus passing at the same time. We checked all the thirty-one buses around the time Edwards was hit and there's one of interest. The driver didn't see anything but the CCTV camera that scans the downstairs back seat has picked up a black Volkswagen Golf, 2007 reg. The Golf follows the bus for a good six minutes, then, on Selwyn Avenue, where Philip Edwards was run over, it suddenly overtakes at speed.'

'Does it show the actual collision?'

'No, but we've got the number plate and the DVLA are going to get back to us with a name and address. The witness, who heard but didn't see the collision and who ran to Edwards' aid and called 999, confirms she saw the black Golf breaking the red light at the top of Selwyn Avenue and turning left onto the high street.'

'Excellent work, DC Kelly. Well done.'

'Thank you, boss.'

*

It took Benedict and Jessica fifty minutes to drive the nine miles from Camden Town north to Southgate, one of north London's quieter suburbs, centred around one of the most attractive underground stations on the network, a fine specimen of 1930s Art Deco architecture, a circular building with a flat roof and featuring a lot of glass. Mr and Mrs Woods lived on Burnside Avenue, a two-minute walk from the tube station. The night was drawing in now, the traffic getting heavier as people made their way home from work.

Mr and Mrs Woods' house was a routine brick terraced house. Still pleasant but, thought Benedict as he parked up on the street nearby, a far cry from the house in Camden. He wondered how they felt about this.

A Family Liaison Officer (FLO), Michelle Garvey, opened the door to them. 'How are they? All things considered?' he added, for fear his question was as crass as it was stupid.

'All things considered? Pretty fucked-up.'

'Are they prepared to talk to us?' asked Jessica.

'Yes, they're keen to help.'

Garvey led them through to the living room, again a far cry from the previous home, a narrow, claustrophobic space with bright red wallpaper that served to make the space seem even smaller. Mr and Mrs Woods sat on the settee, holding hands. Adjacent to them, a woman in her mid-twenties perhaps. She introduced herself as Olivia, Dominic's sister. Michelle Garvey did the rest of the introductions.

Mr Woods invited the detectives to take a seat. Garvey

offered to make everyone a pot of tea.

'First of all, Mr, Mrs Woods,' said Jessica. 'Please accept our condolences on the terrible loss of your son.'

They thanked her.

'Tell us about Dominic,' said Jessica. 'What sort of son was he?'

'Oh, the best, the absolute best, wasn't he, Ted?'

Ted didn't respond, perhaps not realising he was expected to. Then, seeing the expression on his wife's face, made up for it. 'Oh yes, indeed, absolute best. We couldn't have asked for a better son.'

'He was attentive as a son,' agreed his wife. 'And always so generous. Oh, the presents he gave us for birthdays and Christmas and Mother's Day, always so generous. What was it he got me for my last birthday, Ted? A day of wine-tasting.'

'Which you haven't used yet.'

'No but... I will. And Christmas last, he got me that exercise bike.'

'Still in its box, Mum,' said Olivia, speaking for the first time.

'Yes, but it's the thought, and the expense.'

'How did he get on with people generally?' asked Jessica.

'People loved him. Dominic was always the life and soul, wasn't he, Ted? Ted?

'Oh, yes, life and soul.'

'Wherever he went, people would say, aha, here comes Dom with that lovely smile of his.'

'He had friends then?'

'Friends? Oh my, everyone was his friend. Like I say, sergeant, people loved him. He couldn't do enough for people, and people couldn't do enough for Dominic.'

'Any fallouts at work? We know he worked for Safe Hands

Trading.'

'Oh, yes, very high up,' said Mrs Woods. 'Second only to the man who owns the business. What's his name again, Ted?'

'Mr O'Brian.'

'Mr O'Brian, that was it. Dominic almost ran that place single-handed. They all loved him there; he was very good at his job; he knew his stuff.'

'Naturally.'

'You know one of his colleagues died in suspicious circumstances just a couple of days ago?' asked Benedict.

'Oh no, we didn't know that,' said Ted.

'Anthony Browning. Indeed, your son was the last person to see him alive. They had a drink together in the Davenport pub in the hour before Mr Browning's death. Did Dominic ever talk about Anthony Browning?'

'No,' said Mrs Woods.

'Never even heard of him,' said Ted. 'But then he didn't often talk about work, did he, Elizabeth?'

'Apart from how much money he was making,' said Olivia. Benedict watched Olivia from the corner of his eye, and he could see her mother's generous praise of her son was beginning to grate. The question was why?

'Have you any idea who might have killed our son, Inspector?' asked Ted of Benedict.

'Far too early, sir. Apart from your son's cleaner, you're the first people we've spoken to.'

'Ah yes,' said Mrs Wood. 'He liked a clean house. Tidy home, tidy mind, as he used to say.'

'Did he?' said Mr Woods. 'I never heard him say such a thing.'

'Yes, Ted.'

'So,' said Jessica, 'a bit more delicate this, I'm afraid, why would anyone want to do him harm?'

Mrs Woods shook her head. 'I can't think. It's just too awful to contemplate.' She whisked a tissue from inside her sleeve and blew her nose with surprising gusto.

'So, he never mentioned someone he'd fallen out with or perhaps someone he... I don't know, owed money to. Or perhaps they owed him money.'

'No, no, nothing like that.'

'Did he have a girlfriend?'

'One a night, I think,' squeaked Olivia.

'Don't be so crude, Olivia. He was certainly popular with the ladies, wasn't he, Ted? But he was a gentleman, an absolute gent. And so good looking, of course. He got his looks from me.'

Ted grimaced on hearing that.

Garvey entered the room bearing a tray of tea and crockery. 'Here,' said Mr Woods. 'Let me give you a hand. Shall I be mother?'

The pouring of so much tea took an age. After a long while, Benedict turned to speak to the daughter. 'What about you, Olivia? Can you think of anyone who'd want to harm your brother?'

'What, darling Dominic? No, not Dom. Like Mum says, everyone loved him.' The sarcasm positively dripped from her. They needed to speak to her alone. 'Do you take sugar, inspector?'

'Just the one. Thanks. So, you all lived together as a family in your Camden house on Faversham Avenue until...?'

'Seven years ago,' said Olivia. 'I moved out to go to uni when I was eighteen and by the time I came back three years later, Mum and Dad had moved to this... to here.' Turning to her parents, she said, 'And, you know, after all this time, I still don't get it. The three of us cramped in here while Dom had *the* house all to himself. Maybe you should tell the kind detectives why, Mum, Dad.'

'He needed his own space, Olivia,' said Mrs Woods. 'You know that. A young man needs his space.'

'Yeah, but the general idea is that the *young man* finds his own space, not pushing you out to this shithole.'

'Olivia, your language, please. Anyway, it's not so bad here. The neighbours are very nice.'

'It's about sacrifice,' said Mr Woods. 'One day, Olivia, you might understand the word.'

'Oh, I beg your pardon for breathing. *Sacrifice.* Of course, silly me.'

'When was the last time you saw your son, Mrs, Mr Woods?' asked Jessica.

'Months,' snapped Mr Woods.

'No, not months, Ted,' said Mrs Wood. 'But a while perhaps. He's a busy man, so many friends to keep up with. I was loath to make further demands on him. The young have to live their lives, wouldn't you agree, inspector.'

'Oh yes, madam.'

'How's everyone's tea?' asked Michelle, brightly.

Mrs Woods sipped her tea. 'How was he killed, Inspector? Do you know?'

It was always a question Benedict dreaded, especially so soon after the fact. 'I'm afraid someone hit him on the back of the head with something hard.'

'Would he have felt anything?'

'Probably not.'

'Can we go see him?'

'Certainly, Mrs Woods. I'll get the pathologist people to

give you a ring. He'll need you to identify the body anyway.'

'Thank you, Inspector. Will you be wanting anything more from us?'

'No, at least not for now. We do appreciate your time. I know it's not easy for you.'

Benedict and Jessica replaced their tea cups and stood. Garvey handed them their coats and said she'd see them out. Stepping up to Olivia, Benedict asked, 'Could we have a word alone?'

'Sure.'

After another round of thank yous, they took their leave of the grieving parents.

Standing outside, Benedict said, 'Your brother sounds quite the saint, Olivia.'

'Actually, that's what I used to call him, Saint Dom of Camden. You didn't fall for all that guff, did you?'

'You tell me.'

'Mum and Dad, Mum especially, have never hidden their preference. As you can see, the sun shone out of Dom's arse as far as they were concerned.'

'And as far as you were concerned?'

'Dominic was a bully. He used people. He didn't have any friends; he was only nice to people while they were useful. Once they'd served their purpose, he dropped them like a stone. And he was awful with women, used them and discarded them. He made no secret of it. Bloody insatiable, that man. And if people liked him, it's because they thought him stinking rich, what with that house and that posh job of his.'

'Did you keep in touch?'

'No way.'

'And how did he procure your parents' house?'

'You know, if Mum wasn't such an arse, I'd feel sorry for her. Dominic basically pushed them out. One minute, he'd play the soppy son act, *oh I so need my space, Mum. A man my age shouldn't be seen living with his parents.* But he never had any intention of moving out; oh no, not Dom, he wanted *that* house. Next minute, he was so horrible to them, they couldn't wait to leave.'

'Maybe you'll get the house now?' said Jessica.

'You're joking. No chance of that. They'll probably sell it and spend the rest of their lives going on cruises reminiscing on how lovely a son they had, and boring the pants of all their fellow passengers.'

'Well, thank you, Olivia. Most enlightening.'

'Sure. Oh, you ought to have a sniff around a club he used to go to pick up girls. A place in Camden called The Flamingo. You know it?'

'Oh yes,' said Benedict. 'I know it well. As a copper, I mean, not as a customer.'

Olivia looked at him with a wry smile. 'No, I guessed it wouldn't be the sort of place you'd hang out in.'

And with that, Olivia returned indoors.

'In other words, boss,' said Jessica. 'You're too square.'

'Being square, Jessica, has never hindered me yet.'

'You don't know that, boss. You're just too square to see it.'

'And in that, you might well be right.'

Chapter 31: Elise, 2018
Five years earlier

The day after their awful drink at The Three Bells when William showed up out of the blue, Dominic did not contact Elise. She wasn't sure whether to be relieved or not. His behaviour could be troubling but, hell, William was way off when he said Dominic was 'dangerous'. That was simply absurd. She took her butterfly necklace from its box and held it up to the light, admiring it. It really was a lovely piece of jewellery, so wonderfully designed. It must have cost a fortune. How could she ever doubt a man who bought such things?

That evening, she rang Sharon and told her all about the evening, the necklace and the confrontation with William. 'Bloody hell, El,' Sharon said. 'I've never had a fella get jealous over me. He's obviously into you big time, girl.'

'You think so?'

'Fuck yeah. You say he looked like he might hit William? I mean, come on, I'd bloody love it if two blokes fought over me. Think about it.'

'I guess so.' But she wasn't convinced.

'When do I get chance to meet him?'

'I invited him to Amara's do but I don't reckon he'll come. He certainly won't want to go to Nando's; he's a bit…'

'What?'

'Let's just say Nando's isn't really his style.'

'God, this gets better by the minute. Remember what I told you about posh boys – charming on the outside, twats on the inside. But he is rather dishy. What's he like under the sheets?'

'Sharon!'

'Come on, you tell your old mate.'

'If you must know, he's… well, he's amazing.'

'Fuck, no. Really? I've gotta meet him. I didn't really clock him that night. Get him over to Amara's.'

The day after that, however, Elise was inundated with texts from Dominic. The first one arriving soon after she'd woken up for work. It read: *I'm such an idiot at times. Pls forgive me.*

She didn't respond.

'You need to tell me,' her mother said as Elise ate her honey on toast at the kitchen island, perched on a stool. 'Are you still going out with William or not?' She busied herself emptying the dishwasher.

'No. We split up a while back now.'

'A while back? And you didn't think to tell me?'

'I'm sorry. I knew you'd be upset so I kept putting it off.'

'Of course I'm upset.' She stacked a pile of dinner plates in the cupboard. 'You finished with him, didn't you?'

'Can I just eat my breakfast?'

'No, you cannot. Answer me, Elise.'

'Yes, Mum, I finished with him, and I'm sorry I didn't tell you.'

'Why not? Don't you trust me any more?' She stacked the coffee mugs away.

'It's not about you, Mum.'

'But why did you finish with William?'

'Because... you know, it's my business, isn't it? You don't need to know.'

This hurt her, she could tell. Her mother turned and walked out of the kitchen.

A second text pinged: *Can we meet? I miss u so much*, followed by two heart emojis.

Her mother returned, looking flustered. 'You could have told me. I feel so hurt, Elise, that you feel you can't talk to your mother now.'

'Is that what's upsetting you the most? Or the fact I'm not going out with William any more?'

'I... both. I don't know. Both. William's so nice, he's—'

'Yes, he's lovely but I didn't...'

'Yes?'

'I didn't *fancy* him. He was just... there. He'd come round and we watched TV and talk about the soaps and it felt so middle-aged.'

'Sounds very cosy.'

'I don't want cosy.'

'What do you want then?'

'What anyone else my age wants, Mum. I want a man that makes my heart flutter, that makes me feel special.'

'So, are you seeing someone now? Someone who makes your *heart flutter and makes you feel special*.' She spat out the words, annoying Elise.

'I need to get to work,' she said, sliding off the stool.

'Tell me,' said her mother, looking like she might stamp her foot any moment.

'Why is it so important to you?' she shouted.

'Because I am your mother, in case you've forgotten.'

'No, you're more like a guardian, actually, more like a bloody warden.'

'Don't talk to me like that.'

'So stop trying to interfere with my life. You don't need to be so… so damn *protective* of me. I can look after myself.'

She ran upstairs to her bedroom, conscious that time was against her now and that she needed to get to work.

As she was about to leave, her mother called after her. 'Elise, before I forget, your dad and I are going out to a talk at the library on Friday evening.'

'Anything interesting?'

'Local history.'

'Nice.'

'Are you back for dinner tonight, or are you out gallivanting?'

Gallivanting? What sort of word was that? 'Yeah, I'll be back normal time. Gotta go.'

'Do I not get a kiss today?'

Elise slammed the front door behind her without bothering to answer.

She caught the bus to work, listening to an album by Arctic Monkeys on her earphones. She so needed to move out. Even the thought of returning home to her mother this evening filled her with dread. Always so many questions, so much probing, she never stopped.

Her father once, half-jokingly, blamed 'Suzanne'. Suzanne was the name her parents gave to a still-born baby her mother had eighteen months before her own birth. As a result, Mum had spent her second pregnancy in a state of fear, worried sick in case she lost this one too. She hadn't.

202

Elise was born robust and healthy. Twenty years later, she was just as robust and just as healthy but her mother lived her life in a state of anxiety worrying about her, treating her like a delicate vase, terrified that she might fall and break.

After Elise, according to her father, Mum had been desperate again to have another baby in order to 'complete' the family. But, despite a lot of trying and a lot of tests, it never happened and Elise remained an only child. Elise imagined if she had a brother it wouldn't have diminished her mother's protective streak because boys get it easier, but had she had a sister, things might have been easier for her.

And so her thoughts returned to her need to move out, to 'fly the nest'. But with rents so damn expensive, how could she afford it? All her friends were either, like her, still living at home or shacked-up with friends or a boyfriend. A few months back, Sharon had asked Elise if she wanted to flat share and Elise, giving it no thought, turned her down. William had just come on the scene and at that point she was more than content to carry on as she was. Also, living at home is so much cheaper, of course. But boy, did she regret that now. Shazzer, bless her, could be a bit loud, especially after a few drinks, and living with her might have destroyed their friendship, but she still regretted not taking the chance when it was there. Amara too had been looking for someone but Elise had been too slow off the mark and that opportunity also fell through. She'd got to a stage now where paying super-expensive rent seemed preferable to remaining at home under her mother's watchful eye.

A third text arrived: *U R the most beautiful women I've ever met. Speak 2 me.*

An idea popped into her head – an absurd idea but an idea nevertheless. Dominic's parents had a spare room. It'd belonged to Dominic's sister but she'd recently moved out. Could she face living at the Woods' house? She imagined living under the same roof as Dominic, it'd be easier to placate him somehow. They might not even charge her anything. But could she placate him, control him? He'd shown his true colours in the pub the other night; the way he looked at William was, frankly, frightening. What was that about? Had she seen a glimpse of the true man within? Perhaps it wasn't such a good idea, after all.

She got off the bus and walked the short distance from the bus stop to the salon when another text arrived: *Cant get u out of my head. Wish I cld see u.*

This time, she answered. *Me too.*

Chapter 32: Benedict

Benedict and Jessica were back in the office, having just updated DCI Lincoln. 'Is it fair, do you think, Jessica, to suggest Dominic Woods killed Anthony Browning?'

'Not until we have some evidence, boss.'

'Evidence? That old hindrance again. Our job would be so much easier if we could just base it upon what we think is the most likely scenario. Still, you're right.'

Benedict had two whiteboards on show now, one dedicated to the beating up of William Grant, the other to the murders of the two Safe Hands employees. He pondered the boards now, looking at the photos, the notes and the lines between them. But nothing made sense.

He received a call from Diana Pettigrew, the station's most senior forensics officer. He found her in her office, crouched over her computer chewing on the end of a pen.

'Well, Ben, something interesting for you to think about. I think we've already found a prime suspect for you in the Dominic Woods case.'

'Aha. Go on.'

'We found two sets of fingerprints on the kitchen work surfaces and various door handles. We have no match for one set but we do have a match for the second set. They belong to a gentleman by the name of Nathaniel Turnbull, got previous for a run of car thefts and burglary about six years ago. Spent ten months inside.'

Returning to the office, Benedict saw Jessica at her computer. 'Jessica, I think we need to visit this club that Woods frequented. What did Olivia say it was called again?'

'The Flamingo.'

'That's the one.'

'I was just thinking about Dominic's sister, boss. Interesting what Olivia said about him.'

'Yes, no love lost there. Quite the Jack the Lad, wasn't he? Sounds a thoroughly unpleasant sort.'

'Yes, but can we believe her? I mean, she seemed very bitter about the house and how Dominic procured it, and how her mother loved her brother while, basically, ignoring her.'

'His mother certainly loved him.'

'A bit too much, almost creepy. She could see no wrong in him. To what extent was she prepared to cover for him? Did she and her husband really not know of Browning?'

DCs Kelly and Prowse sauntered into the office, arguing over a football game. Was the disallowed goal really a hand ball? Wasn't it accidental, hand to ball, and all that? They ceased their conversation on seeing Paige and Gardiner.

'Hello, boys, any updates?'

'As it happens, yes,' said DC Prowse. 'Quite a biggie, actually. So, we traced the woman in the pointy hat, the one Dominic Woods said saw him leave the pub. Her name is…' He checked a slip of paper. 'Victoria Almond. So, yeah, she and her boyfriend did indeed bump into Woods as they walked into the pub. He was leaving and headed off towards the car park. But… here's the thing. She and her boyfriend were only just popping in. And had a half each and then left. They were getting into their car when Ms Almond saw Dominic again. She remembered because he was dressed so nicely and was, according to her, very handsome. This time, he was passing the main door of the pub, but he wasn't coming out of the pub, he was coming from the direction of the canal.'

'Aha! And she's sure of this.'

'Yes. She was going to mention it to her boyfriend but thought it might sound as if she was eyeing up good looking men so she didn't say anything.'

DC Kelly took up the story. 'So, as a result of this, we had a look at Woods' muddy shoes that DS Collins brought in, then checked the pub's exterior CCTV cameras. And here's the thing, boss. Yes, we see Woods leave the pub, bumping into Ms Almond and heading left towards the car park but… ninety seconds later, the camera picks up someone walking towards the right at the top of the screen. Blink, and you might miss it, but it just about catches these shoes walking by. So, we blew it up and they look like the shoes Woods was wearing.'

'But have they analysed the mud on his shoes yet?'

'Yes, they came while you were out, boss. The mud is a match for the mud on the canal's towpath.'

'Whoa,' said Jessica.

'I think we need to speak to more people associated with Anthony Browning,' said Benedict. 'If one of his friends suspected Woods of killing Browning, they may have killed Woods in return, a revenge killing, if you like. Good work,

207

Prowse, Kelly. Thank you so much.'

The two detective constables smiled.

'Also, boss,' said Kelly. 'We got the CCTV footage from that club Mr Woods was at on the night before he died. He was only there for about half an hour and spent all of it with a woman who laughs a lot. You'll see what I mean when you look at it. But at one point, some bloke comes over and talks to him for a couple of minutes. Here's a screenshot of the two of them together, and a close-up of the bloke's face.' Kelly handed Benedict two A4 printouts. 'Looking at the footage, you can tell they're not comfortable with each other. The bloke doesn't sit down and looks quite agitated.'

'Excellent. Thanks, DC Kelly. Have you run a check on Dominic Woods yet?'

'No,' said Kelly. 'Just about to.'

'OK, make that your next priority if you would.'

*

'Do you still go to nightclubs, DS Gardiner?' Benedict asked Jessica as they waited in traffic on their way to The Flamingo. The day had turned wet again, the rain lashing down.

'Sure. Love a good dance, me. I can't do those that start at midnight and go on to six in the morning.'

'They *start* at midnight? Good God, I thought that was just a myth to make old people like me feel even older.'

'I went to one once on a Saturday night, up in Manchester. The only way to survive is to drink water, no alcohol.'

'No alcohol?' He turned the wipers on. 'Does that even count as a night out then?'

'It still took me until about Tuesday to fully recover. Good fun though. Brilliant music. It gets right into you, you know? Into your core.'

'Yes.' He was not convinced in the slightest.

'Clubs in London are so expensive though. Even without the alcohol. We go to these bars, you know, the ones like warehouses, massive places, thousands of people.'

'Not sure whether Sonia and I would enjoy that too much.'

'No. I dare say you wouldn't.'

Benedict drummed his fingers on the steering wheel. 'So much traffic today.'

There's always something rather depressing about a night club during the cold light of day, thought Benedict, as he and Jessica entered The Flamingo. Jessica asked a cleaner if they could see the manager. The cleaner took them around the back and knocked on a door. A gruff voice within answered.

'Mr Etherington?' asked Jessica, holding out her ID. 'You were told to expect us.'

Mr Etherington, a bald-headed man in a suit too tight for his bulging chest, told them to sit. 'You want to know about one of my regulars, don't you? Dominic Woods.'

'Was he one of your regulars then?'

'Yeah. Strange to relate, a posh boy like him. But he liked to pick up girls here. They were always easy prey to his soft boy charm.'

'What about drugs?' asked Benedict.

'What about drugs? We don't do drugs here at The Flamingo. We're clean, right? I operate a zero tolerance policy when it comes to drugs.'

'Did Mr Woods ever give you cause for concern?'

'Over what?'

'I don't know, his behaviour, his drinking, anything like that?'

'Nah, good as gold he was, never asked for credit, nothing like that.'

'Mr Woods was here the night before he died. Did you speak to him?'

'Me? I don't think I ever spoke to him except maybe to say good evening or whatever. Never had a proper conversation with the fella.'

Benedict passed him the first of his two screenshots DC Kelly had provided him at the station. 'Do you recognise the woman here?'

'Yeah, I've seen her. Couldn't tell you her name though. She usually hooks up with some bloke or other.'

'Is she a prostitute?'

'No! We don't allow prostitutes here at The Flamingo. We have a zero-tolerance policy on–'

'Yes, yes, thank you, Mr Etherington. And what about the gentleman in this shot?'

'Oh yeah, that's Nat. He works here.'

'Nat?'

'Nathaniel Turnbull.'

Nathaniel Turnbull? That was the name Diana Pettigrew mentioned – the fingermarks found in Woods' kitchen. There were connections here.

Mr Etherington continued, 'Nat works in an office two doors down the corridor. He monitors the CCTV cameras, makes sure everyone is behaving themselves. Any hint of trouble, drugs or whatever, he radios through to security and they deal with it. Zero tolerance, like I said.'

'You did indeed. Is Nathaniel Turnbull in today?' asked Benedict.

'No, but he will be later. Nat works every night Wednesday to Sunday from half eight to two in the morning. Come back then if you want to speak to him. He also does a bit of bricklaying although how much of a going concern that is, I wouldn't know.'

'Is Nat friends with Dominic Woods?' asked Jessica.

'You'd have to ask him.'

'We will,' said Benedict. 'Thank you for your time, Mr Etherington.'

'That's all right, inspector. Anything to help the long arm of the law.'

Sitting in the car as Benedict drove back to the station, Jessica rang the office. 'Jamie? Hi, listen, a job for you. See what you dig out on an individual called Nathaniel Turnbull. Lives locally, works at The Flamingo Club… Yes, Nathaniel with an "el" at the end… You got it?… Yes, any previous, that sort of thing. Oh, and he also works as a bricklayer… Yeah, that's it. Cheers, Jamie. Bye, see you later.' She finished the call. 'DC Kelly's on the case.'

'Great.'

Chapter 33: Benedict

Early afternoon, Benedict and Jessica returned to the office from their visit to The Flamingo club to find DC Prowse waiting for them with that expectant, excited look both he and Kelly always had when they had something new or important to pass on. Indeed, what Prowse had to say interested Benedict no end.

'Three years ago, a woman called Caroline Wozniak accused Dominic Woods of raping her. Police at the time even interviewed Woods under caution and they started building a case against him.'

'Anyone else involved?'

'Nope. A case of her word against his. It was always going to be difficult to prove, you know, he said it was consensual, she said it wasn't.'

'A familiar story, sadly.'

'Yeah. Then, his mother came forward with an alibi for him, and Ms Wozniak threw in the towel. She withdrew everything. That was the end of that. Anyway, good news, I tracked down Caroline Wozniak, she works as a self-employed *something*, I forget what it was now, web design or some shit, and she said if you wanted to pop by, today would be good. She lives in Willesden, so not far. Here's her address.'

'No, not far at all. What do you think, DS Gardiner; worth checking out, do you think?'

*

Caroline Wozniak welcomed Benedict and Jessica into her flat, an arty, sand brick residence with low-hanging lampshades that she shared, she said, with her boyfriend. He worked in town, she from home coding websites. So, DC Prowse wasn't too far off. She was about thirty and wore a smock as if about to start painting, not coding.

'I understand Dominic Woods is dead,' she said as she passed them their coffees, one sugar for Benedict.

'How did you feel on finding out?' asked Jessica.

She sat at her desk and shrugged. 'I'm not going to pretend I was upset or anything. The man was a scumbag. A charming one, and very handsome, but a scumbag, nonetheless.'

'How did you meet?'

Her phone pinged but she ignored it. 'He picked me up in a bar. I was flattered. I remember, the friend I was with was jealous as hell. Like I say, he was handsome and charming and rich. He was perfect – on paper.'

'And once you got to know him?'

'He was a manipulative, cunning, two-timing bastard, if you must know. I mean, OK, yes, he could be generous. He threw his money around but not in a flash, look-at-me way, he did it because he had it, it was just there, loads of it. So he'd buy me a necklace or a bracelet or something that I would never, in a hundred years, buy for myself. At first, it was nice, lovely. But it's funny how quickly the novelty wears off. I felt like I was *owned*.' A little black cat appeared out of nowhere and jumped up on her lap. She stroked it. 'Is your coffee OK?'

'Oh,' said Benedict. 'Very nice, thanks.'

'It's Columbian, a small independent company nearby. I like to support them, you know? It's a bit too strong for me, but hey! Now, you see, that reminds me of the sort of thing Dom would do. Let's say, we were in a small, independent food store and they had like a charity box next to their till or whatever. Dom would pay for his purchases and then a couple of twenty-pound notes in the charity box, and he'd do it without looking for praise or glory, he'd just do it without really thinking about it.'

'Nice.'

'Yeah, and, to this day, that's what makes me so sad when I think about Dom. He had the potential to be... well, the nicest bloke you could hope to meet.' She smiled at the cat. 'But he could also be difficult and possessive and clawing. He had a definite dark side, and once you saw that side, you knew you had to get out.'

'Can you tell us, Ms Wozniak, about the alleged rape?' asked Jessica.

'Ha! Alleged. You sound like a news reporter, assume innocence until proven guilty. I can tell you there was nothing alleged about it. We got drunk, we came back to mine, not here, my old flat in Camden, and he wanted sex, and I didn't because I was too pissed. So he forced himself on me. Do I need to say more? I'd rather not.'

'No, no, it's fine. Thank you. But you went to the police?'

'Not straight away, and I don't think that helped.' The cat

jumped off her lap. 'Oh, Muso, come back, sweetheart, come back. I couldn't work here all day by myself without Muso. He's such good company, I love him to bits. I thought about it. I guess I was waiting for him to apologise or something but he never did. It was almost as if it'd never registered. So, yes, I went to the police.'

'But we know you didn't go through with it.'

'No. I couldn't face it. It just mushroomed in no time at all. It sort of grew a life of its own, and I realised I couldn't control it. And it was him against me, fifty – fifty, and I just didn't fancy the odds. I thought at the time, I'm putting myself through the ringer here and for what? A fifty per cent chance the jury might believe me, but not before every part of my bloody life was scrutinised. No, call me weak, but I couldn't do it.'

'How did your relationship with Dominic Woods end?' asked Benedict.

'On that night. I finished it. Told him I didn't want to see him again.'

Benedict finished his coffee. She was right – it was too strong; the stuff would keep him awake the rest of the week. He coughed, 'How did he take it?'

'Surprisingly good. He just accepted it. I had these terrible scenarios that he was going to spill his own blood and declare his undying love for me.'

'Very Shakespearean.'

'Yeah, and in truth – nothing! It was like, OK, fair enough, see ya then. Bye.'

'Ms Wozniak, do you know the name of Anthony Browning?' asked Benedict.

'No.' She shook her head. 'Never heard of him.'

'OK, well, Ms Wozniak, we'll leave you and Muso to get on

215

with your work.'

'Actually, the reason Dominic wasn't too bothered about when I ended it because I was just a passing girlfriend, a fuck buddy even. I knew I wasn't the love of his life; he told me once. He was drunk and it came out, the woman he truly loved.'

'Oh? Do you remember her name, by chance?'

'Oh yeah. Her name was Elise. Elise Tanner.'

Benedict almost dropped off his chair. Jessica's mouth fell open. 'Did you say Elise Tanner?'

'Yes. Why? You look like you know her.'

'We do. We most certainly do.'

Chapter 34: Benedict

Benedict and Jessica sat in the pool car not too far away from Caroline Wozniak's flat taking in what they'd just learned. They sat watching a woman struggling to tie her toddler into its pushchair. The toddler wasn't having it and squirmed and fought his way out. 'So,' said Jessica. 'Hans Tanner, the man we suspect beat up William Grant, is the father of a woman who once went out with Dominic Woods.'

'It appears so. But what, exactly, is the connection?'

'We need to speak to Hans Tanner again, lean on him, bring him in under caution, if necessary.'

'Yes, I think that's a plan.'

The young mother, aware she was being watched, finally, through brute force, managed to secure the toddler into the pushchair. She straightened, relieved perhaps, exhausted for sure. The toddler jammed his thumb into his mouth. The woman looked over at Benedict and Jessica and gave them the middle finger.

'Charming,' said Jessica.

'I've been there. I appreciate her frustration.'

They watched as the woman marched off, pushing the pushchair.

Benedict switched on the ignition. 'Can you give him a ring? See if he's available now.'

Jessica made the call. Benedict, easing his way back to Camden through the heavy traffic, could hear Tanner's phone ringing. Eventually, it went onto his voicemail. Jessica left a message.

Twenty minutes later, they were back at the station, rushing back in to avoid another downpour. Shaking the rainwater from his coat, Benedict asked DC Kelly whether he'd found anything yet on Nathaniel Turnbull.

'Hell, yeah, boss. That Volkswagen Golf that hit Philip Edwards?'

'Yes?'

'It only belongs to Turnbull.'

'Seriously?'

'And it gets better. I heard back from my mate in financial forensics. Dominic Woods transferred a hefty sum of ten grand to Turnbull on the night he was killed.'

'Wow? On the night he was killed?'

'Yep. No reference on the transfer so no clue as to what the payment was for.'

'Did it leave Mr Woods short?'

'Far from it. It still left him over twelve thousand just in his current account.'

'Was it the first such payment?'

'Actually, no. A couple of days before he also transferred one thousand, one hundred.'

'Not much of a motive though, is it? You might kill someone if they owe you lots of money, but not if they've just paid you. So, what was it for?'

'All the more reason to go back to The Flamingo, boss,' said Jessica.

'Indeed, it is. No time to waste, I'd say.'

*

Eight fifteen in the evening. Benedict and Jessica had both been home to eat and freshen up, before meeting back at the station ahead of returning to The Flamingo to speak to Nathaniel Turnbull. 'All set?' asked Benedict.

'Ahuh.'

'Great. Let's go a-dancing.'

'Yes, boss.'

'So, to recap, boss.' said Jessica as Benedict drove to the Flamingo. 'This guy, Nathaniel Turnbull appears to have been the one who almost killed Philip Edwards and received ten grand from Dominic Woods on the night Woods was killed?'

'Yes, by the looks of it. Mr Turnbull seems to be the key here.'

Eight forty, and The Flamingo was still quiet. Benedict, showing his ID, asked the biggest bouncer whether Nathaniel Turnbull had turned up for work yet. 'Just got in,' came the gruff reply. 'He'll be out the back.' He looked up at the CCTV camera above the door and waved at it. 'He'll be watching us, unless he's gone for a piss. Mr E, the boss, allows his staff three pisses a night.'

'Really?'

'Oh yeah.'

Benedict had the distinct feeling the chap was pulling his leg. 'We'll go through, if that's all right.'

'Be my guest, sir.'

Beyond the security guys and a couple of youngsters

behind the bar, the place was virtually empty, the music quiet. But it was still early. Benedict said a cheery hello to the bar staff as he led the way through to the back, Jessica behind him. 'I'll be back later for a dance,' he said.

He could hear Jessica groaning.

He pushed open the door marked 'Staff Only' and saw in the dingy light, a man heading rather quickly for the fire exit at the back. Benedict shouted at him. 'Stop!' The man glanced back, just for a second, but long enough for Benedict to recognise Nathaniel Turnbull from the CCTV footage. 'Mr Turnbull, we're police officers and we need to speak to you.'

Turnbull pushed the bar down on the fire exit door and was out. Benedict chased after him. 'Stop. Police.'

Benedict followed Turnbull out and found himself on a cobble passageway, high walls everywhere. Looking left and right, he saw Turnbull running towards the left. Benedict chased after him, trying not to lose balance on the slippery cobbles, still wet from the earlier downpour. Turnbull grabbed a bulging black bin liner and threw it behind him where it exploded on the cobbles spilling its foul contents. Benedict jumped over it but his left foot landed on something slippery and his leg gave way beneath him. He fell awkwardly. The jarring pain in his coccyx told him he was on his arse. His right hand, in trying to stop his fall, landed squarely on something mouldy and squashy. The stench was rank. Cursing, he struggled up. But by the time he'd righted himself, Turnbull was nowhere to be seen. And nor was Jessica. Hadn't she followed him? As quickly as he could, he ran anyway along the passageway until it came to a sort of crossroads. Again, he looked left and right but by now, Turnbull had gone. With a mental flip of a coin, Benedict turned left, along another narrow passage. His back was stinging now, where he'd landed on it, impeding his progress. It was like a rabbit warren along here. No street lamps, only the occasional light from an overhead building, casting long, sinister shadows. He limped along, wondering what had happened to Jessica. Finally, he could see the main street up ahead. He finally got there, relieved to be back in civilization and away from that Victorian warren. Wiping his right hand on the seat of his trousers, he looked around, not expecting to see Turnbull. And yes, there in the distance was Turnbull walking leisurely up the street. Girding himself, he ran. He caught the man up. Turnbull, aware of something, glanced behind his shoulder and, on seeing Benedict, began sprinting. Benedict gave chase but he knew he'd never catch him; he was getting too old for this sort of thing. But then, up ahead, he saw Turnbull smash into someone and fall over. 'Heck,' he said aloud. Was that DS Gardiner? By God, it was! The two of them, Turnbull and Jessica, wrestled on the street. Benedict ran as fast as he could muster to help. Jessica somehow flipped Turnbull over and with deft movements, handcuffed the man while reading his rights. Turnbull, face down on the pavement, swore but didn't struggle.

'Come on, up you get, Mr Turnbull,' said Jessica. 'On your feet, please.'

'Good work, DS Gardiner. I wondered where you'd gone.'

'Thanks, boss. Mr Etherington advised me where to go. Cut him off at the pass, that sort of thing.'

Benedict rubbed his coccyx and tried to stretch away the pain. Limping still, he followed DS Gardiner and Nathaniel Turnbull back to The Flamingo. The bouncer greeted Turnbull with a gleeful grin. 'Been out for a run, Nat?'

Turnbull, still catching his breath, didn't answer. Jessica led him through to Mr Etherington's office who, on seeing the trio, said, 'What's he been up to? Cos, I'm telling you, Nat, anything dodgy and you're out on your ear.'

'Mr Etherington,' said Benedict. 'We need to speak to Mr Turnbull.'

'Really? Right, OK.' He rose reluctantly from his chair.

'No,' said Benedict. 'Not here. We need to take him to the station.'

'You're bloody joking. He's working.'

'We can't help that, Mr Etherington. We'll try not to detain him too long.'

'Can't you do it tomorrow?'

'No.'

'Shit, all right then. I'll keep an eye on the CCTV. I'll do your bloody job, Nat. But I'll tell you this for nothing – I'll be deducting it from your wages.'

Chapter 35: Elise, 2018
Five years earlier

Tonight, a Saturday, was Amara's birthday bash – a few drinks at The Three Bells, followed by a meal out at the local Nando's, a far cry from DiMaggio's, thought Elise, but so be it. The girls talked about hitting The Keys nightclub afterwards but that'd make it a costly evening so soon after Sharon's do. Also, Amara wasn't much of a club girl. But the question that troubled Elise as she wrapped a bracelet she'd bought Amara as a birthday present, was – would Dominic turn up? If he did, she'd be on tenterhooks the whole night worrying about how he'd get on with her friends. She wasn't too worried about Amara; Amara was a classy girl, she had manners and elegance, the polar opposite to brassy, loud-mouth Sharon. The thought of Sharon and Dominic together made her blood run cold. While she did want to see Dominic, it might be better, she thought, if he didn't turn up tonight. She'd certainly have a more relaxed evening if he didn't.

She and Dominic had been out a few times in the last

couple of weeks and he'd been the epitome of charm each time. It was what she liked about him, what she loved about him, that effortless charm he had. They'd eaten out and even gone to the theatre to see *The Woman in Black* in London's West End. Elise had never been to a proper theatre production before and hadn't been looking forward to it, thinking she might be bored. Far from it, she loved it, the acting, the atmosphere, the story; she was transfixed by it all.

Elise had bought a new outfit for Amara's do tonight – a knee-length black and white skirt and top. The tiny crop-top showed off her taut stomach nicely. And of course, she had to wear Dominic's necklace. Did she look hot, she asked herself, looking in her mirror. Yeah, she looked darn hot!

She texted Dominic, asking if he was coming. *Not sure atm*, came the immediate reply.

She arrived at The Three Bells near eight and, being a Saturday night, the place was already full to the gunnels, The Kaiser Chiefs blaring out over the speakers. She heard Sharon's loud laugh and, following the sound, found her friends crowded around a couple of tables already weighed down with countless glasses. There had to be about twenty girls. Yes, boyfriends had been invited too but, looking around, Elise couldn't see any.

'Bloody hell, Shazzer, I could hear your cackle out in the street.'

'Hey, El, at last, you've made it!'

'You really have the loudest laugh.'

'Ha, you know me, love, she who laughs loudest laughs last.'

'Is that actually a saying?'

'Nah, just some shit I just made up. Good though, isn't it?'

'Amara, hi, happy birthday.' She hugged her friend and

gave her her present. 'God, you look fantastic.' *Even if your skirt is so short, you can see your bloody knickers*, she added in her mind. And she was showing too much cleavage. What was that saying – either tits or arse but never both.

'Oh, Elise, you're such a darling, thank you.' She unwrapped Elise's present and showed surprise but Elise did wonder whether her reaction was genuine or simply good manners. It didn't matter. It's the thought that counts, as they say. 'Elise, I've got to slow up. I'm pissed already. Drinking on an empty stomach, never a good idea. At this rate I'll pass out at Nando's and probably end up getting shagged by some tramp.'

'Where's Mr Posh Boy then?' called Sharon.

'I'm not sure if he's coming, to be honest.'

'He'd better,' said Amara. 'I've heard a lot about him. I so want to meet him now. Is he really that loaded?'

'Bloody hell, Shaz. What have you been saying?'

'Me? *Moi*? Darling, you know me, the soul of discretion, that's me.'

'Bollocks it is. Remind me to never to tell you anything ever again.'

'I love your necklace, El,' said Amara. 'Actually, it's beautiful.'

'Dominic bought it for me.'

'Bloody hell.'

Elise wanted to change the subject – Amara's bracelet looked horribly cheap compared to Dominic's necklace. Luckily, Neil Diamond's *Sweet Caroline* came on and all the girls raised their glasses and sang along.

Half an hour passed, an hour, and it was almost time to leave and hit Nando's. It was obvious that Dominic wasn't coming and, truthfully, Elise was glad about that; she was already too pissed to worry about him.

And then he turned up.

'Bloody hell, Dom,' cried Elise. 'What time do you call this?'

'Well, hello,' said Sharon in her best flirty voice. 'The evening's just got a whole lot better.'

Dominic smiled but Elise could tell he felt uncomfortable.

'Is this the famous Dominic?' asked Amara, bouncing over. 'Pleased to meet you.' She offered her hand. 'I'm Amara.'

'Lovely to meet you, Amara. I understand it's your birthday. Many happy returns for the day.'

'Oh, thank you, dear sir. May I say you're even more handsome than Elise here said.'

He looked down, embarrassed, and muttered a thanks.

'Here,' said Amara, passing him a glass. 'Have a glass of Prosecco.'

'Get that down you quick,' said Sharon. 'You've got a lot of catching up to do.'

And he did, swigging it back in just a few gulps. 'Bloody hell,' said Sharon.

'Top up?' asked Amara, refilling his glass without waiting for an answer.

'Elise tells me you're going to Nando's.'

'That's the idea,' said Amara. 'But you know, we're having such fun here maybe... hang on, I'll take a vote.'

After a lot of shouting and cheering, the girls decided *not* to go to Nando's after all and, instead, continue drinking here. The fact that Abba's *Dancing Queen* came on helped sway the vote. Elise, who was starving, was not happy.

'So, what exactly is it you do?' asked Sharon. 'Elise tried to tell me but she didn't make any sense.'

Dominic tried to tell them but only Amara understood.

226

'And Elise says you live in a nice big house up St John's Wood way.'

'Yes, it is too large for a family of four...'

'Have another drink.'

'Erm, yes, OK. Thank you.'

'Tell us all about it,' said Sharon, swaying slightly.

No soon as Dominic started describing the house, Amara interrupted. 'Do you live with your parents?'

'Yes, I–'

'Oh, so did I until recently. It stinks, don't you think.' Amara told him all about her living arrangements.

This continued for a while, Sharon, Amara and a couple of the other girls drawn to Dominic like bees to the honey, flies to shit, firing questions at him, hardly giving him a chance to answer before asking another, each question more personal than the last, as if they had a right to know. But Elise could tell he was enjoying all the attention, But then, she thought, what man wouldn't?

I Wanna Dance With Somebody by Whitney Houston came on. 'Hey, girls,' said Elise. 'Sing-along.' But they ignored her, too transfixed by Dominic to pay her any attention. It struck Elise that she'd hardly spoken a word to him since he'd arrived, nor him to her. Eventually, the other girls peeled away, while Sharon came to speak to her. 'You've done well there, darling. He's a dish and so rich too. And you say he's amazing in the sack. Christ, El, I can see why you've got your claws into him, you've got the Holy Trinity there, you lucky cow.'

Elise forced a laugh but she wasn't feeling too well disposed towards her boyfriend right at that minute. In fact, she wished he hadn't turned up at all. 'By the looks of it, Amara's trying her best to get her claws in too.'

'Nah, don't worry about her; she wouldn't do the dirty on you.'

'She'd better not.'

Come On Eileen by Dexy's Midnight Runners blared out. 'Oh, girls,' shouted Sharon. 'Time for another sing-along.' This time, they all responded and sang along drawing admiring looks from any men in the vicinity and appalled looks from the women.

'Excuse me,' said Elise. 'I need the loo.' Elise disappeared to the ladies, her feathers ruffled. Dominic hadn't even commented on her new skirt yet. Why was he paying so much attention to Amara? Yes, it was her birthday and she was undeniably a beauty but that was no excuse. She didn't blame Dominic; Amara had cornered him. She needed to go back and stake her position, get her away from him. The woman could have any man she wanted; she wasn't bloody well going to have hers. Re-fortified and freshened-up, Elise returned to the fray.

Amara and Dominic were still talking, Amara playing with her hair, twisting the ends around her finger, a sure sign she was moving in on him. She laughed heartily at something he said. 'I'm sure it wasn't that funny,' said Elise to herself. 'Cow.' Holding onto a glass of red wine, Amara looked utterly pissed – but still stunning.

Standing next to him, Elise linked her arm into his. 'Dom, you're ignoring me, darling.'

'Amara is training to be a paralegal.'

'Yes, I know that. She's a clever girl.'

'So are you,' said Amara. 'Which is why it baffles me why you still do that shitty job.'

Elise hoped Dominic would rise to his defence but he failed to, instead reaching for another top-up of the sparkling stuff. 'I enjoy it.'

Amara laughed. 'What, you enjoy being poor and still living with your parents? Pull the other one, darling.'

'Dom still lives with his parents.'

'To be fair,' said Dominic, 'it's more a case that they live with *me*.'

'See?' said Amara. 'So, come on, El, ditch the shit job and get yourself a proper job. Be a paralegal like me; you'll make a fucking fortune, believe me, then you'll be on par with your classy boyfriend here. I mean, a hairdresser? For fuck's sake.'

Elise had had enough. 'Fuck off, Amara. Don't tell me what to do with my life. At least, I know when to back off my friends' boyfriends.'

'What are you talking about, you daft bitch?'

'Hey,' said Dominic. 'Steady on, Elise.'

'Yeah, piss off, Elise. We were just talking.' She gulped the last of her wine.

'Talking, my arse. You're all over him like a rash.'

'That might be because he needs someone with a bit more ambition in life.'

'I'm not staying to listen to this shit.'

'Yeah, that's right, Elise, you run back to Mummy and Daddy.'

'Dominic, will you take me home?'

'Actually, I'm rather enjoying myself. I think I'd rather stay.'

She stared at him, astonished by that. 'You bastard.'

Amara laughed again. Elise picked up her coat from the back of a chair.

'You all right, darling?' asked Sharon.

'No, I'm bloody not.'

'Hey, you're not leaving, are you? What's up?'

'Ask fucking birthday girl. Dominic, you coming or what?'

'No. I said.'

Elise stormed out, bumping into a woman who told her to mind where she was going. Elise stepped outside, bracing herself against the cold wind, the tears streaming down her face.

Chapter 36: Benedict

Benedict and Jessica had taken Nathaniel Turnbull back to the station and had deposited him in a cell. He only spoke when spoken to. Benedict told him the interview the following day would be a preliminary interview and offered Turnbull a solicitor. Turnbull declined.

The following morning, they reconvened in the office and over a coffee and a Danish pastry each tried to work out the connection between the murders of Anthony Browning and Dominic Woods, and the running over of Philip Edwards and the assault on William Grant. Somehow, all four cases seemed to be linked – but the question remained, how?

Benedict received a phone call from Dick Evans in forensics. The metal pig that killed Dominic Woods was made of cast aluminium, sixteen centimetres in length, and available online for a hundred pounds. And, yes, to confirm, the killer had used their left hand. Evans had also inspected the two champagne glasses and the bottle that had been on Woods' kitchen island that night. No fingermarks apart from Woods'.

They met Turnbull in Interview Room 3. Turnbull sat at the table, his eyes cast down, ignoring the bottle of water on the table in front of him, the very image of a dejected man.

'I hope you slept well, Mr Turnbull. All things considered,' said Benedict. 'We have a lot to discuss so we'd better get on. DS Gardiner?'

'Yes, thank you. Mr Turnbull, why did you resist arrest last night?' asked Jessica. 'What is it you're hiding?'

No answer.

'I'd advise you to speak to us here, Mr Turnbull. I really would, you know.'

The man sighed.

'OK, let's try this from another angle – you spoke to Dominic Woods here in this club just gone midnight on the night before he died. Did you speak to him again around eight on the actual night he died? Did you go to his house, Mr Turnbull? Was that when he transferred that sum of money to you? Ten grand is a lot of money.'

Still no answer. 'Did you *kill* Dominic Woods?' asked Jessica.

'No! No, I never, right? OK, I admit I went to his house. That's because he told me to when I spoke to him the night before at the club. He owed me that money, see?'

'Was it drugs?'

He shot a glance at the door. 'No. It was legit. I re-built his garden wall. I'm a brickie. I knocked down the old one that'd been there for years, and started again from scratch. It didn't need knocking down, I could've patched it up. But Mr Woods insisted, like. Wanted it all new. It'd been three weeks and he still hadn't paid me, and he wasn't exactly what you call short of money.'

'No. Was there anyone else in Mr Woods' house at the

time?' asked Benedict.

'No.'

'I see.' Benedict drummed his fingers on his knee. His back was still aching from the previous night's chase down that cobbled passageway. 'So, what was the other one thousand, one hundred pounds for? The amount he paid you a few days before.'

'Hey? Oh, erm, that was also for the wall. Part payment, you know, for the bricks. Although one hundred of it was for the tip.'

'Ten thousand pounds for a brick wall? I don't know about these things but I have to say that sounds like an awful lot of money.'

'It was a big job.'

'Must have been. And you did it all by yourself? No help?'

'Yeah. I always work on me own.'

'Do you do any painting and decorating?' asked Jessica.

'Have done.'

'Recently?'

'No.'

'So why did you buy thirty-two pounds and ninety-eight pence worth of emulsion paint from B&Q a couple of days ago?'

'What?'

'Emulsion paint, Mr Turnbull?' said Jessica. 'Two gallons of it. That's quite a lot of paint.'

'Well, yeah, I've got a job coming up.'

'Oh, yes? What's the name of the client?'

Turnbull rubbed his nose vigorously. 'There isn't one. It fell through.'

'What *was* the name of the client then?' asked Benedict. 'We'd like to speak to them.'

'I... I can't remember. I didn't keep a record of it as it, you know, fell through.'

'You see, we have another case on our hands at the moment. A flat nearby was broken into, an empty flat, and the person who broke in, threw paint all over the walls, the ceiling, the furniture, everywhere. Red emulsion paint, Mr Turnbull, the exact paint you bought two gallons of at B&Q. Are we to take this as a pure coincidence?'

The man remained silent, looking down still.

'Mr Turnbull?'

'No comment.'

Benedict nodded at Jessica.

Jessica passed Turnbull a print-out from a CCTV still. 'Is this your car, Mr Turnbull?'

Turnbull stared at the photo but seemed unable to respond.

'OK,' said Jessica. 'Let me change that from a question to a statement – this *is* a photo of your car. A 2007 Volkswagen Golf, seen here from the back of a thirty-one bus, just off Warboys Avenue, and here...' She passed him a second photo. 'Turning into Selwyn Avenue, and this last one taken from the traffic light at the junction of Selwyn Avenue and the High Street. In fact, in this last one, Mr Turnbull, where you're breaking a red light, we can see your face.'

'So what? I drive my car around.'

'You see the time on these printouts? The exact time you rammed your car into an unfortunate gentleman by the name of Philip Edwards. Mr Edwards is in hospital right now, having sustained some very serious, potentially life-changing injuries. Nasty, nasty stuff. You can imagine how his parents are feeling right now.'

'That wasn't me.'

'We think it is, Mr Turnbull,' said Benedict. 'We'll be sending someone over to have a look at your car, see if there's any damage to the front of it. We'll also be checking B&Q's CCTV.'

Turnbull sighed.

'And then there's the matter of *another* coincidence.'

He waited to see if Turnbull would react to that. The man didn't, turning his attention back to his lap.

Benedict continued. 'You see Philip Edwards has a girlfriend, a fiancée in fact. This same woman used to go out with Dominic Woods, the man whose house you were in on the very night he died. Now, that *is* a coincidence, don't you think?'

'I don't know.'

'And to add to the mix, the empty flat that was vandalised with that red emulsion paint was the very flat that Mr Edwards and his fiancée were due to move into that same day. Now, bear with me, I'm just thinking out loud here but did Mr Woods pay you to vandalise Mr Edwards' flat *and* run him over?'

'No.'

'Is that what that money was really for? Because, like I say, ten grand is a lot of money for a garden wall, however big.'

'No comment.'

'I think that's exactly what it was.'

Benedict paused for half a minute, allowing Turnbull to think about his situation.

'Now, try and see it from our point of view, Mr Turnbull. You were at Mr Woods' house around the time someone bludgeoned him to death. Now, if you were in my shoes right now, how would you interpret this?'

Turnbull didn't answer.

'It doesn't look good, does it?'

'I'm telling you, I didn't kill him,' he said, looking directly at Benedict for the first time. 'Why would I? He paid me the money.'

'Perhaps he didn't pay all of it?'

'I wouldn't kill someone for a couple of grand.'

'Perhaps you stole a wad of cash lying around.'

'No. I'm not a murderer and I'm not a thief. I work hard for my money.'

'You used to be a thief,' said Jessica. 'To be more precise, you were arrested for stealing cars and burglary. You pleaded guilty and served ten months.'

'That was years ago.'

'Six years ago.'

'So what did you do after he paid you?' asked Benedict.

'I left. What else would you expect me to do? Hang around and eat canapés or something?'

'You went home?'

'No, I went to work. Mr E will tell you.'

'Did you see anyone as you left? Someone loitering outside, perhaps?'

'No.'

Benedict glanced over at Jessica. She nodded. 'OK, Mr Turnbull. We'll wrap this up for now. But don't go far. No holidays in Ibiza for the next couple of weeks.'

'Chance be a fine thing.'

'Like I say, we'll be checking out your car and running a few more checks, namely your relationship with the deceased Dominic Woods. Once that's done, I imagine we'll be arresting you for at least vandalising Mr Edwards flat and running him over in your car. I hope you still think that money was worth it, Mr Turnbull, because I'll tell you this for nothing – there's no way you'll get away with such a light sentence this time.'

Nathaniel Turnbull looked like he was about to be sick.

'Do you need the bathroom, Mr Turnbull?' asked Jessica.

He wiped his mouth with the back of his hand.

'Oh, before we go,' said Benedict. 'Does the name Hans Tanner mean anything to you?'

He shook his head. 'No.'

'You sure?'

'Should it?'

'No, no. Just wondering.'

Chapter 37: Benedict

The following day, Benedict and Jessica were on their way to see William Grant for the third time. Halfway there, stuck in traffic on Camden High Street, Benedict's phone rang. Being on speaker, he answered it.

'DI Paige.'

'Hello, DI Paige. O'Brian from Safe Hands Trading here. Have you got a moment?'

'Sure.'

'I've got a confession to make.'

'Oh yes? I'm all ears, Mr O'Brian.'

'Dominic Woods was having one over on me. Have you heard of Ponzi schemes?'

'Yes, named after a corrupt American financier from the 1920s. 1930s perhaps? Charles Ponzi. Is that right?'

'Spot on, inspector. You should be on Mastermind. But you do know what a Ponzi scheme entails.'

'Erm... some sort of trading scam? Remind me.'

'In a nutshell, you pay off your initial tranche of investors with money put up by the second tranche. Then you pay off the second tranche with the money put up by the third tranche and so on and so on forever, or at least until you fail to attract any new investors.'

'It's totally illegal.'

'Of course. And I'm ashamed to say Dominic was running his own Ponzi scheme right under my nose.'

'Oh, I say.'

'Exactly. I felt he'd been slacking off recently. But he was always such a high performer that I considered it rather natural. After all, we can't always maintain such a high level of success before you burn out entirely, so I took it as part of the job's natural ebb and flow. Then, at the point I noticed a red flag or two, I allowed myself to be distracted by Anthony Browning's inappropriate behaviour which I told you about. I'll admit it was a bit more involved than I may have let on.'

Benedict got stuck behind an extremely slow milk float.

O'Brian continued. 'But now with both of them gone, I took the opportunity to have a deep dive into their accounts and I came across Dominic's nefarious dealings. I admit, I'm flabbergasted. I'm disappointed in him, of course, but most of all I'm most annoyed with myself. I also noticed that Anthony had managed through our IT people to gain managerial access to his accounts as well, despite the fact he had no right or permission to do so. I mean, if he was still here, that would be an on-the-spot sacking offence.'

'And Dominic too, presumably.'

'More than that. I'd have sacked him and called you guys in. I mean, he was messing with people's lifetime savings here, totally putting them at risk, while making a huge buck for himself. I am mortified. Thankfully, he didn't use the name of Safe Hands otherwise I'd be the one being held to account. It's embarrassing enough as it is.'

'I can imagine.' Thankfully, the milk float turned right and disappeared.

'So anyway, I thought I'd better come clean and tell you.'

'But if Browning got wind of Woods' dubious dealings, is it the sort of thing you'd kill for.'

'You tell me, you're the copper, but frankly, when you're talking about one, maybe one and a half million a year, I'd imagine it might well be. Look, I'd better go. I've got a call coming through from my solicitor.'

'Sure. Thanks for letting us know, Mr O'Brian.' He rang off.

'Looks like a classic case of the blackmailer being killed by his victim,' said Jessica.

'It's like a black and white Hollywood film with Edward G Robison.'

'Who?'

'I think it's going to rain again.'

*

William Grant made them each a cup of tea, putting far too much sugar in Benedict's. He tried not to grimace. 'How are you feeling, Mr Grant? You look better.'

'I feel better, thanks. I'm moving back with my girlfriend and stepdaughter next week.'

'Kate Hamilton? Oh now, that *is* good news.'

'Yeah.' He didn't look overjoyed but then again, maybe he was just a man who didn't enjoy speaking to the police so often. Benedict noticed the goldfish bowl was empty and dry. 'What happened to Goldie?'

'Goldie? He died.'

'Oh, I'm sorry to hear that. Do you think you might replace him?'

'What? I don't know. It's still too early.'

'Of course. You haven't got over the death of Goldie yet.'

'Look, I don't mean to be rude or anything but why are you here again?' he asked, emphasising the last word.

'Does the name Hans Tanner mean anything to you?'

'Hans Tanner?' His eyes darted to the empty goldfish bowl. 'No. Never heard of him.'

Benedict caught Jessica's eye. She didn't believe him either. 'Mr Grant, it might help if you told us the truth now. Mr Grant, please...'

He ran his fingers through his hair. Looking down at the carpet, he said, 'I went out with his daughter once. Years ago.'

'Elise Tanner?'

'Yes.'

'I see. Years ago, you say?'

'Yes. Around 2018.'

Jessica, clearing her throat, asked, 'So why did her father beat you up like that?'

'It's a long story.'

'We have all day.'

'I don't—'

'You do now.'

He considered the implied threat. He took a large gulp of his tea. 'OK. I'll tell you. Maybe then, you'll leave me alone.'

'We can't promise that.'

'But we'll try our best,' added Benedict, still trying to swallow down his super-sweet tea.

'Elise and me were going out. Not for long though when she dumped me for this other bloke. Anyway—'

'Sorry, to interrupt already, Mr Grant,' said Benedict. 'But what was his name?'

'Erm, Dominic something.'

'Thank you.' He stole a glance at Jessica. 'Do carry on.'

'I think they were steady but then they split up, I don't know why.'

'Were you upset when Elise dumped you?' asked Jessica.

He took a while to answer, swirling the dregs of his tea around the bottom of his cup. 'Yes, I was. Can't lie. I liked her. She was decent.'

'Did you ever meet her father?'

'Yes, of course. I used to go round there, watch TV with El, that sort of thing.'

'So why did he beat you up then, Mr Grant?' asked Jessica.

'I told you before – mistaken identity.'

'He thought you were Dom Woods.'

'Maybe.'

'Didn't you tell him?'

He looked up finally. 'I couldn't, could I? I had that bloody strip of gaffer tape over me mouth.'

'Did he say anything to you?'

'Only four words – *this is for Elise*. That's why I knew it had to be mistaken identity because I never did anything to Elise, nothing that deserved that sort of punishment.'

'This is for Elise,' repeated Benedict. 'And that's when you realised who he was.'

'Yes.'

'What sort of voice does he have? Does he have an accent perhaps?'

'He does, yes. Sort of German or Dutch or something.'

'Did you see his face?'

'No. It was dark and then he'd got that hood on me.'

'But the other day, when we showed you that photofit, you *did* recognise him.'

'Suppose.'

'Suppose? What's that meant to mean, Mr Grant?'

'Yeah, all right, it was him. I heard his voice and I recognised him from that... that drawing.'

'OK. OK, Mr Grant,' said Benedict. 'No need to upset yourself.'

'Why didn't you tell us?' asked Jessica.

'Why do you think? If he's capable of doing something like that once...'

'Did he ever show signs of violence while you were going out with his daughter?'

'No. Never.'

'Think of the future now,' said Jessica. 'Moving back in with Kate and your stepdaughter.'

'Yeah, that'll be nice. I just want to put this behind me now.'

'Of course you do.'

'We will be charging Hans Tanner, Mr Grant,' said Benedict. 'And unless he pleads guilty, you might have to appear in court.'

'I'll face that when the day comes.'

'Good man. And like I say, it might not come to that.'

'Here's hoping, eh?'

'Yes, Mr Grant, here's hoping.'

Chapter 38: Benedict

Benedict and Jessica returned to the Tanner house on Harriet Avenue first thing in the morning. Hans Tanner was already out at work but Nicola Tanner, his wife, was at home and Elise was about to go to work. 'I can't stay,' said Elise. 'I've got to get to work.'

'If we could ask you to phone your place of work and tell them you'll be late,' said Jessica. 'We do need to talk to you.'

She looked flustered but did as advised, going into the kitchen to make the call. Nicola Tanner offered them coffee, which they gladly accepted. 'You've still not put the painting up, I see,' said Benedict.

'It's not for here,' said Nicola. 'It was meant to be for the flat Elise was supposed to be moving into with her fiancé. It fell through, unfortunately.' Nicola pulled on her earlobe. 'And then, last week, Elise's fiancé was hit by a car and is in hospital with some terrible injuries.'

'Yes, we do know about that,' said Benedict. 'Two of our detective constables spoke to your daughter at the hospital.'

'When's your husband due back from work?' asked Jessica.

244

'Today? He works different shifts. Today, it's... let me see, today, he'll be back about three. Why do you ask?'

'We need to speak to him as a matter of urgency.'

'You already have.'

'We need to speak to him again. But we can come back this afternoon.'

'Not so urgent then. Can I help?'

'Not at this stage, thank you.'

'Yes. Anyway, I'll make you that coffee.' She walked off towards the kitchen.

'They're not happy,' said Elise, back from making her call. 'I've taken too much time off recently.'

'We'll try not to detain you any longer than necessary,' said Jessica. 'Shall we sit? Here, let me write you a note,' she added, tearing a sheet out of her notebook.

'Why?'

'For your work. Tell them why you're late. It might help.'

Benedict watched his colleague write a note, wondering why on earth she felt the need to do that.

'Here,' said Jessica, passing the sheet of paper to Elise. 'Might be best if you sign it.' She handed Elise her pen.

'I'm not sure this will help, to be honest.' But Elise signed Jessica's note, nonetheless.

Playing with her necklace, Elise glanced at the painting.

'We know this is a difficult time for you, Elise.' said Jessica. 'We're sorry to hear about your fiancé.'

'Have you found the person who hit Phil?'

'All I can say at this juncture is that we have a man who is helping us with our enquiries.'

'Oh, that sounds hopeful.'

'We'll let you know in good time, don't worry.'

'They almost killed him. They need to be held to account,

they can't just… get away with this.'

'How is Phil?'

'Not good. Not good at all. It's horrendous.' She looked close to tears. 'He's got a broken leg, a broken arm, five broken ribs, two broken collarbones and a fractured neck, and he's got a collapsed lung and a bleed on the brain. I don't even know how serious those two things are.'

'He's at St Cuthbert's. They'll take good care of him there. Miss Tanner,' said Jessica. 'Are you aware that Dominic Woods is dead?'

'Argh,' she screamed, her hand clamping over her mouth. 'Dead? Dominic? Seriously?'

'Yes. I'm afraid he was found… well, murdered, in his own home yesterday morning. His cleaner found him. He'd been killed the evening before.'

Elise had turned pale. 'Murdered?'

Her mother came through from the kitchen bearing two mugs of coffee. 'Is there something wrong?' she asked, handing the detectives their coffees.

'Someone's murdered Dom,' said Elise.

Nicola Tanner's hand went to her heart. 'Oh my. Oh. That is shocking. How… how was he k-killed?'

'Unfortunately, he was hit on the back of the head. There was no sign of a break-in so we're thinking the perpetrator could well be someone he knew.'

'This is just awful.'

'Where were you Sunday night, Elise?' asked Benedict. 'About eight, nine o'clock.'

'Why are you asking her that?' shouted Nicola. 'You can't seriously be suggesting Elise was involved with this. Elise would never do something like this; I know my daughter, she's—'

'Mum, it's all right. Calm down.'

'Calm down? You ask me to—'

'Mum, just stop, will you? Please, just this once, stop.'

'I'm sorry,' said Benedict. 'But we need to ask these questions. So, Elise, Sunday night?'

'Erm, yes, Sunday night. About eight, nine o'clock. I was here, wasn't I, Mum? I'd just come back from the hospital visiting Phil. I was tired after that. I came home, had something to eat and went to bed early. That was it.'

'I can vouch for that,' said Nicola. 'And I'm telling you, Inspector, my daughter could never—'

'Mum, please.'

'Elise,' said Benedict. 'You and Dominic Woods were in a relationship together for a while.'

'Yes.'

'It finished?'

She shrugged. 'It just fizzled out.'

'Fizzled out? But he considered you, to quote another of his girlfriends, as the love of his life.'

'That was Dom for you. He could be... intense. Who was this girlfriend?'

'Someone who came after you.'

'Elise,' said Jessica. 'Did Dominic ever... shall we say, hurt you?'

'No.'

'I'll put it more bluntly – did he ever sexually assault you?'

'No,' she snapped.

'Do you have to ask these questions?' said Nicola.

'I'm afraid we do, Mrs Tanner,' said Jessica.

'Elise, when was the last time you saw Dominic?' asked Benedict.

'Oh, now you're asking. At least five years.'

'You didn't keep in contact?'

'Oh God, no.'

'That's quite adamant.'

'I have Phil; he's my fiancé now. I don't tend to keep in touch with my ex boyfriends. Why would I?'

'Was William Grant an ex-boyfriend?'

'William?' She appeared genuinely surprised by the question. She shot a look at her mother. 'How do you know about him?'

'He was your boyfriend though?'

'Yeah. For a while. Why do you ask?'

Jessica described what had happened to William Grant.

'Oh my God,' said Elise. 'Is he OK?'

'Yes, he's fine. Rather shaken up, as you can imagine. But he's already on the mend, at least physically. I think mentally, it might take some time.'

'What's happening to everyone?' asked Elise, holding onto a handkerchief. 'Phil run over, Dominic dead and William attacked. It's like someone's got it in for me. This is awful.'

Her mother took her hand. 'It's just a coincidence, love, an awful coincidence.'

'Now,' said Benedict. 'This is where it gets awkward, Miss Tanner, Mrs Tanner.'

The two women swapped concerned looks.

'You see, William has accused your father, Elise, of being the man who assaulted him.'

'Dad?' she cried.

'Hans? That's plain ridiculous,' said Nicola. 'How dare he say that? You asked us about this the other day, and we told you.'

'His alibi is weak, Mrs Tanner,' said Jessica. 'And he's a big guy, your husband.'

248

'That doesn't mean nothing.'

'Secondly,' continued Benedict. 'Like I said the other day, a witness came forward and described your husband, creating that photofit we showed you.'

'Yes, and it looked nothing like him.'

'It's rather subjective,' said Jessica.

'And thirdly...' Benedict almost felt sorry for them, piling on this amount of evidence. 'Another witness recognised the photofit as being Hans.'

'Who?' snapped Nicola. 'Who recognised him?'

'We can't tell you that,' said Jessica.

'No. I don't believe it. It's impossible.'

'Why would William make it up?'

'I... I don't know. You'd have to ask him.'

'We did,' said Benedict. 'He said that the only words Hans said to him during this prolonged assault were, *This is for Elise.*'

'I d-don't believe it,' said Elise, the tears pooling in her eyes.

'He said your father spoke with an accent – German perhaps or Dutch.'

The two women slumped. They obviously hadn't known but the evidence was too much to deny.

Benedict continued. 'William believes your father got the wrong man, that he meant to attack someone else, perhaps Dominic. If that was the case, why would your father have reason to attack Dominic Woods, Elise?'

'I don't know!' she shouted. 'I honestly don't know.'

'Did they know each other? Had they met?'

'I can't remember. No, I don't think so.'

'I met him,' said Mrs Tanner. 'But I think Elise is right – Hans never did.'

'OK. Thank you both for your time. Tell your husband, Mrs Tanner, that we'll be back soon after three. We'll need to question him at the station, and it's not always the warmest. So tell him to wear a jumper.'

'Will you be arresting him?'

'Yes, I'm afraid we will be.'

*

As Benedict and Jessica drove back to the station, Jessica said, 'Elise is left-handed.'

'How do you know that?'

'The note I got her to sign.'

'Oh! So that's what you were doing. And our killer is left-handed. Good work, DS Gardiner. Sneaky but good.'

Jessica smiled.

Chapter 39: Elise, 2018
Five years earlier

Sunday afternoon, Elise went out for a walk across Greenfield Park; she needed to clear her head. Her mother had picked up on her misery and quizzed her incessantly to the point Elise wanted to scream at her. She knew she'd lost Amara as a friend, possibly forever, but, if truth be told, they'd never been the best of friends, just part of the same friendship groups, it was no big deal. Amara had always had a high opinion of herself. But had Elise also lost her boyfriend? Her heart churned with the anxiety of it all. She'd texted him twice now and received no response; she wasn't going to text again. In fact, she regretted texting him now; it wasn't for her to make the first move. He should be the one grovelling to her, begging her forgiveness. She'd also tried ringing Sharon but received a text saying she was too busy to talk right now.

She wondered what happened after she left The Three Bells. No doubt, they all had a good laugh at her expense. Not Sharon though. She was too good a friend. Surely,

Shazzer would have stuck up for her, told Amara where to get off. Elise wouldn't put it past Sharon to tear a strip off Dominic too. Boyfriends were important but your friends came first. Wasn't there a Spice Girls lyric to that effect? But obviously it was not something Amara believed in.

Deciding it was too cold to be wandering around a frosty park, Elise headed for a nice café she knew on the high street, a place called Berties. Relishing the warmth, she ordered a latte and a ham and cheese Panini. She scrolled through her Instagram feed but found her attention waning. What had Sharon called Dominic? The Holy Trinity of a boyfriend. And she was right. Yes, he could sulk for England, she knew that now, but she reckoned she knew what to do now to avoid that.

Her phone rang – it was him.

'I'm sorry, Elise.'

'Are you?'

'I had too much to drink and I wasn't thinking straight. I was an idiot. Let me buy you dinner tonight by way of apology.'

'Dominic, I'm not sure.'

'I can understand that. But please, I want you to know how sorry I am.'

She held her breath, trying to decide what to do for the best.

'Elise, please say yes.'

She exhaled. 'Yes, OK, I'll meet you for dinner.'

'Thank you. Thank you so much.'

*

Dominic embraced Elise on seeing her, whispering 'I'm sorry,' several times in her ear and Elise knew she'd forgiven him. He took her to a different restaurant, this one, a Spanish restaurant called Hermosa, which, according to Dominic, was Spanish for 'lovely'. They ate well, and drank an expensive bottle of red Spanish wine, and the more they ate and drank, the more relaxed Elise felt. No mention was made of Amara.

Afterwards, Elise returned to Dominic's house. His parents were already in bed but Elise met his sister, Olivia, who sat watching TV, her feet on a pouffe, and vaping, leaving a hint of a sweet strawberry aroma in the air.

'Ah,' said Olivia on being introduced to Elise. 'So, you're the famous Elise.' She turned the TV volume down on the remote. 'You really do exist; you're not just a figment of my brother's imagination.'

'Do shut up, Olivia,' said Dominic.

'Just saying, that's all. So how long have you guys been hanging?'

'A while now,' said Dominic.

'We've been to a lovely Spanish restaurant, Hermosa.'

'One of Dom's regular haunts. You are honoured. So what is it you do, Elisa?'

'Elise. I work in a hairdressers' salon.'

'Oh, do you? I suppose someone has to. Anyway,' she said, drawing on her vape. 'Don't let me keep you.'

Dominic and Elise went to his bedroom. 'Don't mind her,' he said, drawing the curtains. 'She's always like that.'

'Like what?'

'Spiky. Can you stay the night?'

Elise hugged him. 'Would you like me to?'

'Hell, yeah.'

*

Monday morning. Elise woke up early in Dominic's bed

naked. But Dominic wasn't beside her. She could hear someone along the landing having a shower, presumably him, unless it was his 'spiky' sister. She stretched and smiled with the warmth that comes from remembering a wonderful evening. The delicious food, the engaging conversation, the sex. Ah yes, the sex; it'd been incredible. Dominic took her to places she'd never been before; made her feel things she never knew could exist. How did he become such a great lover? She'd never felt so spent but it had left her a little sore and she feared she wouldn't be able to walk properly for a week!

Dominic returned from the shower, a towel wrapped around him. 'Ah, she's awake,' he said on seeing her sitting up in bed. 'Good morning, my love. A lovely, frosty day out there. Do you want a shower?'

'I think perhaps I should.'

'Here, use this.' He threw her his dressing gown. 'Oh, I meant to tell you last night. I've booked us a table at DiMaggio's for Thursday. Seven o'clock.'

'Oh, that'd be… No, I can't make it. I'm sorry.'

'Why on earth not? I've booked it now.'

'I've arranged to go out with Shaz, just the two of us.'

'So what? Rearrange it.'

'I can't do that, Dom.'

He sat on the bed next to her, placing his hand over hers. 'You know, I've been thinking about this, about your friends.'

Elise snatched her hand away. 'What about them?'

'This Sharon woman is too… too common for the likes of you, Elise, and–'

'Hang on, you can't–'

'And Amara…'

'What about Amara?'

'A bad influence.'

Elise guffawed. 'A what?'

'And the others, well, what can I say? I think you should stop seeing them.'

Elise's mouth fell open.

'I know. You look shocked but I think you'll thank me long term. I mean, I certainly won't want to set eyes on any of them again, and you shouldn't either.'

'You are joking, right?'

'No, I'm being deadly serious. I'll leave it up to you. Think about it and you'll see them for what they really are.'

'I can't believe I'm even listening to this.'

'And then you can decide.'

'Decide?'

'Decide what's more important to you – them or me. Because, I'll tell you this, you can't have both.'

Elise stood beneath the cascade of water in the shower, trying to wrap her head over what Dominic had just said. What century were they living in? He couldn't make demands like that. How dare he? There was no way she'd ever comply. All the positivity she'd woken up with had, along with the shower water, drained away leaving her hollow.

She returned to Dominic's bedroom to find him sitting on the edge of the bed on his phone, wearing a shirt and boxer shorts. Removing Dominic's dressing gown, she reached for her clothes that she'd hastily threw on a wicker chair the previous evening. She didn't expect Dominic to clasp her from behind, his hands squeezing her breasts. 'We've got time,' he whispered in her ear.

'Oh, Dom, no, we haven't.'

'Of course we have.' Taking her hand, he dragged her over

to the bed. 'Just a quickie.'

'I can't, Dom, please, I'm too sore after last—'

He pushed her down onto the bed. 'It'll be fine.'

'Dom, what the fuck?'

'Do this for me,' he said, pressing his weight down on her and hitching down his boxers.

She did, she complied. She clenched her eyes shut and braced herself and allowed him to fuck her. Thankfully, it was over and done with quickly, but boy, it hurt.

Once done, Dominic dressed quickly, checking his phone and humming to himself. He didn't speak or look at her once until he was ready to leave. 'Help yourself to breakfast. We might have some honey in the cupboards. If you're quick you should miss my parents and Olivia. See you later. I'll give you a call. Bye.'

'Don't I even get a kiss?' she said aloud after he'd gone.

She lay on the bed, still naked, her chest heaving, wanting both to go back to sleep and pretend none of this had happened, *and* to get out of this house as quickly as possible. Everything had been so perfect last night and now, in a stroke, it'd all gone leaving her feeling empty and sullied.

Chapter 40: Benedict

Benedict came into the office to find DCs Kelly and Prowse arguing what was worse – men who wore a ponytail or a mullet. 'At least, with a ponytail,' Prowse was saying, 'you only looked like a twat from behind. With a mullet, you can't escape it.'

'Men in the eighties had no zero style,' agreed Kelly. 'I mean, what made a bloke think, I know, today I'll get myself a mullet and make myself more attractive to women.'

Benedict logged onto his computer and began reading his emails. He'd received one of those compliance courses that everyone in the organisation was obliged to take, this one about how to spot a phishing email. Believing it to be exactly that, a phishing email, he deleted it.

'I think yuppies had ponytails,' said DC Prowse. 'Blokes who worked in the City and carried around those, what do you call them things, Filofaxes, and those mobiles that looked like bricks.'

'Ah, those were the days,' said Kelly.

'Don't be an arse, Jamie,' said Jessica. 'You weren't even

born.'

'Yeah but imagine carrying one of those bricks. *Hello, yes? I'm on the train.*'

DC Kelly's desk phone rang, making him jump.

'You'd better get that, Jamie,' said DC Prowse. 'It might be your hairdresser booking you in for a mullet.'

'Hello, DC Kelly here. Good morning. How can I help?'

Benedict worked his way through his emails, remembering the days that he, as a young man, had a Filofax and how much he loved it.

'Boss,' shouted Kelly.

'Jeepers, Kelly. I'm only here. Yes, what is it?'

'Listen to this, in November 2018, Elise Tanner accused Dominic Woods of rape.'

'Did she, begads? Are you sure?'

'Yeah, PC Stevens decided to root around a bit and he found it.'

'Good man, PC Stevens. And? What came of it? I presume nothing did, otherwise we'd have found out sooner.'

'Yes, she dropped it.'

'Why?'

'The police at the time interviewed Woods and he had an alibi so Tanner withdrew the allegation.'

'Who was the alibi?'

'His sister. Olivia Woods. Apparently, she had him over for dinner that evening while her parents were away for the weekend. So, Elise was making it up.'

'Where were the parents?'

'PC Stevens did tell me, erm, it was on the Eurostar.'

'Paris?'

'No.'

'Amsterdam?'

'That's the one!'

Why did Kelly say it as if he'd never heard of it? Benedict glanced over at Jessica. 'DS Gardiner, give Olivia a ring, please. See if she's available. We need to talk to her. Meanwhile, DC Kelly, I've got a job for you.'

'Sure but can I do it later? It's just that—'

'No, DC Kelly, you cannot do it later. I need this information five minutes ago.'

*

Mrs Woods opened the door to them. 'Oh, hello, inspector,' she said with a nervous smile. 'Were we expecting you?'

'Olivia is, Mrs Woods. We rang earlier and arranged it.'

'Oh dear. I'm afraid she's out at the moment. Would you care to come in and wait for her?'

Benedict and Jessica sat in the Woods' narrow living room with its bright red wallpaper.

'How are you, Mrs Woods?' asked Jessica.

'Oh, you know, not too bad all things considered. Your pathologist woman rang yesterday to say we could have Dominic's body back so now I'm arranging the funeral. I've sent Ted out to the florists.'

'Mrs Woods, I've got to ask you a difficult question now.' He could see her brace herself. 'Were you aware that four years ago, a woman accused your son of raping her?'

'Yes, but it was such nonsense. I met the girl a couple of times. A little gold-digger, that one. And everything fake, her nails and eyelashes, and I suspect her... you know, her bosom. I couldn't see what Dom saw in her. But what she said was utter rubbish.'

'Your son was very wealthy,' said Jessica. 'Do you think that perhaps Dominic paid her off?'

'Absolutely not.' She pulled on her necklace. 'I shouldn't imagine he did. He had no reason to. He was innocent!'

'Did the accusation affect Dominic?' asked Jessica.

'How do you mean?'

'I mean, did the accusation of rape upset him at all, or make him angry? Perhaps, it affected his relationship with subsequent girlfriends?'

She shrugged. 'I don't think so, no. It was a long time ago.'

'Only five years, Mrs Woods,' said Benedict. 'Not so long ago. We had arranged to meet Olivia, Mrs Woods. She's running late. Can you phone her? Tell her we're here waiting for her.'

'Oh yes, good idea. Of course. She had a hair appointment but she should have been back by now.' Mrs Woods made the phone call but no one answered. 'I'm sorry. I'll try again in a bit. I'm sorry; I haven't offered you tea or coffee. Would you like one while you wait for Olivia?'

They both opted for coffee, one sugar for Benedict. The three of them sat sipping their coffees. Benedict, for want of something to say, asked Mrs Woods where she planned to have Dominic's funeral. She explained in detail, and the problem of not knowing whom her son's friends were, therefore not knowing who to invite. Benedict knew that at some point, Mrs Woods would find out that her son stood accused of murdering Anthony Browning but, until they were sure, he decided to spare her that torment for now. However appalling your offspring turn out to be, you still loved them, still wanted to protect them. Even more so if they could no longer defend themselves.

Twenty minutes later, Benedict was getting impatient. Where was Olivia Woods? He knew Jessica was feeling the same. No one likes to be kept waiting. What's more, they had to drive back to Hans Tanner's place.

He finished his coffee. Mrs Woods, however, oblivious to their discomfort, continued singing the praises of her son.

'Will your old house become yours again, Mrs Woods?' asked Jessica.

'Oh, it was never *not* ours. We never sold it to Dominic.'

'Will you move back?'

She thought about this for a while. 'Ted and I have talked about it, and you know, we rather like it around here now. We've got used to it. The neighbours are pleasant and Southgate is a nice area. I think we'll probably just end up selling it.'

'You could rent it out?' suggested Jessica.

'No, too much of a faff.'

Benedict looked pointedly at his watch. 'Well, look, Mrs Woods, we're going to have to go. We need to get back–' They heard the front door.

'Ah, this could be Olivia now. Or it might be Ted.' She listened for the footsteps. 'That's Olivia.'

Oh the relief. Benedict and Jessica stood on seeing Olivia Woods.

She looked flustered and apologised for being late. The hairdresser had overrun, she said.

'Your hair looks nice,' said Jessica.

Benedict couldn't see any difference from the last time he saw her but he smiled diplomatically. 'Mrs Woods,' he said, turning to her mother. 'We'd like to speak to Olivia alone.'

'Oh yes, OK, that's fine. I'll just go and… erm, prepare some lunch. Are you hungry, Olivia?'

'Starving.'

'There we are then. If you'll excuse me…'

Benedict waited until Mrs Woods was out of earshot. 'Miss

Woods, you remember the name Elise Tanner?'

She rolled her eyes. 'Of course.'

'She accused your brother of raping her on the night of 18th November 2018. But she later retracted the accusation on account he had an alibi for his whereabouts that evening – namely you. Is that correct?'

'Yes. Yes, it is.'

'Do you recall what the two of you were doing?'

'Erm, let me see, it's a long time ago,' she said, repeating her mother's phrase. 'I… I don't really remember, to be honest.'

'Dominic came round here for something to eat. You were alone that night, your parents were on a weekend break in Amsterdam. So, being alone you decided to have your brother around for dinner?'

'Yes, yes, that's absolutely right. Did I tell you all this at the time?'

'You did. And in light of such overpowering evidence, Ms Tanner withdrew her allegation.'

'Well, she would, wouldn't she? On account she was making it up.'

'Why would she make it up, Miss Woods?' asked Jessica.

'I've no clue. You'd have to ask her.'

'We intend to. I just wondered whether you had your own theory on the matter. Did you ever meet Elise Tanner?'

'Perhaps once but I don't really remember her. I met her mother. She came to the house once. Bloody barking, that woman. Anyone would think *I* bloody raped her daughter. She actually scared me. Mum and Dad met Elise. Actually, I haven't the faintest about Dad but Mum did.' She pulled on her hair and Benedict could see now that it was slightly blonder than before.

262

'You see,' he said, 'what we find puzzling, Miss Woods, is that before we came here today, we got one of our detective constables to do some donkey work on your parents' weekend away. They did indeed go to Amsterdam that weekend.'

'I know. I just told you.'

'But you went with them, Miss Woods.'

'What?' She turned red in an instant. 'D-did I?'

'Yes, you did. Three return tickets to Amsterdam that very weekend. How was it, the city of Van Gogh?'

'Oh shit, I must've got my dates confused.'

'That's quite some admission to make, Miss Woods. If you were away that weekend, your brother had no alibi. Maybe, just maybe, Elise Tanner was telling the truth.'

'No. I d-don't believe it for a second.'

'Perhaps, you had dinner with Dominic the weekend before or the one after?' suggested Jessica.

'Yes, yes, that was probably it. Like I say, I got my dates confused.'

'Miss Woods, Olivia, piling one lie on top of another isn't going to help you. You lied to the police then, you're lying to us now. You appreciate that's perjury, and that's a serious matter, Miss Woods. I'm going to ask you a question now and I'd think very carefully on how you remember this.'

'Can I just nip to the loo?'

'No, you can't. Did your brother ask you to provide him with a false alibi, Miss Woods?'

'Let me see, erm...'

'The truth, Miss Woods.'

The puff went out of her. 'I told you before – Dominic is... was a bully. He bullied people and he bullied me. He bullied me into saying we were having dinner together that night.'

'Didn't he think you might get caught out on account you were on the other side of the Channel?'

'We got away with it, didn't we?'

'Until now.'

'What will you do?'

'As far as Elise's allegation is concerned, we will ask her about it, but there's nothing we can do – not now that your brother is dead. But, as far as you're concerned, Miss Jones, well, that's an entirely different matter.'

'I'm sorry,'

Benedict shook his head. 'It's Elise you should be saying sorry to, not us.'

Chapter 41: Benedict

Late afternoon. Benedict and Jessica paid their third visit to the Tanner house on Harriet Avenue. This time, Hans Tanner was at home, having got back from work. Nicola Tanner showed them through to the living room where they found Elise sitting on the sofa on her phone. 'Have you come for Dad?'

'Yes,' said Benedict. 'Where is he?'

'Upstairs. Don't worry, he's not going to run away. He'll be down in a minute.'

'Any news on Phil?'

She sighed. 'Not good. He's going to be in hospital for weeks, maybe months.'

Her father came trotting down the stairs. 'I believe you want to speak to me.'

His wife approached him, the two linking arms.

'More than that, Mr Tanner,' said Benedict. 'Hans Tanner, we're arresting you on the suspicion of stealing a vehicle and aggravated assault. You do not have to say anything but anything you do say may be recorded and used at a later stage in court. Do you understand?'

He looked down. 'I understand.'

'If you could come with us, please, Mr Tanner.'

'Can't we do this here?'

'Not now you're under arrest.'

'Will I have a solicitor?'

'If you wish, we can supply one.'

Tanner kissed his wife. 'I'll see you later, Elise.'

'Good luck, Dad.'

*

Interview room one, late afternoon. Hans Tanner opted not to have a solicitor representing him. He sat on the other side of the Formica table from the two detectives, a glass and a bottle of water in front of him. Benedict switched on the tape recorder, recording the time and who was present. Jessica passed him a sheet of paper to sign, a declaration that he was being interviewed at the police station.

'Mr Tanner, we've arrested you on the suspicion of stealing a white Ford transit van on the night of the 15th February, and on the same night you assaulted William Grant, and that you stripped down, gagged and tied Mr Grant to a tree in the woods next to Greenfield Park in the early hours of the morning. A witness came forward and, based on his description, we put together this photofit.' He placed the photofit on the table. 'Of course, we've already shown this but I'm repeating it now that we're under more formal circumstances and for the benefit of the tape. Like I said before, as a result of this photofit, someone came forward to say that they recognised you. Now although Mr Grant didn't see you during the attack on account he had a hood over his head, he also recognised you from the photofit. He also

266

recognised your accent when you said to him, *This is for Elise.*
He said you spoke with a German or Dutch accent. What do
you have to say to all this, Mr Tanner?'

He looked down at his hands but didn't speak, as if
weighing up his words.

'Mr Tanner?'

He took the bottle of water and. unscrewing the lid, poured
himself half a glass. He took a sip. 'He's wrong. I'm not
German or Dutch. I'm originally from Austria. But I can
understand his confusion. People often get confused.'

'What are you saying here, Mr Tanner. I'm a little confused
myself.'

'Yes, I did steal that van and yes, I did assault Mr Grant.
I'm sorry.'

'OK.' Benedict hadn't expected the confession to come so
readily. But then, the evidence was fairly damning.

'Why, Mr Tanner? That's what we don't understand.'

'I got the wrong man.'

Aha, thought Benedict, exactly as William Grant had said.
'The wrong man?'

'Grant went out with my daughter for a while. And then
she got raped. My wife told me only recently but she said she
didn't know who did it, although actually she did. The bugger
got away with it. I assumed it was Grant who'd done it.'

'But it wasn't.'

'No.'

'So, once you knew about the rape, you sought William
Grant and assaulted him.'

'That's about the measure of it. How is he?'

'William? He'll live. The injuries he sustained were fairly
superficial but you caused him quite some anguish there, Mr
Tanner. He truly thought he was going to die up there. That's

267

upsetting for a person. And, naturally, considering he'd done nothing wrong.'

'Yeah, OK, make me feel worse, why not?'

'This is no laughing matter, Mr Tanner. You will be going to court for this. And you risk being put back in prison. I'd be surprised if you weren't.' The man didn't appear overly perturbed, thought Benedict. 'But, to confirm, it wasn't Grant who raped your daughter. The man who raped Elise was called Dominic Woods. Not William Grant.'

'I know. That night I did Grant, I told my wife what I'd done and that's when she finally told me it was this bloke, Woods. I wished she'd told me first time. I was so mad, I can't tell you. So that's why I *killed* Dominic Woods.'

The room went silent. Benedict stared at the man. Was he being serious? The way he just came out with it, so casually. It didn't seem credible. He exchanged puzzled looks with Jessica.

'Sorry, Mr Tanner, could you repeat that?'

'You heard. I killed Dominic Woods. I killed the bastard who raped my daughter.'

'You appreciate what you're saying here?'

'Of course I bloody do.'

'When and where did you kill Dominic Woods, Mr Tanner?'

'Sunday night, at his house. I killed him.'

'How did you get in the house?'

He took a large gulp of his water and wiped his mouth with his fingers. 'I rang the doorbell and he let me in. As simple as that.'

'What time was this?'

'Around nine o'clock.'

'He knew you?'

'No, but I introduced myself. Told him I was Elise's dad and he let me in, offered me a coffee, turned his back and I smashed the bastard's head in. And then I left. There was no point hanging around; it's not as if I wanted to rob him.'

'And you went home.'

'I then went home.' He took a large drink of water. 'Listen, I know what you're thinking, that you're talking to a cold-blooded murderer here, and perhaps I am. But let's give this some context. Are you a father, Inspector Paige?'

'I am.'

'To a girl?'

'Yes. She's fifteen.'

'Right. You might understand then. Imagine how I felt knowing that my little girl had been violated. The fact they'd been, or were, in a relationship, makes no difference. No means no. Imagine how that would make you feel, Inspector. You know how it is, you want to protect your children, whether they're fifteen or twenty-five or whatever age, girls especially. So when I learned that this man... this sorry excuse of a man had done what he did to Elise, it gets to you right inside, you know.' He thumped his chest, the tears welling in his eyes. 'It makes you mad. How dare he do that to my daughter? How *dare* he? You can understand that, Inspector.'

'Did you mean to kill Dominic Woods?'

'No, I really didn't mean to. I went there to teach him a lesson. But he was so arrogant. I hated him, what with his attitude and his big house and his... his sense of entitlement. I meant to hurt him but I saw red. I'm not proud of it.'

'You bludgeoned him to death. It was not for you, however you felt, to dispense justice. You didn't have that right.'

'You think I don't know this?'

'OK,' said Benedict. 'We're going to have to terminate this interview at this point. We can't continue without a solicitor being present, Mr Tanner.'

'I don't mind.'

'No, but we do. You have to have someone here.'

'Can I go home then?'

'No, not at this stage. You'll be kept here overnight in the cells. Tomorrow morning, you can call your solicitor or, if you don't have access to one, we can help. Then you can make a full confession, and, just to let you know, we'll want to know every detail.'

Jessica popped out and beckoned a uniformed officer. 'Can you take Mr Tanner down to the cells, please? He's staying overnight.'

'Can I phone my wife?'

'Yes, you can phone your wife.'

'Well, I didn't expect that,' said Benedict, once Hans Tanner had been escorted away. 'The way he just came out with it, *yes, I killed Dominic Woods*, so casually, as if he was guilty of some minor offence.'

'He didn't do it though.'

'What do you mean?'

'He's lying, boss.'

'How do you know?'

'He's right-handed. He signed his name with his right hand.'

'Did he? My word, you're right. But why would he lie?'

'Because he's covering for someone. And given how much he knew about the circumstances of Dominic Woods' death, I suggest we need to speak to Elise again.'

'Begads, DS Gardiner, I think you're right.'

Chapter 42: Benedict

Next morning, Benedict and Jessica went to see DCI Lincoln to tell him that Hans Tanner had confessed to killing Dominic Woods in revenge for the rape of his daughter in 2018. But they had a problem – according to the Diana Evans' pathologist report, Woods had definitely been killed by a left-handed person. Elise Tanner was left-handed. Her father, as far as they could tell, was right-handed. Was Hans Tanner covering for someone? But to take the blame for murder was, surely, thought DCI Lincoln, a stretch. After all, Tanner would know of the consequences – twenty years at least behind bars.

Benedict and Jessica were about to finish their meeting with the boss when a knock sounded on Lincoln's door. It was DC Prowse looking positively worried about interrupting the meeting. 'I'm so sorry to barge in like this but something's come up regarding the Woods case.'

'Aha,' said Lincoln. 'Fire away, DC Prowse.'

'Yes, well. It's like this... We got Uber and Bolt to do a search of their transactions for the local area for the night that Woods was killed, and something's come up. Bolt didn't have anything but Uber did. They received a six-pound, forty pence payment from one Elise Tanner who ordered an Uber from her house on Harriet Avenue to Dominic Woods' house on Faversham Avenue at eight fifty that evening.'

'Whoa!' said Lincoln. 'Well done, DC Prowse. Did you track down the driver?'

'Thank you, sir. We did. They had the driver's details so yesterday afternoon, me and DC Kelly went to see him. I nabbed a photo of Elise from her Instagram account, and he remembered her, he remembered thinking how pretty she was.'

'Bingo!'

'Well, yes, she is rather nice.'

'No, I mean… it doesn't matter. Did she catch a taxi home?'

'No. No record of that.'

'So, the question is, what was Elise Tanner doing at Dominic Woods' house at the very time he was killed?'

'Helping her father,' suggested Benedict, realising how lame that sounded.

'No,' said DC Kelly. 'You see, there's one other thing, sir,' said DC Prowse, addressing DCI Lincoln. 'Elise phoned her father at half nine.'

'Oh? Did she now?'

'It doesn't seem possible,' said Benedict.

'What's that?' asked DCI Lincoln.

'That a young girl like Elise could kill a man.'

'Why, Ben?'

'I don't know; it just doesn't sound credible.'

'Again, I ask why? Is it because she's young and pretty, perhaps? Are you allowing yourself to be blinkered by a stereotype, per chance?'

Jessica side-eyed him and he knew he'd been rumbled. 'Maybe I am. I apologise, sir.'

'Unlike you, Ben, not to keep an open mind. She has the motivation and now, thanks to DC Prowse's fine work, you can place her at the scene at the right time. There is a set of unidentified fingerprints in Woods' house. If they match Miss Tanner's, we can arrest her. I suggest you go see Elise straightway and bring her in for questioning. I'm not sure we have enough to arrest her for now but we can bring her in and interview her under caution.'

'We're on our way, sir.'

'And take her fingerprints while you're at it,' he called after them.

*

Benedict and Jessica made their way to Harriet Avenue for their fourth visit. Benedict was still smarting a little for allowing himself to make such crass assumptions about Elise Tanner. 'Of course, what I meant was she doesn't seem strong enough to kill Woods.'

'Yes, boss. Although with the element of surprise—'

'I mean mentally tough enough.'

'She's a woman on the edge, boss. This time last week, she was celebrating at her engagement party and now her fiancé is in critical condition in hospital with every chance he might be severely impaired for the rest of his life, their flat has fallen through and her father's been arrested for assault and murder. I think I'd flip under the circumstances.'

By the time they got to Harriet Avenue it was approaching ten a.m. Nicola Tanner answered the door. Elise, she told them, was at work. 'What now?' she asked. 'Why are you

273

keeping my husband?'

'We need to interview him with a solicitor present, Mrs Tanner,' said Jessica. 'Hopefully, later this morning.'

'He hasn't done anything wrong.'

'We'll find out.'

'Mrs Tanner,' said Benedict. 'Where was Elise last Sunday evening, the night Woods was killed?'

'Oh, you're back to her now. She would have visited Phil in hospital. She's done so every night so far. Then, she would have come home. She was very tired; she's had a difficult week.'

'Thank you, Mrs Tanner.'

'And where was your husband?' asked Benedict.

'He would also have been here with me. Shall I tell Elise you called?'

'No, we're going to see her now. What's the hairdresser's address?'

'It's called The Finest Cut, on the high street just a few shops up from the station, on the same side.'

They thanked her.

'I think you might be right, Jessica,' said Benedict as he manoeuvred the pool car up Camden High Street. 'Hans could well be covering for his daughter.'

'Well, we might find out by lunchtime.'

'Here we are: The Finest Cut.'

The hairdressers, all pink and gold, was busy. The young woman on reception pointed to Elise who was in the process of applying hair dye to a middle-aged woman's hair.

'Elise,' said Jessica.

Elise turned pale on seeing them.

'Can we have a word? Do you have a staff room we could talk in?'

'Hey, hey,' said another woman, approaching. She wore a black tabard, and had her black hair piled high on her hair. 'Who are you and what are you doing here?'

The detectives showed her their IDs. 'And you are?' asked Jessica.

'Mary Angelopoulos, this is my salon. What do you want with Elise? Can't you see she's busy? I can't have you coming in and upsetting my customers. I'm so sorry, Mrs Wilson,' she added, addressing the woman in the chair.

'Who are they?' snapped Mrs Wilson. 'Are they social workers?'

'I'm sorry, Ms Angelopoulos,' said Jessica. 'But we need to speak to Elise.'

'Can't it wait? She's missed enough work already.'

'I'm afraid it cannot. Elise? Please…'

'Sorry, Mary,' said Elise, placing her tinting brush and bowl on a table. 'Won't be long.'

'For goodness' sake, Elise.'

'I said, who are they?' repeated Mrs Wilson. 'Are they bailiffs?'

Elise led them into a small kitchen at the back of the salon. 'Is it my dad?' she asked. 'Or Phil?'

'Right now, neither,' said Jessica. 'It's you we need to speak to. We need you to come with us to the station.'

Elise began shaking. 'No. No, I can't,' she shouted. 'You saw Mary, she's not happy with me as it is.'

'You have no choice here, Elise.'

'You can't do this; you're not arresting me?' She glanced at the back door as if thinking about making a run for it.

'You either come with us quietly,' said Jessica. 'Or we'll cuff you.'

'No, please. Don't do this to me. Not now.'

'Yes, now. Come on.'

'No.' She backed away.

She glanced from Jessica to Benedict, the panic written all over her face.

'Don't do anything silly here, Elise,' said Benedict, edging closer to her.

She seemed to deflate, knowing she had no escape, no option but to do as told. 'How long will we be?'

'As long as it takes,' said Jessica. 'Are you going to come or do you want me to cuff you. Because I will, Elise.'

'OK. OK.'

Jessica led the way back into the shop, Elise, her eyes to the ground, in the middle, Benedict behind.

Mary Angelopoulos was waiting for them. 'What's happening? You're not taking her away, are you?'

'Yes, we are,' said Jessica.

'For Christ sake's, Elise. What now? I can't keep carrying you. You can see how busy we are.'

'I'm sorry, Mary.'

'What good is that to me?'

Benedict flashed her a smile which, somehow, just seemed to make matters worse.

'It's no laughing matter, you idiot.'

'No, of course not. I do apologise.'

'How long you're keeping her?'

'Hard to say at the moment.'

'Listen, Elise, I want you back here at nine o'clock tomorrow, otherwise you're looking for a new job. Now, Mrs Wilson, where were we?'

'You've not told me who those people are. Are they tax inspectors? Have you been fiddling your affairs again, Mary?'

'Not now, eh, Mrs Wilson?'

Benedict, as usual, drove. Jessica sat in the back with Elise, making sure her seat belt was fastened.

'What is it you want?" asked Elise. 'I've not done anything wrong.'

'We'll speak when we get to the station.'

'You heard what Mary said, I'll lose my job.'

'Well, if you tell us the truth, we can try and avoid that.'

'I can't afford to lose my job.'

'We'll try our best for you, Elise.'

Elise stayed silent for a while as Benedict drove back to the station. Then, he heard her say quietly, 'Why has everything turned to shit?'

Chapter 43: Elise, 2018
Five years earlier

Thursday morning and Elise was having her breakfast. She'd already ordered a pair of earrings on Amazon, due to be delivered the following day. Nothing like an online purchase to put you in a good mood.

'Good morning, lovie,' said her mother, coming into the kitchen. 'Do you want a cup of tea?'

'No, thanks. Don't forget I'm going out tonight with Sharon.'

'Oh yes, you said. Going anywhere nice?'

'Yes, we're going to an Indian.'

'Not DiMaggio's this time?'

'Huh, I wish. It's a few doors down. Maybe we'll go there for pudding.'

'Dessert.'

'Whatever.'

'And don't you forget, your father and I are going to that local history talk at the library tomorrow.'

'Cool.'

Her mother flicked the kettle on. 'How are you, lovie? I'm worried about you. These last few days, you've seemed–'

'I'm fine, thanks.'

'OK. Are you sure?'

'Yes, Mum, stop worrying about me.'

'If you say so, love. Oh, I meant to say, I saw William in the supermarket yesterday.'

'Oh yeah. How is he?'

'He's got a new girlfriend.'

'William? Has he?' The punch in the gut took her by surprise. A girlfriend? Already?

'I didn't speak to him but they are definitely an item, as you say.'

'Bloody hell.'

Nicola made her tea and declared she was going upstairs to get changed.

The doorbell sounded. Elise went to get it to be handed a small Amazon parcel. She hadn't ordered anything but it had her name on it. Taking a pair of scissors, she opened the Amazon box to reveal two colourful boxes. 'What the heck?' She opened the first box and pulled out a jar with a cork lid and inside a large, blue hand painted butterfly. Attached to the lid was a label: *To my beautiful girlfriend, all my love, Dom. xx.* It was lovely, the detail on the butterfly impressive. The second box contained a jar of honey and another note: *Amazon don't sell chocolate éclairs but 2 out of 3 ain't bad!* Of course, she'd told Dominic that her favourite things were butterflies, chocolate éclairs and honey. She smiled. A few days before she might have been overjoyed, as she had been when Dominic gave her her butterfly necklace, but now, today, she viewed her gifts with little enthusiasm.

She tucked the honey away in the pull-out larder behind

various other pots and jars and, going to her bedroom, hid the butterfly jar at the back of her wardrobe. She knew her mother sometimes poked around in her things and she didn't want her finding it. She got ready for work, wearing something a bit smarter than usual as she was meeting Sharon after work. At the last moment, she decided to brighten her outfit with Dominic's butterfly necklace.

Waiting at the bus stop, shivering in the cold, Elise received a text from Dominic, the first since the morning when they'd had sex. *Dont forget tonite. Dimaggios 7. Cant wait to c u. Hope u like the pressies!*

Damn it. He was not going to force her to blow Sharon out. This, she knew, was important, if she and Dominic were to have a future together he had to know he couldn't simply push her around and bend her to his will. She had to make a stand here, the principle mattered.

The bus came. Sitting on the top deck, she texted back: *Luv the pressies. Thank you! Going out with S tonight. I did say. Sorry. Maybe tmr if u around??*

She held her breath, waiting for his response, her leg jigging with nervousness. He remembered him asking her, *Are you purposefully trying to undermine me, Elise?*

The bus reached her stop. She jumped off the bus and quickly made her way to the salon, keen to get out of the cold, expecting her phone to ping any moment and, despite her determination to make a stand, dreading it.

*

Elise met Sharon at St John's Wood underground station. They hugged. 'I love that necklace,' said Sharon. 'Is it new?'

'Yes. Got it in a sale.'

'Nice, very nice. Now, I've heard great things about this

Indian,' said Sharon. 'Although with the food you've got used to lately, it might seem a little… inferior.'

'Don't be silly. I'm really looking forward to it. I'm so hungry; I've not eaten today.'

Elise didn't like to say she'd been too worried about Dominic's text to eat. As it is, the text never came, and now, near seven o'clock she refused to worry about it any more. Sharon was perfect company for a night like tonight. All one had to do was ask her a question and, like winding up a toy, she was off, talking non-stop, plucking off subjects at random. Sharon was always a breath of fresh air, no pretensions about her, just a simple, easy to talk to friend.

They linked arms and, using Sharon's phone as a guide, found their way to the restaurant. Halfway there, Elise stopped short. 'Oh God, this is DiMaggio's.'

'Oo, really?' Sharon peered in, cupping her hand against the window.

'Sharon, what are you doing? You'll put their customers off their dinners.'

'Are you saying I've got an ugly mug, or something? Looks nice, bloody nice actually. Not that busy. Suppose it's still early. Hey, shall we go here instead?'

'Sure. Good idea. Got a spare couple hundred of quid knocking about?'

Sharon scanned the menu in the restaurant window. 'Bloody hell, I see what you mean.'

'I told Mum we might stop here for pudding.'

'Yeah.' She looked closer at the menu. 'No. I don't think so. Not at those prices. I think we'll stick to the Indian.'

'Thought so.'

Two hours later, Elise and Sharon emerged from the Indian restaurant, their stomachs aching from too much food and too much laughter. But it'd been a smashing meal; just the tonic, thought Elise; she so needed that.

'Hell, it's freezing tonight. How about warming ourselves up with a nightcap at The Three Bells on our way home?' said Sharon.

'Now you're talking.'

Walking back towards the underground station, again arm-in-arm, Elise said, 'I didn't tell you this but Dominic invited me to DiMaggio's tonight. He'd even booked a table.'

'You're joking. Why didn't you go?'

'Because I'm with you, silly.'

Sharon stopped. 'You're telling me you turned down dinner in a posh restaurant with your dishy boyfriend for an Indian with me? Are you mad?'

'We'd already arranged it. So I said no.'

'Bloody hell, I'm honoured. What did he say?'

'He was a bit pissed off, to be honest. But I thought, no, I'm going out with Shazzer and I'm not blowing her out just because he clicks his fingers.'

'Good on yer, girl.'

'That's what I thought. Girls together.'

'Yeah, fuck 'em. God, I'm so cold. Let's hurry. Oh look, here we are again, the infamous DiMaggio's. Let's see if it's any busier.' Again, Sharon pressed her nose against the glass. 'Oh yeah, it's a lot busier. Hey, there's a bloody great big tree in the middle. How did I not notice that before? What's it doing there? Did they build the restaurant around it?'

Elise laughed.

'Oh fuck!' screamed Sharon, jumping back from the window, her hand over her mouth.

'Christ, Shazzer, don't do that. What's the matter?'

'Nothing. Nothing, darling. Come on, let's go. I'm freezing

my tits off here.'

'No, what did you see?' Elise went up to the window but Sharon positively yanked her back by the arm.

'It's nothing, darling. Please let's go. I'm so cold.'

Freeing her arm from Sharon's grasp, Elise peered through the window. But there was nothing untoward happening, just wealthy people enjoying their meals. What had made her swear like that? Silly woman. And then she saw her striding across the restaurant, a spring in her step, a clutch bag in her hand. 'Oh my God, that's Amara. What the fuck is she doing there?'

'Probably nothing, Elise. Why don't we—'

'She's with Dominic!' Her heart jumped up her throat. 'She's... They're...' She couldn't find the words. They were together, as a couple, having a meal, laughing, flirting, sitting at the same table she'd sat at with him. She spun away from the window her hand pressed against her chest. 'Oh my God. Oh my God. I don't believe it. I don't fucking believe it.' She was finding it hard to catch her breath.

Sharon looked terrified. 'Look, let's sort it out tomorrow.'

Elise stared into the distance, trying to absorb what she'd just seen, and an anger simmered within her, getting more intense by the second, until it threatened to erupt. She knew what to do.

'Elise? No! Stop!' Sharon tried to prevent her from going in. 'Don't do this, El. Don't give them the satisfaction.'

'Get out of my way.' She pushed her friend to the side, surprised by her own strength, and marched in. No one was at the welcome desk but the maître d she remembered before came leaping over. 'All booked up for tonight, I'm afraid, Miss.'

Sidestepping him, she marched up to Dominic's table,

aware that people were already looking at her. Dominic saw her, a dessert spoon in his hand, his puzzled expression morphing into a half-smile. Amara, following his gaze, clocked Elise and shrunk back in her chair, terror-struck, her hand going to her mouth.

'It seemed such a waste to let the booking go,' said Dominic, coolly but his blinking eyes belied the panic within.

'Elise,' whispered Amara. 'I'm sorry. I'm so sorry…'

'Hello, Amara,' said Elise. 'I always thought you were a bitch and now I know for sure.'

'Elise—'

'Don't fucking speak to me.'

'Madame, please,' said the maître d appearing next to her.

'Go away. Dominic…' With deft fingers, she removed the butterfly necklace and slammed it loudly on the table. Her eyes filled with tears, damn it.

'Elise, stop being so dramatic; you're making a show of yourself.'

'You need to leave, miss.'

'Have you fucked her yet?' She heard the collective gasp from around the restaurant.

'Is it your business?'

'Security. We need security.'

'I'm leaving,' she said, her eyes still on Dominic. 'I don't ever want to see you again.'

He actually bowed his head. 'As you wish, Elise. I shall miss you. You were a good fuck.'

The words struck her like an arrow. Was that all she was to him? A good fuck? Was that it? She couldn't see through her tears, she needed to sit down, the room was spinning, spinning so fast. She heard Amara's voice. 'Are you OK, Elise? Can we get some water here?'

'It's fine, I've got her,' said Sharon, taking her by the arm. 'I've got a bottle in my bag.'

'You must take her away, madam.'

'Oh, piss off, you.'

'Will she be OK, Shaz?'

'What do you care, you two-timing bitch?'

'I'm so sorry about this, Amara. Are you OK?'

'Shut up, Dominic, will you?'

Elise's world stopped spinning for a moment and Dominic's smug face came clearly into view, looking up to her from his chair, just him, no one else, nothing else. Her words, although quietly spoken, cut through everything, all the clamour, all the noise: 'I hate you so much, Dominic. I hate you from the depths of my soul. You've used me all this time. All this time. I hate you. You're nothing, nothing but a cunt.'

Chapter 44: Benedict

Benedict and Jessica put Elise in interview room 2, offering her a coffee which she refused. Jessica popped over to update DCI Lincoln. Prepared, the two detectives went to see Elise Tanner.

'Do help yourself to some water,' said Benedict. 'We're going to be recording this interview,'

Turning the tape on, he recorded the time and the names of those present.

'Miss Tanner, first of all, I have to tell you that your father has admitted to assaulting William Grant.'

Elise groaned, burying her face in her hands. 'Oh, Dad, what have you done?

'We will be charging him today.'

'Will they send him back to prison?'

'Highly likely, I'm afraid.'

Benedict paused while Elise digested this. She looked down at the table, picking at a cuticle, her breathing heavy.

After a while, Benedict continued. 'Now, moving on. Miss Tanner, could you tell us about your relationship with

Dominic Woods?'

Elise told the detectives about how she met Dominic; how she totally fell in love with him but then things started to go wrong, small things at first. But with time, he became more and more controlling, forcing her to cut out his friends, becoming jealous if she should just look at another man. In the end, she knew she had to cut herself off from him. Then, when she finally did, he raped her.

'He raped you?' asked Jessica.

'Yes. Yes, he did.'

'But when I asked you the other day if Dominic had hurt you in any way, you said he hadn't.'

Elise held her breath. Breathing out, she said, 'It's not something I like to think about. Surely, you can understand that?'

There followed, she said, a couple of dark years when her mental health plummeted and she could see no way out. Dominic, now out of her life, continued to dominate her thoughts, affecting her ability to pursue a 'normal life'.

'Were you ever suicidal during this time?' asked Jessica.

Elise took a while before answering. 'Not really,' was her eventual answer. Slowly, she said, she pulled herself out of her gloom, and began living a healthier life. Then, six months ago, she met Phil Edwards and she fell in love with this kind-hearted, considerate man. Getting engaged was, for Elise, the best thing ever. It had, she said, 'brought closure'.

'Elise,' said Benedict. 'We've got something we need to tell you at this stage.'

Benedict could sense her bracing herself.

'We now know that it was Dominic behind the hit and run on Philip Edwards. He paid a man to damage Philip's car, to vandalise the flat you were moving into and, ultimately, to

287

run Philip over.'

'I know all this. He told me. You see what I mean. Dom was, well, he was deranged. Dangerous. I thought, after all this time, he'd moved on from me but...' She left the sentence hanging.

'Elise,' said Benedict. 'In November 2018, you accused Dominic Woods of rape.'

'I just told you – he did.'

'But Dominic claimed he didn't rape you and said he had an alibi, didn't he?'

'Yes. He got his sister to lie for him.'

'So, you withdrew the allegation?'

'Yes.'

'Can I ask why? If he raped you, you knew he was lying about his alibi.'

She rubbed her eyes. 'I knew it'd come down to his word against mine and he got his so-called alibi, and I had no proof.' Benedict remembered Caroline Wozniak saying exactly the same, neither woman could face Dominic Woods in court. 'After it happened,' said Elise, 'I made that classic mistake – I had a shower. I just had to.'

'The sad thing is, Elise,' said Jessica. 'We know that you were right – Olivia Woods was lying. She wasn't even in the country on the night in question.'

'The bitch. I knew she was lying but I didn't know that. My mother knew she was lying too. She hated her; she was livid. I had to stop her from confronting her. God knows what she'd have done.'

'She's very protective of you, isn't she?' asked Jessica.

'Protective? You could say that. I'm her only child, after all.'

'Are you OK with that?'

Elise twisted her engagement ring around her finger. 'It gets a bit much, to be honest. I guess… you see, Mum lost a baby. This was a couple of years before me. Dad says it messed with her mind, so when I came along, she was super-protective, you know? Always has been. I wish I never told her about what Dom did to me. It made her so angry and depressed. She went bloody loopy, had a bloody melt down over it. It affected her so badly, I ended up being the one looking after *her*. I should never have told her. A huge mistake that.'

'How did your mother feel about you moving out?'

'She likes Phil but now I'm not moving any more, I think she's happy about it. I've got to be honest, I couldn't wait to move out. I mean, I love her to bits but she gets…'

'Too much?'

'Yeah, exactly. It's suffocating at times. Sounds horrible of me, I know, but it does my head in.'

They paused for a moment.

After a while, Benedict said, 'Elise, I know we've asked you before but now that we find ourselves in more formal circumstances, I ask you again – where were you Sunday night, about nine o'clock?'

'What I said before – I went to visit Phil in hospital and after that I came home. Mum had made me something to eat and because I was so tired, I went to bed early.'

'You need to tell us the truth here, Elise,' said Jessica.

For the first, Elise Tanner lost her composure, her cheeks turning red, her eyes darting to the side. 'It *is* the truth.'

'We also asked you the other day when was the last time you saw Mr Woods,' said Benedict. 'If you remember, you told us that you hadn't seen him for at least five years. Do you still stand by that?'

'Yes. I hadn't seen him since *that* night.'

'But that's not true, is it?'

'Yes, it is,' she snapped.

'Elise, last Sunday evening at eight fifty, you caught an Uber to Faversham Avenue where Dominic Woods lived. Not only is the financial transaction recorded by Uber, but your driver recognised you from a photo one of our officers showed him. There's also an unaccounted set of fingerprints in Mr Woods' kitchen. If I was a betting man, I'd wager that those prints are yours. What do you have to say, Elise?'

With her elbows on the table, Elise put her face into her hands and remained still.

'Elise,' said Jessica. 'You need to answer the question.'

'I want a solicitor.'

Benedict managed to suppress a groan. 'That is your right. We can arrange that. I'm not sure whether we have a duty solicitor at hand today, do we, DS Gardiner?

She shook her head.

'So what I suggest is that we stop the interview now and reconvene tomorrow morning.' He and Jessica stole a surreptitious glance at each other. 'I'm afraid, you won't be able to let you go. We will have to place you in a cell until tomorrow morning.'

'Tomorrow?' groaned Elise. 'You want to put me in a cell? Christ. You heard what my boss said.'

'Our hands are tied, Miss Tanner,' said Benedict. 'I'm sorry. So let's stop the tape now and return to this tomorrow. The time being—'

'I didn't kill him,' she whispered.

'I'm sorry,' said Benedict. 'I didn't catch that.'

'I said I *didn't* kill him,' she screamed, the tears now streaming down her face.

'But you went to see him at the very point he was killed. Miss Tanner. What do you think a jury would make of that?'

'I didn't kill him though. I was angry with him, yes, but I can't *kill* someone. Who can?'

'Someone did, Miss Tanner, someone who was there at the same time, or very close to it, as you.'

'What were you doing there then on the very night he was murdered?' asked Jessica.

'I wanted to confront him, ask him why he was trying to hurt me so much. He said it showed Phil was a loser and not fit to be my future husband, that I deserved better, a proper man who'd look after me and made sure I was never short of anything.'

'Rather old-fashioned views,' said Jessica.

'That was Dominic for you. If you didn't have a six-figure salary it made you less of a man.'

'He was earning seven figures.'

'Fuck, was he? There you are then. I told him I was going to report him to the police.'

'What did he say to that?' asked Jessica.

'He laughed in my face, told me not to be so *silly*,' she said, using air quotes to emphasise the last word.

'Where did this conversation take place?'

'In his kitchen. He poured us out a glass of champagne each. Not that I touched mine.'

Benedict nodded at Jessica. It was time to play their next card. 'Elise, your father has admitted to killing Dominic Woods.'

'Dad?' She sprang out of her chair. 'Fuck, no! That's impossible. That's… no, no, you're lying.'

'Please sit down, Miss Tanner. He confessed to us just yesterday afternoon, Elise.'

'I don't believe it.' She paced the length of the interview room. 'He fucking did not confess.' Returning to her chair, she slumped on the table and broke down now, talking incoherently, words coming fast that Benedict couldn't make out.

'Have some water, Elise,' said Jessica.

'I don't want any fucking water. This is mad. There's no way Dad could've killed Dom. No bloody way.'

'He sat where you are now, Miss Tanner,' said Benedict. 'And he told us that he had. Is there any reason why your father should lie to us?'

She gripped her hair.

'You see,' said Benedict. 'This is what we think. We believe your father *did* kill Dominic Woods but he did it with your help.'

'No.'

'After all, you were there.'

'No, I… I didn't. I told you.'

'OK, so assuming you were alone in that house with its owner, why did you phone your father at half past nine?'

'I didn't.'

'You did.'

'Oh, shitting hell. I don't remember.'

'Try to remember.'

She stretched her head back and stared up at the ceiling. 'I honestly do not remember. Christ, I can't take much more of this.'

'That's fine, we've finished now.'

She breathed out and swore under her breath.

'So, let me tell you what's going to happen now,' said Benedict. 'I'm prepared to let you go home or return to work, it's up to you. On condition that you are back here tomorrow morning at–'

'I can't! Mary said–'

'I don't care what Mary says. If you don't promise, I'll lock you in a cell for the rest of the day right this minute.'

'Oh, hell.'

'By then we'll have a solicitor for you. Right now, an officer will take your fingerprints. If they match the ones we found in Mr Woods' kitchen, and we'll soon know, you will be arrested alongside your father for the murder of Dominic Woods. Do you understand?'

She didn't answer.

Chapter 45: Benedict

This time, Hans Tanner had a solicitor present, representing him, Mr Newman, whom Benedict and Jessica had met before. An angular man with wire-rimmed glasses and cheeks spotted with pink as if over the years, he regularly enjoyed a drink or three.

'Have you had time to talk to your client, Mr Newman?' asked Benedict.

'Yes, thank you, I have.'

'We'll begin then.' He pressed 'record' on the tape recorder and introduced the interview. He passed Hans Tanner a pen and a blank sheet of paper. 'Mr Tanner, could you write the words *Mary had a little lamb, its fleece was white as snow* on this sheet of paper, please.'

'What?' said Mr Newman. 'How absurd. Why does my client need to do that?'

'Humour me. Mr Tanner, please, if you'd be so kind.'

With a shrug, Tanner did so, writing the phrase with his right hand.

'Thank you,' said Benedict. 'Now, could you write it again

but this time using your left hand?'

'Really?'

'Yes.'

'I hope this is going somewhere,' said Newman.

Tanner did as asked and then slid the sheet of paper back across the table. Benedict picked it up and passed it to Jessica. 'You are definitely right-handed then, Mr Tanner. You're certainly not ambidextrous.'

'I never said I was.'

'No, but you said you'd killed Dominic Woods by smashing his head in. Mr Tanner, Mr Woods was killed by a left-handed person, there is no doubt about that.'

'Just because Mr Tanner is not ambidextrous with his writing,' said Mr Newman, 'that doesn't mean anything.'

'There, I beg to differ,' said Benedict. 'Your adrenaline is pumping like never before, you're probably very frightened, and you want to get the act over and done with as quickly as possible. So, you're not going to think, *I know, just for a change, I'll use my weaker hand.* Are you, Mr Newman? But, moving on. What was Dominic Woods wearing that night, Mr Tanner?'

'Eh?'

'You heard the question. What was he wearing?'

'I... I have no clue, I can't remember.'

'Was he wearing jeans and a hoodie perhaps? Or was he still in his shirt and tie? You must remember, surely?'

'You're not proving anything here, Inspector.' said Newman. 'Do you remember what your wife was wearing last Sunday?'

'No, but I see her every day. Your client, Mr Newman, by his own admission, had never met Mr Woods before. If you've only met someone once you tend to remember them by what they were wearing on that one occasion.'

'And you think a jury would run with this? I think not.'

'It's a strange situation we find ourselves here, don't you think?' asked Benedict. 'Normally, we accuse you of the crime and you, the accused, Mr Tanner, and your solicitor argue against said accusation. But here, we're trying to say you're innocent of killing Dominic Woods and you and your solicitor are maintaining your guilt.'

'We live in a topsy-turvy world, Inspector Paige.'

'Indeed we do. Mr Newman. But what I'm really suggesting here, Mr Tanner, is that *your daughter* killed Mr Woods and you are either covering for her or you were an accessory.'

'Bollocks,' he shouted. 'That's utter bollocks.'

'She was at Mr Woods' house in Faversham Avenue at the *very same time* as you, Mr Tanner. Are you seriously suggesting you didn't bump into each other there?'

'No, because she wasn't there.'

'Oh, but she was, Mr Tanner, she was there all right. She told us herself in this very room not more than thirty minutes ago,' said Benedict, jabbing his finger on the table. 'Your daughter was at Dominic Woods' house in Faversham Avenue on the night he was murdered in cold blood. She caught a taxi, an Uber, from your house to his at eight fifty that evening.'

'How do you know it wasn't me?'

'Do you normally book taxis using your daughter's phone? I know my daughter would chop my fingers off before allowing me near her phone. And, anyway, I wouldn't know her pass code. Do you know Elise's pass code for her mobile, Mr Tanner? What is it?'

'No but–'

'The Uber driver recognised her, Mr Tanner,' said

Benedict, his voice rising. 'He was shown a photo of Elise and he said, yes, that's the woman who sat in my car.'

'Inspector, please stop shouting at my client.'

Benedict took a deep breath. 'I'm sorry. You're quite right. I do apologise, Mr Tanner.' He looked across at Jessica.

Jessica, taking the hint, took over, asking, 'Mr Tanner, why did Elise ring you on your mobile at half past nine that night?'

'No idea. To ask me what's for dinner?'

'Seriously now, sir.'

'OK, I don't even remember her calling me so I've no idea what she called about. Satisfied?'

'No. not in the slightest.'

'This sounds perilously close to harassment, DS Gardiner.'

The two of them glared at each other from across the table.

'Elise killed Woods, didn't she?' said Benedict, having caught his breath.

'No.' He shook his head vigorously. 'No. How could she? She's just a girl.'

'She's a woman of twenty-five, Mr Tanner,' said Jessica. 'She's hardly a girl any more.'

'She's my girl,' he said, jabbing himself in the chest. 'She always will be.'

'That does not excuse perjury.'

'We have the evidence that she went to the house,' said Benedict. 'And, what's more, she readily admits she was in Woods' house, and that she spoke to him in his kitchen. Elise killed him and you, the protective father, are prepared to take the rap for it, even if it means going to prison for so long, you'll come out a very old man. But, hear me out, you will likely be going to prison for the assault on William Grant, plus for stealing a vehicle, and now on the charge of perjury, but *not* for the murder of Dominic Woods because you didn't kill Dominic Woods, Mr Tanner. You are right-handed. There is not a shred of evidence that you were in that house. We have your fingerprints from your previous conviction so we know you didn't leave any prints there. You have to stop lying to us, Mr Tanner.'

'But I know my daughter. There's no way she could've killed Woods.'

'We're due to interview Elise with a solicitor present. Hopefully today.'

'You'll be wasting your time. I've told you, she didn't do it.'

'Right. OK. So let's say we believe you for a moment. But tell us, why should we believe a word you say, Hans, when all you've done from the start is lie to us? From denying your involvement with William Grant to now, you have spun one lie after another.'

'I'll have you for slander if you're not careful, Inspector.'

'It's not slander, Mr Newman. It's the truth. Your client has continually lied to us. But OK, let's assume for one moment, Elise did not kill Dominic Woods and *you* didn't kill him. So, who did, Mr Tanner, who did kill Dominic Woods?'

Chapter 46: Elise, 2018
Five years earlier

Friday, early evening. Elise had never been so relieved to return home from work, and to have the house to herself. Tonight was the night her parents were attending the local history talk in Camden Town library. She kicked off her shoes, found a frozen lasagne meal in the freezer and slammed it into the microwave for twelve minutes. Meanwhile, she had a shower, her second of the day, and put on her favourite silky nightie and a warm dressing gown. She went to her wardrobe and pulled out the jar with the butterfly in it. It was certainly a lovely present but she had to resist the urge to throw it against the wall.

Returning downstairs, she switched on the TV and settled in for a cosy night alone. Hopefully, her parents might go to the pub after the library and make more of a night of it. Her Amazon earrings she'd ordered yesterday morning hadn't arrived. Pity.

She needed this time to herself. Today had been difficult at work to the point Mary asked if she was sickening and wished to go home. Normally, she'd jumped at the chance but she couldn't face seeing her mother. So she grinned and bore it and stayed at work.

The events of the night before kept playing through her mind, seeing Dominic and Amara together in DiMaggio's, sitting at the same table where she'd sat with him. Were she and Amara part of a long string of unsuspecting women he'd lured into his bed having wined and dined them in such plush surroundings? She had little recollection of how she got home except that Sharon, bless her, had been with her every step of the way like the true friend she was. She remembered Sharon swearing at frequent occasions: all men are bastards, Dominic was a prize dick, he didn't deserve someone as beautiful as Elise, etc, etc. Sharon escorted Elise into the house and even managed to bat away her mother's concerns by telling Mum that Elise was drunk and needed to go straight to bed. Her mother, perhaps a little in awe of Sharon's forthright personality, backed down.

She must've got to bed by about ten so at least she'd had a good night's sleep and got to work on time. Sharon had phoned before she left, asking if she was OK, asking whether Elise wanted her to call in sick and come round. Elise thanked her but no, the last thing she wanted was to stay at home mulling over things and having her mother fretting over her. Work was the best place to be.

And then the sex on that last morning. The previous night they'd *made love* and, yes, it was wonderful. But that morning was horrible. Dominic took no heed of her protestations and had thought of nothing but himself. She'd been sore from the night before and that had left her in real pain. Could it be classed as rape? No, she thought. She'd consented, reluctantly perhaps, but she had.

Placing her mobile next to her on the settee in case Sharon phoned again, Elise ate her lasagne while watching some reality show about surviving on a desert island featuring lots of celebrities she'd never heard of, watching them cry, argue and have massive meltdowns on regular occasions.

She'd just finished her meal when the doorbell rang. That would be her Amazon delivery, she thought, springing up from the settee.

It wasn't – it was him. She slammed the door but he wedged his foot in and, with a push, forced his way in. 'Nice way to greet your boyfriend.'

'Dominic, what are you doing here? I want you to go.'

'Elise, come on, don't be so mean.' He walked through to the living room. He considered his surroundings. 'Nice place you have here, very proletariat.'

'My Dad will be back any minute.'

'All the more reason for me to hang around then,' he said, falling onto the settee. He picked up the remote and turned the TV off. 'I'm feeling a bit lonesome, Elise. My parents have gone off to Amsterdam for the weekend. Ever been to Amsterdam, Elise? No? The city of Van Gogh and Anne Frank? I know, let's go one day, you and me. How about it, Elise? Come on, you know you want to. It'd be fun.'

She didn't answer.

'Are you always in your nightclothes so early?' he asked. 'How depressing.'

'Please leave, Dominic.'

'Not until I hear you apologise.' He put his hands behind his head and leaned back.

'Apologise, me? For what?'

'You need me to spell it out? OK, for humiliating me last night. You do know your little antics drew the attention of *every fucking person there*,' he said, screaming out the last four words. 'Paolo told me to tell you you're banned for life.'

'Who?'

'The maître d', of course. I told him not to worry; that you wouldn't be returning – not on your pithy salary. You said some fairly revolting stuff in front of all those good people, things that embarrassed me, Elise. How can you look at yourself in the mirror?'

'You were with Amara!'

'Because you blew me out. You can't book a table at DiMaggio's and then cancel. It's just not done. Besides, it's unfair on them.'

'Oh dear.'

'So what did you expect me to do since you were indisposed? I asked someone out, someone I knew would appreciate a superior night out.'

'So you thought, I know, I'll invite Amara.'

'Frankly yes. I don't see the problem. It's not as if I shagged her or anything. Maybe next time. If I feel like it.'

'Fine, you shag away. I don't care. You've said for piece, now go.'

'Not so hasty, sweetpie.'

'Please don't call me that.'

'The other thing, did I not explicitly say you weren't to see your friends any more? And there you were, gallivanting with that brassy excuse of a woman. Where did you go anyway?'

'We had an Indian.'

'Oh, good God, says it all. You haven't apologised yet.'

'I'm phoning my dad.' She reached for her mobile on the settee but Dominic, sitting next to it, snatched it. 'Give me my phone.'

He stood, pocketing it. 'Look, maybe you were right to be

angry with me. *I* should apologise. I'm sorry I went out with Amara, Elise. I should have thought. It was silly of me. There,' he said, spreading his arms. 'I've said it.'

'Good. I accept your apology. Thank you. Now leave.'

He stepped up to her. She remained put, determined not to back down. She wasn't scared of him. He ran a finger down the length of her hair. 'How about we make up? I mean, properly.'

'No, never.'

'Oh, Elise, come on, stop this. I've apologised, haven't I? And here I was demanding an apology from you.'

'Please go now, Dominic. Just leave me alone.'

It all happened so quickly. He grabbed a fistful of her hair, coiling it around his hand, and yanked her onto the settee. 'Get off me,' she screamed. Kneeling in front of her, he slapped her across the cheek and pulled open her dressing gown. 'No, please, Dominic. Don't do this.'

'Shut up, you stupid bitch. I'll teach you to humiliate me.'

She tried. She tried so hard to resist but he was too strong for her. Everything she did, he easily counteracted it. In the end, she clenched her eyes shut and willed him to finish quickly while the tears poured down her face...

An hour later, Dominic had long gone and Elise hadn't moved, still sprawled out on the settee, her dressing gown open, her nightie hitched up around her waist, still crying. She heard the front door and her parents' voices. This galvanised her. She shot off the settee and, barefoot, ran up the stairs just as her parents came in. Quietly, she closed her bedroom door and collapsed onto her bed.

*

The next morning, Elise opened her eyes and the full horror

303

of what had happened came rushing back. The tears came again. She heard her father leave for work. She didn't move. Eventually, her mother knocked on her door. 'Elise, you're late for work.' She didn't answer. 'Elise, are you asleep? Can I come in?'

Nicola came in. She went to the window and drew the curtains. She turned and saw the outline of her sleeping daughter beneath her duvet. Nicola shook her leg. 'Wakey, wakey, sleepyhead, time for work. Are you feeling poorly? Elise, for goodness' sake, wake up now.'

'I'm not going to work.'

'You are sick, poor girl. What's the matter?'

'He raped me.'

'I'm sorry? What did you say?'

'He came round last night and he raped me, Mum.'

Elise heard her mother gasp. 'Who did? William?'

'No, not William. Dominic.'

'Dominic? Dominic who?'

'I never told you. He was my boyfriend.'

'Are you OK?'

Elise sat bolt upright, screaming, 'Of course I'm not OK. Why would you even think that?' She collapsed into tears.

Her mother sprung over and hugged her. 'Oh my God, I don't believe this. I d-don't understand. Who is this Dominic?'

Elise couldn't answer, burying her head into her mother's chest.

'We need to call the police.'

'No, no, no. I can't face it. Please don't. Not now, not yet.'

'Your father then—'

'No, you can't tell him.' She pulled away from her mother who recoiled on seeing the anguish in her daughter's eyes.

'Mum, I need you to promise me, you must never, ever tell Dad.'

'But, lovie, why? Surely—'

'Promise me!' she shouted.

Elise could see the confusion in her mother's face 'I... I don't—'

'He mustn't know. It'll kill him. Or he'll kill Dominic and be sent to prison for years.' She shook her mother by the shoulders. 'He can never know, Mum. Never!'

'But what happened, Elise?'

'You don't want to know,' she said, falling back onto her pillows.

'No, I need to know. You're my daughter and I love you so much, I'd do anything for you. Anything.'

Elise didn't answer for a while, allowing the tears to seep down her face. 'Later. I'll tell you later. If you promise not to tell Dad.'

Nicola sighed. She took her daughter's hand. 'I promise I won't tell your father.'

'I'll tell you everything then; how I met him, why I finished with William, how Dominic seduced me, how he raped me. I'll tell you every last detail.'

Chapter 47: Benedict

The results from Elise Tanner's fingerprints came back. Yes, they were, as Benedict and Jessica had predicted, a match for the unidentified set found in Dominic Woods' kitchen. Benedict was updating DCI Lincoln. 'The fingerprint match is the icing on the cake, sir,' said Benedict. 'Hans Tanner did not kill Woods. His daughter did. We have absolutely no evidence linking Hans to the crime scene.'

'Apart from his own confession.'

'His confession is simply not credible. Elise, on the other hand, is all over the place – her fingerprints, her own admission that she was at Woods' house, her motive, plus the fact she's left-handed. I think, with your permission, sir, we should arrest her and interview her with a solicitor present.'

'So much for your *innocent young girl who wouldn't harm a fly* theory?' asked Lincoln with a hint of a smirk.

He hadn't actually said those words, thought Benedict. But he took it on the chin. 'I do believe that come tomorrow, another push and she'll crack.'

'OK, Ben. Sounds good. Please proceed.'

'Thank you, sir.'

'Meanwhile, make a start on the report, would you?'

That wasn't such good news. 'Yes, sir.'

Benedict was told a solicitor had arrived. Excellent, he thought. Now was the a good time to interview Elise Tanner. He barely had a chance to sit at his desk when his mobile rang. Unknown number. He answered it. 'DI Paige here.'

'Inspector Paige, is that you? Oh, thank goodness. It's Elizabeth Woods here.' It took him a moment to cotton on that this was Dominic's mother. Why, he wondered, was she sounding so distressed. 'I'm so pleased to have caught you.'

'Something's wrong, Mrs Wood.'

Jessica pricked up her ears.

'I'm not sure. I think so. I've just received a text from Olivia and it says *help me.*'

'Help me? Anything else?'

'No, that's it. I'm worried, Inspector.'

'Does she often text things like that?'

'No, never.'

'Where is she? Where are you?'

'Ted and I are at the funeral parlour. We left Olivia at home. I don't know if she's still there.'

'OK. Look, I'll get the nearest uniformed officers to check your house. Meanwhile, DS Gardiner and I are on our way.'

'What should we do? Should we return home?'

'Erm… no. I think if Olivia's in trouble, you might be better staying where you are. I'll keep you updated.' He rang off. 'Jessica, we need to hot foot our way to Southgate. DC Kelly!'

'Yes, boss.'

He told Kelly to have officers check out the Woods' residence in Southgate as a matter of urgency. He'd barely finished the sentence when he was out of the door, Jessica trotting behind trying to keep up.

Benedict always drove but he knew he wasn't that good at driving fast with a siren. Instead, Jessica drove. And she drove like the clappers. Benedict gripped his car seat, rapidly turning white, closing his eyes as his DS weaved and swerved through the traffic at such an alarming speed. He feared he was about to meet his lunch again. Several times, he had to clamp his mouth to stop himself from swearing or crying out in alarm.

Under normal circumstances, Camden High Street to Southgate would take some twenty-five minutes by car. Jessica did it in less than fifteen. She screeched to a halt outside the Woods' house to find two squad cars already haphazardly parked up, their blue lights flashing silently. Benedict spotted a uniform officer keeping guard at the Woods' front door.

'My God, DS Gardiner, you sure know how to drive.'

'Plenty of practice in Manchester, boss.'

'Impressive, most impressive. Let's see what's happening here.'

He jogged up to the policeman, holding up his ID card. 'DI Paige, Camden. What's going on?'

'Sir, we have a madwoman threatening a resident of this property.'

'The latter will be Olivia Woods. Don't know about the madwoman.'

'Madwoman?' asked Jessica, joining him.

'We have a madwoman on our hands, DS Gardiner.'

'You mean a female with possible mental health issues, boss.'

'That as well. Has anyone called for armed back-up,

officer?'

'Not yet, sir.'

'Is it safe to enter from here?'

'It is, sir. But proceed carefully.'

Benedict eased open the front door. He could hear shouting coming from inside. With Jessica on his heels, he pushed open the door to the narrow living room.

The first thing he saw was Olivia Woods, her back to the corner behind the settee, and the other side of the settee, brandishing a large kitchen knife was Nicola Tanner. Surrounding them, two uniformed policemen and a policewoman, their hands out as if trying to placate Tanner.

'Get her away from me,' shouted Olivia. 'Just get the stupid cow away from me.'

'Mrs Tanner,' said Jessica. 'What's wrong?'

Nicola Tanner spun around. Her face was bright red and soaked with tears. 'If it wasn't for *her*,' she screamed, waving her knife about in her left hand, 'her brother would've been in jail. She lied for him; the bitch *lied*.'

'Why the knife, Mrs Tanner?'

'Justice, that's why. Justice for my Elise. Her brother's ruined her life.' Turning back to face Olivia, she screamed, 'He ruined it when he *raped* her, and now he's come back into her life and ruined it again! Philip's in hospital because of your shit of a brother.'

'You don't know that,' shouted Olivia.

'He told Elise. And she told me. She tells me *everything*, my Elise, so I *know* what your brother did, the little shit. Elise is distraught.'

'This isn't going to help, Nicola,' said Jessica, edging closer to her.

'Get back! All of you, get back now.'

'Put the knife down, Nicola.'

'No, not until this bitch gets what she deserved. If she hadn't had lied, her brother would be rotting in jail and he'd never have turned up to ruin Elise's life *again*.'

'He'd also still be alive,' said Benedict. 'You wouldn't have killed him.'

'He didn't deserve to live, the bastard.'

'You killed my brother?' gasped Olivia.

'And you're next,' She lunged forward. Olivia screamed but the depth of the settee kept her safe.

'What happened, Nicola?' asked Benedict. 'You followed Elise to Dominic Woods' house?'

'Yes. I did.'

'You took a call from Elise on your husband's phone and you went to Faversham Avenue to pick her up. Once there, Elise waited in the car for you, while you knocked on his door, went in and killed him.'

'Aren't you the clever one?'

'We've arrested both your husband and daughter for this.'

'Shows how stupid you are then.'

'You were prepared to let them take the blame.'

'I was going to tell you once I'd finished with this lying bitch here.'

'Look, I'm sorry about Dominic,' said Olivia, the panic in her voice. 'He wasn't a nice person.'

'Nor are you.'

'And I'm sorry I lied.'

'Too late for that now,' she shouted, waving her knife around.

'Nicola, you have put the knife down,' said Jessica.

'Why? Might as well be hanged for a lamb as a sheep.'

The other way around, thought Benedict, deciding that

perhaps this wasn't the time to correct her.

Nicola stepped onto the settee, lifting her arm. Olivia screamed again, covering her eyes. One of the officers yelled and, leaping across the room, rugby-tackled Nicola but failed to secure her left hand. She fell onto the settee. Benedict rushed into help, aiming for her hand. He yelped in pain as the blade ripped through his jacket, slicing the skin on his upper arm. Another second and Jessica waded in and pinned her hand down. 'Let go, Nicola, let go!' She shook the woman's hand to the point Nicola, now shrieking, lost her grip. Jessica prised her fingers off the handle. The knife bounced off the settee and clattered to the floor. The policewoman scooped it up. Nicola Tanner sobbed. Olivia cried. Benedict clasped his arm, the blood seeping through his fingers at an alarming rate, muttering expletives as the pain tore through him.

'Ben, are you OK?'

'Yeah, yeah, it bloody hurts.'

The policewoman gathered the crumpled Olivia in her arms. 'It's OK now, you're safe now. It's OK.'

The first policeman pulled Nicola up to her feet and, handcuffing her, read her her rights.

The third policeman, who'd been standing guard outside, rang for an ambulance.

Working quickly, the second policeman removed Benedict's jacket and eased him flat onto the ground. Jessica placed a cushion from the settee under his head before running off.

'You're fine, sir,' said the second policeman. 'It hasn't touched an artery. It's superficial.'

'It doesn't feel bloody superficial. What's your name, son?

'PC Martini, sir.'

Nicola Tanner began wailing about Elise and the monster Dominic Woods while the first policeman, holding onto her, tried to calm her while the policewoman led Olivia Woods away, promising to make her a sweet tea in the kitchen to help her with 'the shock'.

Jessica returned with a couple of bathroom towels, handing them to PC Martini before disappearing again. Martini used the edge of a bank card to 'seal' the wound. 'You're doing great, sir.' He lifted Benedict's arm, ensuring the wound was positioned above his heart. Jessica returned again, this time with the first aid kit they kept in the car. Handing it to Martini, the policeman quickly swiped away the now half blood-soaked towel, replacing it with a sterile gauze before fastening the dressing with a bandage. 'Done, sir!' declared Martini.

Jessica knelt down next to Benedict. 'Are you OK, boss?' she asked, remembering this time not to call him by his first name.

'I think so, thank you. And, PC Martini, thank you too. You know your stuff.'

'Not the first time, I'm afraid, sir.'

The welcome ring of an ambulance siren sounded. The sound seemed to calm Nicola Tanner. She allowed the first policeman to lead her away. She stopped at the living room door. 'Are you all right, inspector?'

'All fine here, thanks, Mrs Tanner.'

'I'm sorry I hurt you. I didn't mean to do that.'

Benedict craned his neck to better see her. 'It's OK. But thanks anyway.'

'I know I'll be sent to prison and I shall worry about Elise but she's a grown woman now; she'll come out of this OK. She's a survivor. She's learnt to survive before, and she'll do it again. But I don't regret it, DI Paige, and you know I'd do it again. He never paid for what he did to my daughter.'

'I know.'

'He did deserve it, you know.'

'Yes, perhaps he did.'

Epilogue

Benedict

Mid-morning on another cold, drizzly February day. Benedict Paige lay on his settee at home, his feet up, reading a book on the Cold War but finding it difficult to concentrate. Outside, he could hear the garden birds making a racket. He smiled. He had the house to himself. Sonia, having made sure he was OK, went to work, and his children were back at school following their half term break. He had the feeling they were glad to return, thinking it preferable to having to look after their father. That was fine, he wasn't feeling talkative. He hadn't even put the radio on – happy simply to enjoy the peace and quiet, and the birds.

Earlier, DS Gardiner had popped around with a box of chocolates and a bunch of flowers on behalf of the whole office. She made him a cup of tea, chatted a while, then declared she had to get back to work. DCI Lincoln phoned him on his mobile, checking to see if he was OK and congratulating him and his team on wrapping up all three cases in one neat bundle. Benedict thanked him.

His upper arm remained heavily bandaged and it hurt a little if he moved it too suddenly but on the whole it was fine. The wound had been well tended to and hadn't become infected. All was well.

The three cases had resulted in a number of arrests. Nathaniel Turnbull had been arrested for vandalising Mr Sheth's flat and, more importantly, for having run over Philip Edwards and causing significant injury to the man. Hans Tanner had been arrested for the kidnap and assault of William Grant. Mr Grant seemed reluctant to press charges but DCI Lincoln had persuaded him, saying it was in the public interest. And of course Tanner's wife, Nicola Tanner, had been arrested for the murder of Dominic Woods. She'd also have to face charges for her attempt to attack Olivia Woods *and* for wounding a police officer, namely him. All three faced long prison sentences. Yet, despite their crimes, he felt rather sorry for them all.

Nathaniel Turnbull had been motivated by money but not by greed, simply money to survive. His work had dried up, he lived in stricken circumstances and he'd been in debt. He desperately needed money simply to keep a roof over his head and food on the table. Sadly, in trying to improve his situation; he'd made it a hundred times worse. He'd been almost as much of a victim of Dominic Woods as anyone else.

Likewise, Hans and Nicola Tanner. Had Dominic Woods not raped their daughter, neither would now be facing jail time. Both had been motivated by the need to avenge Elise. They'd both been devastated by what Woods had done, perhaps even more than Elise herself. Elise had been rebuilding her life, moving on and looking to the future, while her parents were still trapped by the past and by their hatred of Woods. The rape had destabilized them, made them over-protective of their only child, had even deranged them to the point they went too far in trying to mete out their own form of justice.

And then Elise herself. The poor girl. She'd almost escaped her past when Dominic Woods returned and devastated her life anew. Both her parents were now in prison on remand and soon to be incarcerated for years to come. Her fiancé was still in hospital in a critical condition which he might never truly recover from, either physically or mentally. He'd come out a different man, an embittered and fragile one. Benedict only hoped Elise and Philip could, somehow, still have a future together.

The only person to have escaped arrest was Woods himself. Had he been alive, he would have been arrested for defrauding dozens of people with his financial scam and for the murder of his colleague, Anthony Browning.

Benedict yawned. The last week had been exhausting. Right now, all he wanted to do was read about the building of the Berlin Wall, listen to the birds outside in the garden, drink his tea and perhaps, later, have a snooze.

Perfect, just perfect.

Elise

Sitting at her fiancé's hospital bedside, Elise Tanner was also reading a book. Hers was called *How To Take Care of Your Poorly Loved One*. She'd bought it from Amazon and it had arrived that morning.

It was Elise's day off from work. She almost volunteered to work, to make up for some of the time she lost but she so wanted to spend time with her fiancé. Phil lay in his bed, his eyes closed, his breath steady. A nurse had just finished taking his blood pressure. Elise thanked her.

She was dreading having to return home to an empty house. She simply couldn't wrap her head around the fact that *both* her parents were in prison. It didn't seem possible. Why had they taken it upon themselves to fight her battles? She felt sorry for them but resented it at the same time. They'd always been suffocatingly protective and now it had come to this. She hadn't asked her father to beat anyone up on her behalf and she certainly hadn't asked her mother to kill Dominic. She wished she'd never told her mother about what Dominic had subjected her to. But she was upset, distraught. Sometimes, a girl needs her mother. Had she imagined, even for a second, that it would have led to this, she'd never have told her.

She knew now that her mother had never truly recovered from losing her baby all those years ago. Would it have made a difference had the baby lived? A little girl, eighteen months older than Elise. Yes, perhaps. Probably. They'd named her Suzanne. Suzanne Tanner.

She leant forward and rested her hand over Phil's, the small diamond on her engagement ring catching the overhead lights. They didn't need to rent now, they could live in her parents' house until her father was released, because there was no doubt he'd be serving a shorter sentence. It frightened her how old her mother would be when they finally released her. She'd be an old woman, probably in need of care.

She'd already postponed the wedding indefinitely but that was fine. People were understanding. She had more important things to worry about, namely, to help Phil on his road to recovery. They'd move into the house and together they'd start again. She'd managed to keep her job – just. And Phil's bosses at the supermarket had been so sympathetic, saying that however long it took, Phil's job was safe, and he could initially return on a part-time basis and still be paid full-time. One couldn't ask for more from one's employer.

She still berated herself for having had that wobble recently, when she thought for a moment that Phil was not the man for her. Because that was all it'd been – a wobble. For she knew now with utmost certainty that Philip Edwards, in whatever state he was, *was* the man for her – for now and forever for she loved him like never before.

An hour later, Elise put her book in her shoulder bag, kissed Phil goodbye and, leaving St Cuthbert's, returned home.

How long, she wondered, would it take her to get used to this? Returning home to an empty house, no Mum, no Dad. No hearty welcome, no questions about how her day had been, no hot dinner awaiting her. The place seemed so quiet without them, four walls stripped of its soul, a house but not a home. God, she was going to miss them.

The painting was still there, 'Country Dawn', propped up against the sideboard. No one had moved it since the day it'd arrived. So recent but it felt like a lifetime ago. So much had happened since. So much had gone wrong. She picked it up and placed it *on* the sideboard, better to view it.

Stepping back, she stood there in front of it for some time, admiring it. Yes, it was a fine piece of art, a beautiful painting of the countryside at its bucolic best. England, my England.

She imagined strolling down the path hand in hand with Phil, the sun on their backs, love in their hearts, a picture of utter contentment and serenity. Just looking at it, losing herself in it, calmed her, slowed down her heart. Her life may have been turned on its head but there was still such beauty in the world.

Elise padded through to the kitchen and, opening the cutlery draw, took a long, sharp carving knife. She weighed it in her hands. She wondered what went through her mother's mind when she picked up that metal pig. Did she also weigh it up in her hand, did she know what she was going to do with it, had she already planned it? What made her go through with it? Her love for her daughter or her hate for the man that had violated her? Perhaps, both.

Elise returned to the living room, the knife in her hand. With quick, sudden movements, she slashed at the painting. Blinded by her tears, she tore at it with the blade, from top to bottom, from left to right, diagonally across, every which way, a frenzy of violence. Thirty seconds later, it had been demolished.

The knife slipped from her grip, landing with a loud clunk on the laminate floor. Breathing heavily, her heart pounding, she wiped away her tears. In front of her now, a large rectangular frame and within it, numerous pieces of torn canvas, limp and flapping, gone forever. Once upon a time, not so long ago, an artist called Justin Travers had created this work of art, and now she, Elise Tanner, had destroyed it.

She had destroyed *it* and much more. So much more.

And she felt a whole lot better for it.

Elise went upstairs to her bedroom and retrieved the butterfly jar from where she'd hidden it in the wardrobe. The blue butterfly inside had been beautifully painted, it truly was exquisite.

She read the label: *To my beautiful girlfriend, all my love, Dom. xx.*

She placed it on her bedside table and lying on the bed on her side, she smiled.

THE END

Novels by Joshua Black:

The DI Benedict Paige Novels

Book 1: And Then She Came Back
Book2: The Poison In His Veins
Book 3: Requiem for a Whistleblower

To obtain Joshua's short story, *The Death of The Listening Man*, and join his Mailing List and be the first to know of future releases, etc, please go to:

rupertcolley.com/joshua-black/

Rathbone Publishing

Printed in Great Britain
by Amazon

19598125R00189